DANCED OVER THE SEA

Jean Chapman

This first world edition published in Great Britain 2004 by
SEVERN HOUSE PUBLISHERS LTD of
9–15 High Street, Sutton, Surrey SM1 1DF.
This first world edition published in the USA 2004 by
SEVERN HOUSE PUBLISHERS INC of
595 Madison Avenue, New York, N.Y. 10022.

British Library Cataloguing in Publication Data

Chapman, Jean, 1929-
    Danced over the sea
    1.   Farm life - England - Fiction
    2.   England - Social life and customs - 1945 - Fiction
    I.   Title
    823.9'14 [F]

    ISBN 0-7278-6051-8

Typeset by Palimpsest Book Production Ltd.,
Polmont, Stirlingshire, Scotland.
Printed and bound in Great Britain by
MPG Books Ltd., Bodmin, Cornwall.

I had a little nut tree, nothing would it bear
But a silver nutmeg and a golden pear.
The King of Spain's daughter came to visit me,
And all for the sake of my little nut tree.
I skipped over water, I danced over the sea,
And all the birds in the air couldn't catch me.

One

1976

Bess was woken by the noise. It was light but early – five, she confirmed by the bedside clock.

Ian, her husband, still breathed deeply, regularly, by her side, but as the strange, scrabbling, noise came again, she crept from their bed. She went to the window, parted the curtains and slipped into the window alcove.

She could *see* nothing unusual. The dew was an undisturbed sheen on the lawns; the line of poplars backed by silver birches, planted nearly fifteen years ago to screen the lake from the house, were motionless; there was not even a breeze.

The noise came again. It sounded like something trapped, something trying to escape: there was a desperate quality to the noise. The disturbance was too loud for a bird – perhaps a fox? Had one of the dogs cornered a fox, or a badger? But the dogs should not be out. It was definitely something large, something frantic, something quite close. She unlatched the window, pushed it wide, and looked out – and down – and gasped.

Her two sons were engaged in a bitter struggle. Dickie, the older by four years, was sitting on Julian, had one arm twisted in a harsh lock up his back, and was bent over as if whispering into his ear. It was Julian's feet and free hand on the gravel, as he tried to raise himself and escape, that had roused her.

'What are you doing? Dickie! Let your brother go this minute,' she hissed down at them.

'He's not my brother,' Dickie replied and pushed the younger boy's arm harder up his back before standing up. 'He's just an interfering little tyke.'

1

For a moment Bess was chilled by the fury in her elder son's voice and thought he was going to kick at the figure at his feet. 'What are you both doing out there at this hour?' she demanded, noting that Dickie was fully dressed while Julian just had shoes and pyjamas on. She was aware too of Ian stirring, questioning, then coming quickly to her side.

'Fighting.' It was Ian who answered her question, as he took in the figure of his son rising shakily from the ground. 'Come up here,' he ordered.

'You're not my father,' Dickie retorted and before either of them could make further comment he added, 'and believe me I really will bury him one day, if he keeps interfering in my life.'

'At once!' Ian emphasized.

Bess instinctively stepped back from the window appalled by her elder son's words. She turned away, into Ian, his body still hot from their bed, but tense, not unaffected by the threat from the sixteen-year-old – their dismay caused by a shared memory.

Julian had been just a few weeks old. He had been put out in the garden in his pram and four-year-old Dickie had filled the pram with soil from the garden and patted it down flat. The baby had only just been found in time, rushed to the hospital and his nostrils and mouth cleared of soil.

There had been excuses that could be, and were, made for Dickie at the time. He was young, and a new sandpit had been installed in one corner of the gardens, where they had all spent considerable amounts of time showing him how to firm the sand in a bucket to make a good castle. Nannie had felt particularly guilty, for she had left the baby sleeping while trying to catch Dickie, who had run off and hidden in the kitchen garden. She had finally found him as he stood on the pram mudguards, belabouring the soil with the flat of his seaside spade.

The story had been retold at intervals as the boys grew up, but it had been no more than a family story, related without rancour for the amusement of family gatherings, but the fact remained that Julian had nearly died. Dickie's threat today had a totally different ring. Bess was chilled by how fierce and agitated he looked as he stood over his half-brother. What *had* Julian done to deserve such anger?

'I'm going down,' Ian announced, pulling on his dressing gown. 'It'll be some stupid boys' quarrel about Dickie going off early to go fishing or something.'

She nodded but, left alone, she knew this was not so: fishing never brought out such fury and enmity, even on the part of the more mercurial Dickie. She also knew that she could not just wait in bed.

It was not hard to find the trio: the sound of hushed but furious voices came from the room in the far corner of the hall set aside as an office for estate business. She entered to find the two boys on either side of the room, both obviously unrepentant and ready to fall on each other's necks at the first opportunity. Between them, Ian looked equally furious, and hardly more controlled.

'What is going on?' she demanded. 'What are you boys doing out and about at this time?'

'There are more questions than that to answer,' Ian said sombrely and, opening his hand, displayed a locket. Bess gasped – it was the locket he had given her as a girl. She treasured it above anything, more than any other piece of far greater value she had since been bought, or inherited. The trinket was part of the story of their meeting, then their separation; the misunderstanding; then her marriage to Dickie's father before she and Ian had re-met. She took it from Ian's hand and clasped it in both hands over her heart.

'I told you she loved it!' Julian exclaimed at his brother.

Dickie growled at him to shut up.

'You'd better start explaining,' Ian said, 'or I'll pack Dickie off back to school for the rest of the holidays, and Julian can go to his Great-Aunt Grace Topham.'

Bess would have found the looks on their faces comic if she in turn had not been so appalled by the fight, and now the locket. 'Where did you get it from?' she asked, though she knew exactly where it had been. 'Which of you took it?'

Neither boy answered.

'As far as I can make out the fight was because Julian tried to stop Dick taking it.'

3

'Is that true?' she demanded of the younger boy, knowing he was an easier option.

'I know you love it – I can tell when you pick it up – but he said you didn't want it, never wear it and wouldn't miss it,' Julian said, his face white, his jaw pushed sideways with apprehension after the story had poured from his lips.

'What did you want it for?' she asked Dickie.

'He said it was for nothing in particular,' Julian answered.

'Shut it you!' Dickie threatened, then as Ian went to the door and closed it, standing with his back to it and folding his arms, the older boy added, 'I didn't know it was Ma's, she never wears it, I didn't think she set any store by it. I didn't think anyone would miss it.'

'You knew it was not yours,' Ian retorted at the same time as Bess exclaimed, 'So you just went to my desk and took it!'

Dickie was silent, looking down, but his face was red with anger and frustration, not with any sense of shame or guilt.

'Perhaps,' Ian said, 'we might learn more if we approach this from a different angle. *Who* did you want it for? I presume it must be for a girl.'

Now Dickie's face flamed but he remained silent.

'You're dressed, so an early-morning assignation – before anyone is around to see?'

Ian had obviously come close to the truth as Dickie scowled, hunched his shoulders, but watching Julian, she was sure this was not something he had any knowledge off. His concern had been to save her locket.

'Well, I'm not wasting my time on you, young man,' Ian was saying. 'You should think hard of some way of making amends to your mother for such a crass act, and in the meantime you are banned from all the coming hunts and shoots.'

Dickie opened his mouth to protest.

'When I am satisfied you have made sufficient reparation and have shown some sign of repentance, I'll reconsider.' He opened the door and waited for Bess to go first. He then waited for Julian, who walked upstairs with his mother, and lastly he waited for Dickie. For a moment the youth leaned back with pretended nonchalance, but as Ian still stood, eyes fixed on him, he suddenly straightened and rushed out, running past them all, bounding up the stairs and into his bedroom, banging the door.

Bess propelled Julian towards his bedroom.

'I couldn't just let him take it,' he muttered, glancing up at his mother as she stood close opening the door for him.

She struggled to be fair, not wanting to overpraise one at the expense of the other, but instinctively opening her hand to look at the locket, she nodded her thanks.

Going back to her own room, she was surprised to find Ian dressing. 'It's only half five,' she said, surprised herself that such a family trauma had been compressed into a mere thirty minutes.

'I won't be able to sleep again. I'm going for a walk, the dogs'll enjoy it.' He did not add that he intended to have a good look around to see if there was anyone about. Ian remembered his own fascination with the opposite sex at sixteen. It was a powerful force, and to have driven Dickie to take a piece of his mother's jewellery for a present could mean the boy felt he was on the verge of receiving the ultimate favour from a girl – or he had already made the journey and this was payment.

'I can't believe he did such a thing,' Bess said, 'I really can't.'

'Don't take it too much to heart.'

'What?' She sounded aghast. 'Is there something in all this I've missed? I've taken it very much to heart.'

He thought that at forty she was more handsome, far more striking than she had been, even at sixteen when he had given her the locket. Her black hair was more expertly cut to work with the natural curl, her cheekbones appeared more prominent, the hollows beneath more sculptured, more defined.

'We won't let him know, but I did once give you my dad's penknife. The old boy never knew what happened to that.'

'Ian, I always thought it was yours!' she exclaimed.

'I think I thought it was mine, I had it in my pocket so often.'

'You'd scratched your initials on it,' she accused.

'I did too,' he remembered, pulling on his socks. 'So our whole relationship was based on a falsehood.'

'Yes,' she agreed, murmuring, 'How terrible,' and, sliding

5

down the bed a little, felt she gathered their relationship around her like a great soft eiderdown, always comforting, always there. She felt snug – smug for a moment – then she said, 'I've still got it if you want to give it back.' She had. The penknife was in the same desk drawer as the locket had been.

'No, of course not!' he exclaimed. 'You *never* let your father know things like that, and you don't tell your children either, otherwise there'd be no dealing with them.'

'But the threat to bury Julian was awful,' she said, bringing herself back to the moment's problem.

'Sixteen is a bad age to be frustrated about anything, particularly for this "never had it so good" generation,' Ian reflected, stomping his feet into his shoes. 'They seem to want everything, when they want it, no such thing as waiting. Have it now, pay later.'

She was silent as he finished dressing, and he knew she would be agonizing over how to deal with the incident, and with the two boys, *fairly*. It was a constant dilemma for Bess. Her older son was the heir to the estate and farms belonging to his father, Greville Philipps. There had been an endowment from his late grandmother, Lady Clare Philipps, and a place booked at his father's old school from the date of his birth. Julian, his own son, on the other hand, was happy at the local grammar school. The boy had developed a passionate interest in architecture, in the whole process of building. Julian regarded school as something to be seen through until such time as he could be properly apprenticed to his already chosen profession. In the meantime, in his spare time he read about and practised the arts of building – walls and arches – and had found an indulgent mentor in the local stonemason. 'So I can understand what you can do with bricks and stone,' he had told his father, adding with an almost visionary look in his eye, 'and then there's glass.'

After primary school the two boys had, really, grown up like boys from different families, and in a way they were, only their mother was mutual. Her love for them equal – she worried first that Dickie might resent Julian being at home more, then that Julian might feel Dickie was having the greater opportunities. Ian's judgment was that Bess indulged in too much self-questioning; both boys were doing very well, thank you very much – though that morning's incident worried him.

He went to give her a kiss and as he did so, she leaned her cheek heavily against him.

'We'll sort it out,' he reassured her. 'We've survived worse.'

'Much worse,' she agreed and as she smiled up at him he found her lips irresistible. He felt her immediate response, and his own. 'No,' he denied the feeling aloud, but did not add that he felt he must go and have a good scout around – a find-the-lady, or at least the girl, exercise. It would not do for the heir of one of the largest landowning families in the county to be playing some game with a local village lass, which is what he suspected. These days that kind of squirearchy was not tolerated – unless the girl was willing, and, he prayed, over sixteen.

He lifted a hand to Bess as he left the bedroom. 'Love you,' he mouthed.

'Love you,' she echoed and, as the door closed, picked up the locket from her bedside table. She could not believe that she had let all these years go by leaving the precious thing in a desk drawer. It had seemed appropriate to put it there at the time, with her first husband still alive, Dickie a baby, and her resolution to make her marriage work.

Her life, she felt, was still like walking a tightrope, balancing between the two boys and being loyal to the memory of the first husband, who had taken his own life in the lake, and the second, who, if life had been fair, should have been her only husband.

'Sometimes I don't know where my heart should be,' she breathed, aware both of the melodrama, and the truth, of the words.

Ian let the dogs out from the stables, chalking a message on the blackboard provided for such things inside the tack room. He didn't want Tommie, their sixty-year-old stable lad, looking for the spaniels.

He decided to draw a wide circle around the grounds, going first towards the lake, then uphill to where the estate bordered Bess's father's farms. The stretch of his legs, the swishing of his boots through the grass, the keen morning air, were invigorating and soothing. It was probably a futile errand but at least it gave him space to think.

Had Dickie risen early so he could take the locket without fear of being seen? He shook his head. No, it was far more likely it had only occurred to the boy when he was on his way out the door. Dickie could be impulsive to the point of stupidity. The trouble was, such an act committed anywhere outside the family – say at school – would be a criminal act, theft. It had to be dealt with.

He reached the Bennett land, turned left to begin his sweep. He had convinced himself that he would encounter no one, when he was alerted by the stance of the two springers. They stood listening, each with a front paw raised. The next moment, the two were racing off to the far hedge. He whistled, the dogs paused, wagged their tails and looked apologetic for knowing better than he did, and went on. The next moment he saw the reason for the dogs' enthusiasm: Bess's father emerged from behind the hawthorn hedge and stood at the gate looking over towards him. Ian raised a hand and Edgar Bennett waited on his land. Tall, gaunter than when in his prime, Edgar now lived alone on his farm, though Bess was in the process of trying to persuade him to have a live-in housekeeper, rather than just daily help.

'Mornin', Edgar,' he shouted. 'Couldn't you sleep?'

'Me? I should be asking *you* that,' the older man retorted. 'Out by six – what's happened?'

'We were disturbed by something or other, came to have a look round.'

'That's strange,' Edgar said as he reached him. 'George was out and about well before milking time, he said he'd been woken before his alarm went off.' He opened the gate for Ian, adding, 'And one of the men found a load of rubbish dumped in one of the road gateways overnight, and I mean a load.' The old man had a growing exasperation with the litter-louts and the thoughtless who left gates open, or broke down his hedges and fences. 'Come and share a pot of tea before you go back,' he added.

Ian would rather have turned back and continued his survey of the estate, but it had taken him years to build up any kind of a relationship with Bess's father after she had lost her first husband. Even now, Ian felt he must be guarded, was never completely at home with this man who had held his daughter's love and devotion so completely through her growing years – and still held her in thrall, in Ian's opinion. He would see her struggle if she was forced to say or do anything she knew her father might not approve of.

'I can't help it,' she had once explained, 'he summons up the child in me.'

On the other hand, Ian was aware that Dickie used his grandfather as a means to his own ends. Over the years he had more than once heard the phrase 'Grandpa says it would be a good thing if . . .' or 'Grandpa says I can, if you say so . . .' the implication always being that Ian, or Bess, were the spoilers of the fun if they did not agree.

'The boys all right?' Edgar asked, breaking into his thoughts. 'Be seeing a bit of Dickie now the shooting's about to begin, and thought I might ask young Julian to come and do a bit of bricklaying on one of the barns for me.'

'He'd like that,' Ian confirmed, but made no comment about the shooting; that was a conflict that would come soon enough. He thanked heaven that Julian had this overwhelming interest that should take him away from the Hall and the estate in due course. Ian hoped his son would be able to lead a happy, independent, life, fulfilling his ambitions away from any Philipps/Bennett family issues.

Ian Sinclair came from a background uncluttered by family land and estates, uncluttered by family really. His elderly father lived in Cornwall with a lady artist he had befriended years ago. His mother had gone her own way to try to find the good times she craved. He, and his father, had been glad to see her go out of their lives.

He kept a hold on his own identity, and perspective on Bess's obvious belief that the Philipps estate was a divine trust she held for Dickie, by running a garden design business, linked to a small printing firm with which he published 'How-to' books on garden design.

'Want to have a look at my top wheat field?' Edgar announced as they walked across the Bennett land. 'Have you time?'

'Sure. Cereals are usually early up there, aren't they?'

Edgar nodded. 'Good south-facing slope to that land. Six fields when I was a boy – the whole farm'll be one big field before I finish and young Dickie takes over.'

Ian felt a moment's resentment on behalf of Julian. There was the Philipps estate; did Dickie have to inherit the Bennett land too? Then he pushed the thought aside. Julian's creativity would probably thrive better unencumbered by real estate.

They walked, uphill now, Edgar head down a little, putting some weight on the walking stick he habitually carried around the farm – so he did not see the flash of pale colour Ian observed. It was a girl in a pale summer dress. She crouched and ran, flushed out by their approach he had no doubt.

She ran like a young hare, or a scared rabbit, beneath the cover of the hedge towards her home, for Ian had recognized her at once. It was Katie Wright, elder daughter of George and his wife, Colleen. They lived in one of two semi-detached dwellings where Edgar housed his herdsman and George, his senior farm labourer.

Opening the gate, Ian walked in first, turned along the headland under the hedge in the direction the girl had gone – but she was already out of sight. He turned back to where Edgar had thrust his stick under one arm and was rubbing an ear of wheat between his palms.

Was this all coincidence? Ian wondered. Dickie up and stealing a trinket, Katie out and about. Katie must be eighteen or nineteen – but then Dickie was tall, looked older than sixteen, and was certainly up to some secret mischief. Ian felt real distaste for the idea of this public school boy, his stepson, who nowadays mixed almost exclusively with his 'own set', but even so expected to be able to come back and dally with a local girl. A girl whose father worked for the Bennetts and whose family had been linked through friendship and work for several generations. He felt himself breathing faster, as real misgivings caught his heart. It all seemed to forebode ill.

By his side Edgar grunted and stood nodding over his cupped hands, and as Ian looked at him, he raised them towards his son-in-law. The grains of wheat lay plump and golden in his palms, first seeds of a harvest ready for gathering.

Ian calculated that if Dickie was chasing the daughter of one of the old man's workers he feared a different harvest. He hoped the girl knew what she was about. He reviewed what he knew of the amiable girl, with her slim waist and full breasts. She had shunned the idea of working in the village factory, and made her way each day from the farm to the main road to catch a bus into town and the solicitor's office where she worked as a typist.

'Right, home for that tea, then,' Edgar said, adding, 'before another harvest begins.'

Two

Katie paused behind the shelter of the hedgerow. It was not unusual to see Mr Bennett out and about on his land, but office hours were more Ian Sinclair's style. There must be some connection between the non-appearance of Dickie at the early morning meeting *he* had suggested and the arrival of his relations.

She glanced up to her home at the far side of the field: anyone coming out of the back door would see her instantly. She had little option but to go back. She would say she had mistaken the time. She could imagine that 'disapproval' would be a mild description of everyone's judgment of her meeting Dickie at six o'clock in a morning. The immediate comments would be that he was only just sixteen, and she was over eighteen. He was heir to a large estate, she was the daughter of one of his grandfather's farm labourers, but there was so much more.

They had known each other from birth, for years they had been together several times a week, though she had never been quite sure whether her role had been playing with, or looking after the younger boy. Even when Dickie went away to school at seven, and until their early teens, she had seen him regularly through the holidays. Together with her mum and brother, William, she had gone with the family from the Hall to the Philippses' holiday bungalow in Norfolk for at least two weeks every summer, often for longer.

She sighed and began to saunter homewards across the last field.

She had confided her reasons to no one but had opted for a job in a city office for the sole reason that Dickie's mother had started her acquaintance with the Philipps family, and the Hall, by working in an office, the estate office. Her father had

12

wanted Katie to take a job at the village garage, where she could have combined a little office work with serving petrol and cleaning cars. She had felt herself above such menial tasks, destined for something much better. Her dad might be a true man of the soil (an 'honest labourer' her mother called him), but Katie felt his judgments, like his work, were often far *too* down to earth, pulling her down with his blunt uncompromising reasoning.

She was far prouder of her mum's lifelong friendship with the matriach of the Hall and estates, Bess. Bess and Colleen. She had heard her mother say that nothing and nobody would ever come between her and Bess.

She smiled as she thought how they both lit up as they saw each other, and her mother must hug and touch Bess, the lady of the Manor, and how the Lady of the Manor responded to each contact, how hands covered hands, embraces were leaned into.

'What are you doing?' It was her mother's voice that startled her as she lingered between field and kitchen garden. 'You're ready for work early.' Colleen Wright stood quite close, a basket of washing on her hip, her dark-gold hair neatly cropped, cut around a face too mature for the Peter Pan style, but bonny nevertheless.

'I mistook the time.'

Her mother laughed, put the basket down, came to the gate and opened it for her daughter, putting an arm around her waist as she came through. 'You silly! Time for tea and toast then, because you've had nothing.'

'No, I didn't,' she admitted. Then, leaning her head over on to her mother's shoulder, she added, 'You're very . . .'

'Very?'

'You touch people a lot, hug them, take their arm.'

'Do you think so?'

She nodded.

'Do you think I shouldn't?'

'I wish I could do it as naturally as you do,' Katie said. 'It's nice. You do it with Dickie's mother.'

'Bess! I suppose I do, come to think of it. When we were girls she used to say I screwed her dresses up at the back and used her as a shield against the cows.'

13

'You weren't afraid of cows? Mum!'

'I still am, but I put a brave face on it.'

'Don't tell Dad.'

'Oh! *He* knows.'

'You laugh a lot, Mum.'

'What is this? Study Mum Morning?'

She watched her mother as she made toast, poured tea, perhaps it was more Study Herself Day: where Katie stood in the world. Where she stood in relation to Dickie, Dickie Bennett-Philipps, Richard Greville Bennett-Philipps.

'Is everything all right, Katie? You're very quiet these days.'

She shrugged. 'I guess.'

'Everything all right at work?'

'Yes.' She held her cup in both hands and breathed out, making the steam rise around her face. 'Fine.'

'No problems then?'

Only the problem of Dickie, who had sought her out in the last few weeks, had met her from the office one evening, given her tea and a selection of chocolate cakes at Kunzel's cafe. Sitting next to him on the bus home, she had been plagued with two different emotions: one, that she felt so right by his side; and two, that the Bennett-Philippses did not travel on buses. He had got off at her stop and together they had walked the footpath over the fields and through the spinney.

In the teashop their banter had been light-hearted, on the bus there had been what seemed to Katie a moment of truth, as the conductress had singled Dickie out for a 'thank you, sir' when everyone else had received a 'ta, luv'. She wasn't sure Dickie had even noticed, and in the trees the thought of any social niceties faded.

'I've wanted to walk with you like this for years,' he'd said.

'Years!' she had exclaimed, laughing, and, turning to question the statement, she had found his lips coming awkwardly on to her lips and teeth.

'Sorry,' he had said, retreating, 'sorry, I shouldn't have.'

'I didn't expect . . .' she had begun, 'that's all.'

'You think I'm too young to be able to care properly.'

'No, no, of course not,' she had replied but the spell had been broken.

14

'More toast?' her mother asked. She shook her head and hastened back to her thoughts.

It had been too late, too inept, then to tell him that he felt to her, and looked to everyone else, like a man – and above all she felt different being with him. Different to the way she had ever felt with any other boy or man she had ever been near. It was like excitement, and fear, and joy all rolled into one.

There had been other boyfriends, and a married man, a church bell-ringer, who had first offered to pay her fare on the bus 'but don't tell anyone', then had propositioned her after church, offered to take her on a day's outing to Matlock. Intrigued at first and flattered by his attention, she had hastily backed off, afraid of his experience. There had been a previous scandal to do with the bell-ringers and young girls learning the art of church bell-ringing. She had ever since felt guilty when she saw his rather dumpy amiable little wife going about her shopping in the village.

Then there had been boys at the comprehensive school, boys who pretended to have 'had a bit', 'done it', 'gone all the way' with everyone from the school's head-girl to the devastating Ruth Peel, who looked like illustrations of Cleopatra and was head of the History Department. She guessed it had been all talk. She had gone out with some, had wrestled with them as they tried to push their hands either up her jumper, or down her blouse. There had been others who specialized in intruding their hands under girls' tunics as they had to squeeze by the close-packed throng to get off the school bus. She only *just* found them worthy enough of the status of 'having a boyfriend' to bother with them at all. Certainly, she never for one moment considered them worth 'going all the way' with.

'All the way', was a journey she still had to make, and one that, if she was honest, scared her to death, or the possible consequences scared her to death. Boys excited her but the mere thought of having to confess to her mother, or her *dad* that she might be pregnant was enough to cool any ardour – well, almost any ardour. She knew all about 'precautions' – she also knew girls, and married women, who had given birth to babies they certainly did not plan.

'It is time you did set off now, our Katie.'

'Oh! Yes.' She felt herself blush.

'You look quite hot, sure you're feeling all right?'

'It's the tea. See you tonight.' She kissed her mother's cheek, received a friendly slap on her bottom, and set off again.

She peered in every gateway with a bubble of hope in her heart, and the leafy recesses of the spinney twice had her stepping out of her way as she thought a movement made by the wind might have been Dickie. She reached her bus stop with three minutes to spare. She felt deflated by disappointment, exhausted by anticipation, her life diminished by his non-appearance.

The sound of an approaching motorbike drew her glance to the road – she saw the motorbike was followed by a car, and behind the car was her bus. So that was that: so much for Dickie's intentions. It did not seem fair that he could turn up in her life whenever the fancy took him, but she would be hard put these days to just turn up in his.

The motorbike was nearer, slowing down, and the rider in black leathers waved the car past. It was a shock to see that the car was driven by Edgar Bennett, who seemed a little reluctant to go on, but the bus was closing the distance between the vehicles. He pipped his horn and picked up speed. She stood with a hand covering her lips, wondering what all this meant – seeing him twice before eight thirty in the morning – then she lifted her hand to the fast-approaching bus. The motorcyclist had stopped at the far end of the lay-by and was pulling off his helmet.

'Katie!' he called. 'Katie! Don't get on the bus, I've come to give you a lift into town.'

'Dickie?' she queried.

He walked backwards, still astride the bike, and waved the bus by with large high gestures. The driver shook his head in disapproval, his hands and arms circling hard on the steering wheel to take the bus back on to the road proper, to the amusement of those on the bus in a position to see the roadside scene.

'I didn't know you had a motorbike,' she accused as her energy flooded back with all the rush of a spring tide with the wind behind it, 'or that you could ride one.'

'Birthday present,' he announced.

She thought he was certainly what anyone, anywhere, would call a good-looking bloke. 'And look at you in your leathers!' Her own face flamed as she enthused at how well he did look in the tight-fitting, and obviously expensive, gear. He blushed at her open admiration and they both laughed.

'What happened this morning?' she asked. 'Thought you'd sent your dad instead.'

'Stepfather,' he corrected. 'It's a boring story, and I don't want to make you late for the office.'

'You've not passed your test,' she accused, pointing to the L-plates, 'and I've let the bus go.'

'No problem.' He heaved the bike on to its stand and began to remove the learner plates.

'Dickie, you can't do that!' she exclaimed, aware she had heard that one of his great-uncles on his mother's side, the Tophams, was a city magistrate.

'I'm proficient,' he said, 'been riding around the grounds for years on a banger.'

She did not move.

'Come on Katie, I dare you. You've never refused a dare.'

'For some reason I've never refused yours,' she said as she eyed the back of the bike and her own very short tight skirt. She thought of being over an hour late if she waited for the next bus, and asked, 'But shouldn't I have a helmet?'

'Everything's under control,' he said, handing her his helmet.

'And you?' she queried, but he lifted the pannier seat and took out another helmet. 'I borrowed it from one of the men,' he told her and, clamping the ancient battered helmet with the old-fashioned chin strap on his own head, gestured for her to put his on.

She lifted it to her head, but the thought of being inside the metal and glass bubble appalled her. 'No, thanks,' she said, 'I'd rather have the other.'

'It's awfully scruffy,' he protested, but when she insisted he pulled out a clean handkerchief and gave first inside, and then out, a good rubbing.

'Come on,' she protested, 'you've already had it on your head.'

'I didn't mean you to wear it,' he said as he finally helped her buckle the chin strap.

17

The touch of his fingers on her face, the smell of his new leathers, and the prospect of the illegal ride into town was as exciting as their first near kiss had been. The promise of joy and trouble was irresistible to her when it was Dickie who invited.

'Hold on!' he called. 'Arms around my waist nice and tight.'

She tightened her hold a little.

'Tighter,' he ordered. 'Come on, Katie, tighter, I can still breathe.'

Before she could think of a suitable reply she was nearly jerked from the back of the bike and they were away at a heart-stopping speed; after the full two hundred yards to the main road, they came to a jerking halt for the traffic, but before she could remonstrate, the jerk was repeated and they were off again.

Though she was not late at the office, she was not impressed by his handling of the machine either, but as she dismounted she saw his hands were shaking as he took off his helmet.

'Not used to a passenger,' he said. 'First time I've had anyone on the pillion.'

'First time you've ridden this machine in town,' she guessed.

He nodded. 'Need to practise. Pick you up at five thirty then,' he added in a louder voice and looking behind her. She turned to see the firm's bookkeeper lingering on the doorstep.

'Mornin',' Ken North called. 'One-way system all round here – you'll have to go to the top, turn right, then left, then right and out of town by the prison.'

'He *knows*,' Katie retorted, unaware whether he did or not, 'thanks very much.'

'Yes, thanks, old boy,' Dickie added.

She saw Ken's eyebrows rise a little at the 'old boy', then she saw her boss coming down the elegant street of four-storey Georgian houses, now all offices. 'I must go.' She looked at him and his bike with some doubt, but as he frowned a little and urged a nod towards her she added, 'See you at half five then.'

By the time the senior partner of Benbrook & Co. was upon them, he had the old helmet in the pillion, but before he pulled on his own he nodded to Mr Philip Benbrook. 'Good morning, sir.'

'Nice young man,' he commented to Katie as he allowed her to precede him into the office.

By six thirty that evening the offices were all long deserted, the street too – no one lingered too long near their workplaces, going off to their transport home, or into the city centre to the eating places, theatres, cinemas, to meet their dates.

Katie was disconsolate. Would there be another 'long story' to be told about his non-arrival? Then to her mortification she saw Ken North coming back along the street. If there had been anywhere to hide she would have. He was carrying his snooker cue in its black metal case. He paused for a moment aghast to see her still standing there, then he grinned. 'Supposed to be picking you up was he, young Lochinvar?'

She nodded, feeling too downhearted, and seeing no point in trying to make up some story in Dickie's defence. The reason she was still there an hour after the office closed must have been obvious to anyone who saw her arrive that morning. 'Something must have happened,' she said.

'Come and have a drink at my snooker club, they have women members. Could teach you to play if you like.'

'Thanks, but no thanks.' She felt his disappointment and gave him a brief smile; he did try to make friends yet always seemed alone. 'I'll just go and catch the next bus – they'll be wondering what's happened to me at home.'

'As you like. Another time, perhaps?'

She did not answer, but walked with him to the corner where his snooker club occupied the first floor, over a huge electrical shop. Here she had to cross the road to the bus station. 'See you tomorrow,' he said.

She nodded dejectedly, caught the half past seven bus home, cheering herself with the wild hope that Dickie might meet her off the bus. He did not.

She wondered how long he had gone out of her life for this time: an hour, a day, a week, a month, for ever?

Three

The next morning Ian saw his father-in-law swing his jeep round in front of the Hall, get out and, without pausing to retrieve his walking-stick, go across toward the stable block. He would expect to find Bess there having her usual morning consultation with Tommie.

Ian wondered what the old man had on his mind to bring him to the Hall when he had crops to harvest *and* to make him forget his stick. George Wright always had said his boss's walking ability depended on where he was going and his state of mind.

Ian left the estate office and went quickly out by the back way, hoping to waylay Edgar before he found Bess. He preferred to hear what Edgar had to say first-hand, not in reported fashion from either Bess, or Dickie, who would both be guilty of overlaying the old man's remarks with appropriate shades of pacification in the case of Bess, or persuasion in the case of Dickie.

He found Edgar standing in the middle of the yard, fussing over the two spaniels. 'Mornin',' he called. 'Where is everybody?'

'Bess is getting ready for a trip into town, new trousers for Julian, and there's talk of a hat.' There was also talk of a trip to see her Uncle Angus Topham to ask the best way to deal with Dickie's pending summons for riding a motorcycle without L-plates.

'A hat!' Edgar exclaimed. 'That's serious . . . and Dickie?'

'Dickie?'

'Yes, is he going to town?'

'No.'

'Out on his motorbike again? Saw him on it twice yesterday.'

'Twice?'

'Once early in the morning, then he came over to see me in the afternoon, about four.'

'You felt he was managing the machine all right?' Ian asked. The sub-text was that Edgar had given his grandson an extra sum which had enabled him to buy the large Norton motorbike instead of the scooter he and Bess had thought more appropriate for Dickie's debut on the public highway.

'Fine.' Edgar chuckled. 'Swept into a lay-by and waved me on like an old hand.'

'This was early yesterday?'

'Yes, young Katie Wright was waiting for her bus to work.'

'Ah,' Ian breathed – the pieces were fast falling into place.

'Then he rode over in the afternoon to tell me you have banned him from shooting.' Edgar's comment was delivered in the same tone of voice, but his blue eyes were icy, full of interrogation.

'Yes, that's right.' Ian saw no reason to try to gloss over his decision.

'So it is true – bothered me all night – came over to check. He's included in the invitation for Lord Markham's first shoot, knew you wouldn't mind my taking him.'

'Normally, no.'

'What in God's name has the boy done, murdered someone?'

'Did you ask him what he had done?'

'He didn't seem to know,' Edgar answered.

'Then he prevaricated.'

The older man frowned. 'He didn't seem to feel he deserved the punishment.' He waited for further explanation.

'It is a question of the punishment fitting the crime, and he has the remedy in his own hands,' Ian heard himself saying in spite of his resolve to be silent on the subject. 'If he can find a sufficient means of making up for what he did, and of apologizing to his mother, I'll review his punishment – until then . . .'

It was not an opportune moment for Bess and Julian to appear from the house. Bess waved and Julian ran towards them.

'Hello, Grandpa, come to see how Dickie is?'

'How he is?'

'Yes, you know he fell off his motorbike—' Julian began,

then stopped as he saw that his grandfather certainly did not know.

'No one said,' he accused. 'Is he hurt?'

'Not as much as he ought to be,' Ian said, 'young idiot.'

'Just a good many bruises and a limp. He hit a high kerb and the bike landed on his foot,' Bess said, then with the clear intention of changing the subject asked, 'Anthing you need from town, Pa?'

'And Dickie tells me he's banned from all the season's sports,' Edgar said, ignoring the question.

The forced good humour waned, and while Bess raised her chin and stood her ground, Julian dropped behind his mother.

'It's not up for negotiation,' Ian stated.

'But what has he done?' Edgar asked, looking from one to the other. 'It's not too awful for me to hear, is it? Bess?'

Julian looked around his mother at his grandpa.

'Something to do with you, Julian?' Edgar asked.

'No, Pa, I won't have you question Julian,' Bess said. 'We've made our decision on this. I'd like you to leave it at that.'

'There'll be so many questions asked,' Edgar persisted. 'Everywhere I go people will ask where he is. I've already confirmed his stand at several shoots. It'll put me in an embarrassing position. What am I to tell people?'

Ian sensed Bess wavering.

'You want him to move in the right circles, don't you, meet the right people. To do this to him – and me – for whatever cause, will just make for gossip, make us, and the boy, a laughing stock.'

'The trouble is,' Ian responded, 'he does not consider himself "a boy" any longer, so, he must show himself to be the man he thinks he is and face what he has done, make reparation, and then, as I've, we've –' he paused to glance at Bess – 'decided, the matter will be reconsidered.'

'Well, I can't imagine . . .' Edgar began, then his eyes rested once more on Julian. Ian felt the shift in the old man's attention to his son and was suspicious. 'What about my old barn then?' Edgar asked. 'Any chance of doing some rebuilding on it this holiday?'

'Oh, yes, please!' Julian exclaimed, going forward so he stood midway between parents and grandfather. Like a symbol, or a sacrifice, was the thought that skipped unbidden into Ian's mind.

'I could start tomorrow, and you know, Grandpa, it should be possible to clean up some of those old bricks you've got in the corner of the orchard. I'm sure there'll be enough to rebuild. You do mean the end of the old harvest barn, the one with the herringbone ventilation holes? We don't want to have to buy new. Well, new wouldn't do, we'd have to find some reclaimed ones anyway.' He glanced at his mother. 'D'you think I might get some proper working jeans as well as trousers, Ma?'

'Good idea,' Bess said, leaving Ian to put her arm around Julian's shoulders.

'Right, I'll leave that in your hands then, Julian, and you let me know how things go.' Edgar nodded to the boy as he might to any professional builder he was employing to do a job.

Ian was glad he had already known about this idea to keep Julian happy and occupied, or he would have suspected Edgar of just making an opportunity to question his son.

'Perhaps we'll have the matter sorted before the shoots begin,' Bess responded to her father's offer with her own spontaneous goodwill.

Ian closed his eyes for a second. Oh Bess, he agonized silently, why do you always try to be on both sides?

'So that should be all right then.' Edgar was complacent as they waved the pair off.

Ian had no time to concoct a suitable reply as Dickie came limping around the corner of the stable block.

'So what've you been up to, young man?' Edgar called heartily, then taking in the strapped and slippered foot, added, 'And how did you get home afterwards?'

'We picked him up from the city hospital; his bike from a city garage; and his summons, I presume, will come through the post,' Ian listed. 'You'll excuse me, I have work to do.'

Some fifteen minutes later he emerged from the house with a manuscript he had to take to his printers, to find the two still talking, Dickie now propped up with his grandfather's walking stick.

'I'm going over to the farm for the day, OK?' Dickie called to him.

23

Ian waved his bundle of papers, implying a consent as curt as the request, then paused to ask, 'Aren't you busy harvesting, Edgar?'

'I'm going to hold the fort, answer the telephone, and Colleen will be there at lunchtime – ages since I saw her,' Dickie told him.

It was on the tip of Ian's tongue to remind him that Colleen's daughter, however, would be at work; instead he said, 'Give her my love, tell her we'll be over to see her soon.' No harm in letting the young Romeo know the parents were in contact.

'Sure. Come on then, Grandpa,' he urged, rejoicing in the knowledge that he could relay the story of his accident to Katie via her mother, and she would understand he had not let her down without good reason.

He had pop music on the radio when Colleen Wright arrived in the early afternoon.

'Dickie? Hello, my love, didn't think it was your grandpa listening to that lot.'

'You look well.' He stooped to kiss her cheek. 'Like the hairstyle.'

'Well, it's easy.' She put up a hand to touch her short crop, but then noticed his foot. 'What's this?'

'I'll tell you,' he said, ushering her in. 'I've made some tea ready for when you arrived.'

'I don't usually drink tea as soon as I walk in,' she said with a laugh.

'Today we will.' He aligned the cups and began to tell her of falling from his motorbike.

'Oh, my God!' she exclaimed, and sat down at the kitchen table as if her legs would no longer hold her.

'It's only a bruised ankle,' he said.

'No,' she denied it was his injury that was upsetting her, 'a motorbike? What do you want one of them terrible things for?'

'To be independent of course, get about on my own,' though as he said the last words he acknowledged that the main reason was so that he could see Katie more easily.

She waved away the idea as if it was an insistent wasp. 'You'll be having a car before you're much older, a little sports

24

car,' she urged, 'more in keeping with . . .' an arm gestured towards the estate. 'Why can't you wait until then?'

'You know what your George says: "Do it today, not regret it tomorrow."'

'Not about motorbikes he don't.'

'Perhaps your William will—'

'No, and you can wipe that silly smile off your face. "Where angels fear to tread", that's where you're stomping around, Dickie Philipps. My older brother was killed on a motorbike, *and* he killed someone else at the same time. No one in my family is going to come within arm's length of a motorbike, let alone ride one.'

He was aghast, shaking his head, he knew there were several gravestones in the churchyard with the name 'Wright' on them. 'Katie never spoke about . . .' he paused, 'of losing an uncle.'

'I doubt she'd remember him, and we've never talked about him much.'

'Not ever that I remember,' he added, puzzled that this should be so.

'It happened a long time ago,' she said, shrugging him off, and would have risen at once to begin her work.

'Have your tea first,' he urged.

She accepted the cup but paused in the drinking as a thought came. 'Your mother never mentioned you were to have a motorbike.'

'It was going to be a scooter, but Grandpa gave me the extra to get a proper bike.'

'A proper bike!' she exclaimed. 'Why can't he leave things be?'

'Grandpa?'

'Yes,' she retorted, 'your grandpa. He should know better. Just don't bring it anywhere near me, that's all.'

'A lot of my friends—'

'*Your* friends maybe, but not anyone belonging to me!' she emphasized, rattling her empty cup back on to its saucer. He had rarely seen her so adamant: usually Colleen was the one who found the compromises, the peacemaker in their childhood disagreements.

He wondered how she would have taken the knowledge

that he had given Katie a lift, and had been on his way to bring her back home when he had fallen off.

'Remember!' she emphasized.

Her manner was so vehement, her clattering about with pots and pans so different to her normal placid ways, he didn't have too much more to say. He watched as she finished preparing a casserole and put it in the Aga. 'Won't matter what time Mr Bennett decides to eat, it'll be fine,' she said. 'You staying? What're you going to do with yourself?'

'I've some birthday thank-you letters I should be writing.'

'Well, do it then, don't just waste the whole day.'

He pulled a face at her and she smacked him on the shoulder, then they both laughed. Dickie raised his hands, surrendering. She shook her head at him.

'You, young man, have got to pull yourself together. In another year or two you'll have a lot of responsibility on your shoulders.'

He laughed. 'You don't seriously think they'll *ever* let me take over.'

'Oh, believe me, it'll come all too soon. It's what you're being groomed for, schooled for. Listen to your parents – they know what's right for you.'

'By "parents" you mean my mother and my stepfather?'

'Your happiness means everything to *both* of them.'

'You mean, what pleases Mother, pleases him.'

For a moment he thought she might belabour him with the dustpan she had just picked up, but he saw her anger fade to disdain as she stared at him. 'Yes,' she confirmed, 'he worships the ground she walks on.' She picked up a broom and, opening the back porch, began to sweep the step and around the dog kennel. 'There'll be enough casserole for the two of you,' she told him, 'and, if you stay, cut some nice crusty pieces off that new loaf, Mr Bennett likes that with a casserole.'

He had moved into banned territory, he had again lost her goodwill. He had made comment about her life-long friend, his mother, and Ian. He should have known better, now he was put in his place by the simple ploy of Colleen slipping into the role of employee.

He felt lonely when she had gone, and depressed as he reviewed the last two days. Why had he been such a fool as to take the locket from the office desk drawer in the first place?

He had only seen it by chance when he had been in there to answer these same letters that lay on the table now. Julian had come in, as Dickie knew he often did. He was usually after paper for drawing, or carbon paper, or to look at the estate plans of houses; that day it had been for an eraser. Dickie had looked in the drawers for him and pulled out the small black box, and opened it. 'That's Ma's,' Julian had said.

'Ma keeps her jewellery in her bedroom, or the safe,' he had said, but Julian had located a rubber and was away, busy as usual on some project or other.

Dickie had put the locket back and only remembered it on the morning he had arranged to meet Katie. He had felt shy about the rendezvous he had made on the spur of the moment. He had just not been able to think of another time when they could meet without being interrupted, or provoking questions, or when they could be sure of being entirely alone. The idea of giving her the locket had somehow seemed to give a reason for the preposterous timing, so early in the morning before she went off on the bus to work.

Everything had gone wrong. Julian had been awake and followed him downstairs. He was a strange kid, Dickie judged, interested in buildings and bricks, shadows at different times of the day and night. Weird. He had told him so when he had come into the office and found him with the locket. He had thought he had cowed the little tyke, but had suddenly been leapt on from behind as he left the house.

He was at once too restless to write letters, and too irresolute to ring home to see if someone would come and fetch him. The harvesters must be working until late, probably with headlights on the combine. He sighed.

'That came from your boots,' a voice said from the doorway.

'Katie?' He rose and limped towards her. 'Katie.'

'Mum told me what happened.' Her voice was low, subdued like the evening light, and, nurse-like, she took his arm. 'I wondered if you'd still be here.'

'Did you wait long for me last night?' he asked as she tried to lead him back to his chair. 'I kept thinking about you outside that office when everyone else had gone.'

'I caught the half past seven bus in the end,' she said, adding, 'Look, sit down.'

'Katie,' he began, feeling his heart and mind were packed so tight full of things to say he could not quite come on the right one. 'Thanks for coming.'

'That's all right,' she said. 'When I heard you'd had an accident I wanted to of course.'

He took her hand from his arm and held it. 'I find you more special than anyone else I have ever, ever, met,' he said ardently.

The ponderous tock of the grandfather clock seemed to become like a heartbeat, filling the room, and her own heart pounded in unison. 'But you'll meet a lot more people as time goes on,' she told him.

'It doesn't matter. No one will be as special to me as you are, no one. No one.' He took her other hand and held them together inside both of his, as if she was at her prayers and he giving his blessing to them. 'I am sure about that.' He nodded his certainty down to her.

Her stillness became so intense it was more a retreat than a silence, prompting him to ask, 'What did your mother say?'

She cleared her throat but did not answer right away. Her dad had said he had 'grown into an arrogant young bugger'. Her mother had immediately sprung to his defence, as she did about anything to do with the 'big house' as George Wright insisted on calling the Hall. 'He'll have to alter his hand when he comes to running the estate, if he survives that long,' her dad had said.

'Of course he will,' her mother had stated, 'its just a phase he's going through. He'll be fine.'

'Oh! I know your precious Bess *thinks* he will, but you know what thought did.'

'What's the matter with you?' her mother had demanded, making it a personal matter. 'You've no good word to say about anyone these days.'

It was at this point that Katie left the house, leaving them 'having words' and unaware she had gone.

'She was terribly upset when I mentioned the motorbike,' he added when she did not answer.

'That'll be because of my uncle. I don't really remember

him. And let's be honest, Dickie, you're not safe on that bike, not in town anyway.'

'I seem to have proved that,' he said.

'Does it hurt?' she asked.

'It did, not bad now. Can I put my arms around you? That'd help no end.'

She hesitated for a moment, then took a small step towards him. He put his arms very gently around her waist. She could feel the heat of his hands below and over her shoulder blades.

She stood quite passive but every sense aware.

He tightened his arms a little, then she heard and felt him let his breath out in a long ragged stream. His cheek came near, touched hers, he kissed her cheek, then in the most delicate way he released her. 'Thank you,' he said and stepped back. 'I *do* love you,' he said as if the strangely formal embrace had finally confirmed it.

Her dad had also said that Dickie Philipps would have no respect for anybody. He'll take what he wants, and run. No stability, no sense of responsibility. It wasn't true. He had not taken advantage, not embarked on some pawing and mauling session. She felt a little ashamed that she had feared he might do, and so, for her, ruin this their first loving embrace.

'The trouble is that you are too young – not to me, I don't mean, but the way the world sees us.'

'Do we care what the world thinks?'

'You know,' she whispered as he stepped nearer to her again, 'I think we have to.'

'Then,' he said, taking her to him again, and this time his hands were on her back and behind her head, as one might hold a baby, 'I'll have to just ask for you to wait for me. Not that I intend to go away from you ever again.'

'You have your education to finish,' she reminded him with a gentle laugh.

'I intend to do that right here, at home.'

'But they won't let you.'

'They won't stop me,' he said.

At the end of the lane came the sound of a large vehicle.

'They're bringing the combine home,' she said.

'Kiss me, Katie,' he said as the beams of the headlights swung like searchlights across the kitchen windows. She did, stood on tiptoe to add pressure to his gentle touch, getting her lips right this time. The kiss lingered, longer than was wise, but she was away as the machine's engine died and men's voices were heard coming towards the house.

Four

Later the same night, the sound of a vehicle, then lights bouncing across the facade of the Hall, made Ian and Bess look up. 'At last,' Ian said as they heard men's voices. A few moments later the front door banged; a pause, then Dickie hobbled into the sitting room.

'Hi!' he greeted them both with a beaming grin. 'I'm going up. 'Night.' He came over to give his mother a kiss as if nothing untoward had happened, called a second 'goodnight' to his stepfather and went out closing the door behind him.

Bess did not come to terms with this unexpected mood of bonhomie in time to reply. She had that day spent an uncomfortable hour or two being lectured on bringing up boys by her uncle, who had gone on to say that as she had obviously failed to make him law-abiding, he had better turn up in court repentant, well turned out and apologetic.

Ian chuckled at the ambiguity of her expression. 'Guess the accused has had a good day, even if his mother feels reprimanded.'

'Yes,' she agreed sharply.

'Repentance is obviously never going to be Dickie's strong point,' he said on the way to lock the front door. She tossed up her chin; he remembered that gesture from when she had been Dickie's age.

He waited for her at the bottom of the stairs and as they ascended he took her hand – though she did not acknowledge the gesture, she only released his hand when she went to switch on the light in their bedroom.

She hesitated at sight of the moonlight – a full harvest moon – flooding the room, throwing the shadows of the high window frames to make rectangles of light across carpet, walls, bed. Ian walked past her and went to stand at the window, looking out on to a roll of countryside, drawn across by darker lines of hedges and stamped with magnificent spreading oaks, sycamore, chestnut, tapering poplars, black against a world revealed in silvers and greys.

She left the light off and moved to the bed to take off her shoes, stockings, skirt and jumper, admitting she felt peeved. She had spent the evening worrying how to reconcile herself to Dickie's behaviour and how to keep relations good between her father and Ian. It seemed to her that the boys had both gone to bed happy, Julian rejoicing in a pair of jeans well splattered with studs and a leather name-patch on the back the size of a tea-plate, and Dickie – well, she was not sure what he was rejoicing in.

She stood up to pull off her slip and, bringing it over her head, saw Ian had turned from the window and was watching her.

'You look like a dancer on a checkerboard of light and shadow. I feel you should break into ballet,' he said.

'Perhaps a pas de deux,' she suggested and extended her arms making a diagonal cross in the one of the rectangles of moonlight.

She had not intended this to be a prelude to anything, but Ian's sudden and rapt attention came like a tide pushing all and everything else of the day away.

He began to take off his jacket, pulled it almost roughly from his shoulders, dropped it on to a chair. For a second she felt as if she really was a dancer waiting in the wings, her partner just extending his hand for her to join him. She could imagine an echo of music, *Swan Lake* of course. She laughed at her personal drama, and he made a sound in his throat like a predatory growl.

She was drawn to the bed and soon the thought came, as it often had over their years together, that he designed his love-making with the same skill he designed his gardens, always with a surprise, a vista of longing she did not expect. This time he kissed beneath her breasts when she yearned for him to kiss her nipples, but only did he ride up to these when her longing was almost beyond bearing.

When they were still, lying stretched long, naked, pale in the moonlight, she quoted to him: 'Ian Sinclair's designs are always a delight, ever innovatory.'

He laughed and buried his face in her neck. He knew what she meant. He entered their love-making led by desire, but his actions came as insights, responses to her mood, an instinct for what was right, or what would please. So he loved, and so he created his gardens.

Just before she slept she remembered that the first time she had met him, as a ten-year-old girl in her father's harvest field, he had made her feel like a princess in a tower, part of a kind of fairytale. He made her feel so still.

She woke some hours later and the light in the room was quite different – now the patterns were misshapen lozenges on the far wall – and she was cold. She pulled the clothes over them and snuggled carefully into his sleeping warmth, safe.

Ian's mood of pleasure and contentment was dissipated as Dickie breezed down to breakfast the next morning – although breezing was difficult to do with a limp, Ian felt he achieved it.

'I've decided not to go back to school,' Dickie announced as he put his plate on the table, 'ever.' There was a pause, then he asked, 'I wondered if you'd square it with Ma for me?'

His first reaction was to hoot with laughter, but it was quickly swamped by anger. He wanted to shout at the boy, asking how next he would contrive to upset his mother. 'Really,' he said, struggling to keep his voice steady, 'what makes you think I should want to do that?'

'Well, it would save her grief; she takes what you say better, or so I'm told. If you endorse the idea . . . as it were . . .'

'You think you might get away with it,' he finished the sentence and in spite of his anger felt such empathy with this boy, on the brink of manhood, wanting to take charge of his own life. 'So who have you been talking to?' he asked, but this seemed to put Dickie at a loss for words and he merely shrugged.

'Who's put this wild idea into your head?'

'No one, and it's not a wild idea. If I carry on at school it will be a waste of my life, and money that could be put to better use. I'd be better employed here at home.'

'If the last few days are an example, I'm not so sure about that.'

'I suppose that's true.'

The quiet admission softened Ian's tone to their young rebel.

'When you've finished your education, yes, that is what your mother and your grandfather do want. But *don't* rush at it all, at life, too quickly.' He paused, hoping that another meaning might occur to Dickie without him spelling it out. 'Don't want it all at once; enjoy your freedom, travel a bit. There'll be years enough for you to be here after that, a whole lifetime in fact.'

'I want to start living *now*, not in *two*, *three*, *four* years' time. Nobody knows how long their lifetime is going to be, do they? I might not even have *one* year for all we know.'

All the passion was back in the boy's voice. 'That's true,' Ian agreed but thought it strange for a youth to think of death – his experience was that they usually felt and acted as if they were immortal. 'But adults, parents, have to plan for what is normal, for what they see as best for the future of their children—'

'Their children!' Dickie exclaimed. 'I'm not a child. That's the trouble – I am grown-up, it's just that nobody in this house has noticed.'

'We haven't noticed any increase in your sense of responsibility, no.'

'What this?' Bess asked, closing the door to the passage and the kitchen beyond, where their daily help was waiting to see her. 'Why are you shouting?'

'Because I'm fed up with being treated like a child.'

'Perhaps if you acted in a more adult way,' she suggested.

'Perhaps if I got the chance I might.' He suddenly rose and limped to the wall, stood with his back to it. 'My life's slipping by, I need to get on with what I really want to do! I'm leaving school.'

'You are not!' Bess exclaimed and in the space of the three words relived her own rebellion against school, and compromised with a milder, 'For goodness' sake, haven't you caused enough trouble?'

'Perhaps if you sit down and tell us what's made you suddenly think like this,' Ian suggested.

'It's not sudden. I've never wanted to go away to university, so what's the point of staying on, doing more and more exams? I want to be here on the estate to take up the job that's going to be mine anyway, the estate, the farms. I might as well make a start.'

'Dickie, do sit down,' Bess said, 'you are supposed to be resting that ankle.'

'No, I can sit down when –' his glance took in Ian at the table – 'I'm older. I want to get on with things *now*. I'm not going back to school.'

'Has your grandfather something to do with this?' Ian asked.

'Why should you think that?' The question came from both Bess and Dickie simultaneously, and from both with the same amount of indignant ire.

'You did spend the entire day there, then came back late last night – came back in a totally different mood. Something had obviously happened to please you at the farm.'

Dickie scowled down at his feet before answering. 'I'd had a day being able to think for myself for once, make up my mind about a few things.'

'Are you unhappy at school?' Bess asked. 'You've never said, you always seemed pleased to go back to your friends, to go away with them at holiday times when you could have been at home.'

Ian thought Bess had made some good points. 'Perhaps we should get down to the real reason for your behaviour,' he said and saw the panic in his stepson's eyes.

'If you know perhaps you should tell us.' Bess's glance at her husband was suddenly hard, impatient. Her father's daughter. The Bess of the night before a million miles away.

At that moment Julian came into the room. 'Shut in?' he queried. 'What's up?'

'No, let me tell you,' Dickie raised his voice and gestured toward Julian. 'It's fine for him to stay at home all the time, but not me. Why is that? Go on, tell me.'

'No, you are not making Julian your fall guy,' Ian said rising, again closing the door. 'I think there are things you and I should talk about alone.'

'What!' Dickie exclaimed. 'You mean "see me in your study"?'

'The office'll do,' Ian said. 'I can talk about the birds and the bees as well in there as anywhere.' He caught a glance from Julian, who looked fascinated, full of questions.

'No, thanks,' Dickie said, 'unless there's something you need to know.'

'That was cheap, rude, mannerless.' Bess included Ian before her glance entirely focused on Dickie.

'Well, what does he think he can teach me?'

'How to behave,' Ian suggested. 'You've already broken the law of the land twice, we should at least try to preserve some kind of decorum.'

'Decorum,' Dickie repeated, 'gadzooks.'

Ian stood up quickly but Bess was aware that Julian had slid on to the nearest chair, listening intently. She turned her attention to him first. 'Mrs West said you'd had your breakfast.'

'Yes, I came to say I'm going for a bike ride over to Foxton Locks today, five of us, you know, the famous five out of our class. I've got some money, so we'll buy some crisps or something and be back about tea time.'

'Yes, that'll be fine,' Dickie put in. 'You come, go, stay, just as you please.'

'Just mind what you are doing,' his mother said.

'Yes, we don't want *you* falling off *your* bike,' Dickie put in.

Bess kept her eyes on Julian as he still lingered. 'Right, off you go.'

She waited for some seconds after he had left, then turned back on her husband and her son. 'So do you mind telling me what this is all about. Birds and bees, Ian? A locket for a girl, Dickie?' She looked at her husband then added, 'And there's more isn't there? Some things I haven't been told.'

'There's nothing more, Ma, he's just putting two and two together and making five.'

'I can add two and two and make four,' Ian said.

'No, you're making five, six or seven,' Dickie said defiantly.

'Everything that's happened is linked, isn't it, Dickie?' Ian insisted.

'In your mind perhaps.'

'You take the locket; you pull into a lay-by where a certain girl is waiting, ahead of a bus going into town.' He saw Dickie's head go up. 'You were seen,' he added before the youth could damn himself with further lies. 'Then presumably you take off your L-plates to pick up a certain girl. You go, or attempt to go, back into town in the evening to pick that same girl up, but come a cropper.'

'A girl? A certain girl. What girl are we talking about?' Bess demanded.

Ian looked at Dickie – the boy had gone desperately pale, but he did not answer.

'The girl I'm talking about is Katie Wright.'

'Colleen's Katie?' Bess was astonished. 'But she's years older than Dickie, and . . . and . . .'

'And the daughter of one of your father's employees.'

'The daughter of my oldest friend,' she corrected as she turned on her son. 'Dickie, you're sixteen. A lift I could understand *if* you'd passed your test – but the locket? And now not wanting to go back to school. What is this all about?'

'It's nothing to do with . . .' he searched for the words, 'either of you, or with anybody else.' He took them both by surprise by making a sudden lurching run out of the room, across to the kitchen, where they heard him greet Mrs West. Bess followed, but by the time she reached the kitchen he was out of the back door.

'Don't reckon he'll go far on that foot,' Mrs West commented as she arrived post-haste in the kitchen. 'Kids, hey, who'd 'ave 'em?' Mrs West had raised two delinquent sons and was now on the first grandchild in trouble for truancy.

The next moment an engine started up.

''Ere,' Mrs West exclaimed, ''e's never going to try to ride that motorbike with that foot!'

'Oh, no!' Bess echoed her helper's concern as they saw the bike and rider shoot past the window, then she turned back to meet Ian in the doorway.

'I heard,' he said. 'Don't worry, he won't go far – just to your father's, I imagine. He'll get more sympathy there.'

Bess looked at him sharply but Mrs West laughed.

'You can say that again: twists the old man round his little finger, he does.'

By mutual consent and in silence they left Mrs West to get

on with the heavy cleaning she came to do. They walked circumspectly from the kitchen, went along the passage, across the hall to the estate office and closed the door.

'Why do you employ that woman?' Ian asked. 'Talk about the spy in our midst.'

'She needs the money,' Bess answered.

He tutted but pulled her to him; they fitted so comfortably, so perfectly, her arms slipping around his waist, her head high enough to lie on his shoulder.

'I think Dickie had tears in his eyes, that's why he rushed away,' she said. 'Do you think we should go after him in the car?'

'What, make it a chase?' Ian laughed but felt a sudden pang of panic as he sensed her withdrawal. Then she physically pushed herself away from him, as she still tried to grapple with her son's problems. 'Bess,' he urged, 'whatever happens we mustn't let this come between us.'

'No, of course not,' but she frowned at him, answered brusquely, as if he was not part of her current equation. 'I think I should see Tommie about the horses then go straight over to the farm.'

'Let me know if he's there, and stop him riding that bike back. I'll fetch it later in the jeep,' he said and wondered why he should feel quite this bleak, so stony-hearted – so fearful for their future.

There was no one at the farmhouse when Bess arrived. She looked around the yard and sheds for the bike.

She went back inside and wandered through the downstairs rooms, the sitting room where her mother had entertained now much faded and rarely dusted, with only a remembered echo of the hale and hearty occasions when landed gentry and large farmers met there. These days her father lived, ate and mostly entertained his few visitors in the kitchen. In the hall she paused before the portraits of her mother and her grandmother. She reached up to touch the face of her mother: the portrait showed her serenely beautiful.

She remembered her own school leaving, which had not been approved of either. What heartache she must have caused, she remembered with a rueful smile, when she had refused to stay at home. She had gone to live with her grandmother. Perhaps only now, with Dickie the same age, did she realize how much these things hurt one's parents. She had stayed away from home until her mother had become ill. Tears stung her eyes: she had thought mothers lived for ever.

She looked uneasily towards the darker corner of this hallway with the portraits of even earlier Bennetts. She remembered destroying the portrait of the man who had wronged her grandmother, and the trouble there had been afterwards. She never regretted it, but this gloomier end of the hall always gave her the shivers.

It was time this place was redecorated, and if she managed to persuade her father to have a live-in housekeeper, now would be a good time to brighten things up. She would not listen when he played the emotional blackmail card, saying it suited him and he liked it the way her mother had left it. Her mother would certainly not like it now, as clean as Colleen was allowed to make it but *so* shabby.

She glanced at her watch, eleven, another hour before Colleen came to begin her work – and *where was* Dickie? She decided to leave her car where it was and walk across the fields to her friend's house. A heart-to-heart with Colleen was what she needed, and any discussion with Colleen would be open and frank. Sometimes one could be told more than one wanted to hear, but it would be honest, often very enlightening. If Colleen knew anything she would tell her, but Bess knew she would not be keen to tell even her best friend about her son attempting to take the locket.

The smell of fermenting fallen apples was strong as she walked through the orchard behind the farm. Only the cooking apples, the huge Bramleys, larger than a man's spread hand, remained to be gathered. Perhaps, she mused, she would just ask if Colleen had seen Dickie, and tell her about school.

She climbed the hill, leaving Red Pool Spinney on her right, reached the top end of the field leading down to the brook. Hawthorn thickets still overhung parts of the brook where she and Colleen had spent so many hours as children, making bowers, water gardens, fishing, paddling, and where their children, including Dickie and Katie, had also played.

Colleen would immediately know there was something wrong: it was almost unknown these days for her to walk across the fields in the middle of a working morning. In her head she rehearsed censored versions of events.

Colleen, as she guessed she might, saw her coming from the kitchen window.

'This is an honour at this hour of the morning,' Colleen called, coming to the door in a flurry of flapping tea towel. 'What've I done to deserve this?'

'I need a sympathetic ear, another woman to talk to, really.'

'Crikey.' Colleen skipped out of the house and linked arms to lead her back in. 'You'd better come in and we'll have a coffee to fortify ourselves.'

'Your Dickie,' Colleen began and Bess's heart leapt as if ambushed.

'What about him?' she asked cautiously.

'You didn't tell me he had a motorbike. It was a real shock to me when he said.'

'It was not what we intended.'

'He told me.' She shook her head. 'Your father shouldn't interfere. Those are things for parents to decide.'

'You know what he's like, dotes on Dickie.'

'To be fair, he dotes on both his grandsons, neither can do wrong. If I hear about Julian's herringbone bricklaying once more I'll be able to go round and do it myself, no problem.' She placed the cups of coffee on the table with thoughtful care. 'But it is Dickie that's the problem again,' she guessed.

'It is, and not just the motorbike, though he's gone off on it again this morning . . . after a family row. You've not seen him have you?'

'With that foot!' she exclaimed, while shaking her head in answer to the question, but before she could sit down to her coffee the telephone rang in the hall. 'Oh, blow! Won't be a minute.'

Bess heard the formal announcement of the number give way to warmth and familiarity as Colleen's voice rose.

'Hello. Hello, Katie! What's the matter?'

Bess's attention was riveted. She listened unashamedly, holding her breath. She heard the interest in Colleen's *mm*s and *ah*s, the laughter, her mind a turmoil of imagined situations

– all to do with her son. The conversation finished, she took up her coffee cup, but her hand shook so much she returned it quickly to the saucer.

'Our Katie,' Colleen announced unnecessarily, 'be late home, going to the cinema with someone from the office. I thought there was something going on, she's been coming back on the late bus once or twice. I think it's the bookkeeper chap.' She compressed her lips and nodded at Bess with some pleasure. 'Thought she was never going to take any young man seriously enough to go out with him.'

'What makes you think its the bookkeeper?'

'Oh! She's mentioned him a time or two. Ken, his name is, Ken North, know he invited her to go to his billiard hall once.'

'Doesn't sound quite Katie's cup of tea,' Bess said, 'billiards.'

Colleen shrugged. 'You can never tell. I used to say if George was the last man on earth I'd never marry him.' She laughed. 'So there you go. Now, what's your trouble? What's our dear Dickie done now?'

'He wants to leave school, swears he's not going back, unless it's in chains.'

Colleen laughed even as she shook her head. 'I'm worried about our Katie not going out with fellas at her age, and now you're worried about Dickie wanting to leave school at his age. Funny old world, isn't it?' She grinned. 'Mind, when you think about it, at sixteen I'd been working at the factory for nearly a year, and you were planning to set up your own livery stables. We thought we were very grown-up.'

'Dickie obviously does.' Bess went through all the reasons Dickie had given, adding a few theories of her own about him missing out, about Julian being at home all the time. 'He obviously thinks he's ready to take his place "in the real world", but we don't want him to make some awful mistake and regret it later.'

'That's certainly true.' Colleen became very still, staring into the dregs of her coffee. 'I wouldn't want our Katie to have to get married. I still feel ashamed when I think of my shotgun wedding.'

'Colleen,' she protested, 'you married the man you loved.'

'And Katie was born six months and one week later.'

41

'A beautiful early baby,' Bess persisted, forcing her friend to accept the story they had told and her smile. 'Happy troubles.'

Colleen relaxed, shook her head and they laughed together, gently, full of love for each other, affection which had seen them through such upheavals. Colleen pushed her hand across the table and Bess grasped it for a moment.

'So you and George will be having this boyfriend, this young man from the office, over for tea, I expect,' she said, admitting to herself she would just like to be sure.

'We'll have to give him the once-over sooner or later,' Colleen said, adding, 'but here's me going on, and you worried to death about Dickie.'

They worried and speculated but reached no conclusion other than that in 1976 education was more important than ever, and Dickie certainly ought to continue his.

They walked back to the farm together and the discussion with her father went along the same lines, but he looked at her and laughed. 'You all seem to come out all right in the end,' he said. 'Lord Markham's been having the same trouble with his granddaughter. Her mother can do nothing with her apparently, so she's living with her grandfather for the time being.'

Ian was quiet when Bess returned to the Hall, put out that Dickie had not returned or seen fit to let his mother know where he was. He was even quieter when she told him of the Katie telephone call. After some time he remarked, 'She could be making it up, covering for Dickie.'

'You mean you just don't want to believe it.'

'Oh, believe me, I do!' he exclaimed.

'She's mentioned this young man to Colleen several times,' she told him, adding, 'I think I'll ring the Eldridges – their boy is Dickie's nearest school chum.'

'But twenty-five miles away. If I were you, I'd just get on with things and wait.' He caught her anguished look and reminded her, 'Do you remember when Dickie ran away when he was ten. We scoured the neighbourhood, phoned people . . .'

'Found him in the boiler house behind the coke heap,' she finished for him.

'As black as the ace of spades.'

They laughed shakily and Ian folded her close. 'He's not a fool, he knows where he's loved.'

He was to add, 'And he's bloody inconsiderate,' much later in the evening while he watched Bess become ever more abstracted as the minutes, then hours dragged by.

'This,' he said, 'is exactly how we spent last night, sitting, listening, wondering, waiting.'

'I think we should call the police,' she decided as ten o'clock struck.

'I think we'll give ourselves a deadline of midnight. If he's not back by then, well, I'll ring Deric Partridge.'

'Deric, but he's a journalist, what would—?'

'I saw him when I was going to the printers this morning, he's on the night desk this week – he has to make regular calls to the police station and the hospitals for incident reports and casualties. He'd make discreet enquiries if I ask him.'

'So you think something has happened to Dickie?'

'No, I'm thinking of ways of keeping you calm.'

She jumped up and paced the room. 'I *am* perfectly calm!' She went over to the window and peered down the drive.

'I can see you are perfectly at ease.'

'And don't patronize me, I—'

Then they heard the sound of the motorcycle coming up the drive.

'Right!' Ian stood up.

'Ian, I really can't take another argument tonight.'

'Then I'd better go to bed out of the way,' he suggested.

'I wish you would,' she said so unequivocally that, although he had had no intention of doing so, he rose and strode from the room, leaving her to her precious son.

Bess heard him reach their bedroom as the noise of Dickie's bike receded round to the back of the house.

She went to wait for her son in the breakfast room. When she heard him inside, she snapped on the light and called to him. He came in blinking and stooped sideways, having trouble putting any weight on his ankle. She was appalled at how pale he was.

'You're in pain,' she said and he nodded.

'Done too much on the ankle.'

43

'You deserve it then,' she said. 'Where have you been?'

'Just with friends, Ma. Leave it, will you? I know I should have phoned. I feel rotten.'

There was no denying that he looked it. 'I'll get you some aspirin and a hot drink.'

'Just the aspirin, please, Ma.'

'Well?' Ian asked when she went into their bedroom.

'He's not well, in pain from the ankle. I have –' she raised her voice slightly – 'already said he deserves it.'

'Where's he been?'

'With friends.'

'Oh, if that's what he says, that's all right then.' The sarcasm was insulting and heavy as Ian turned on to his side away from her.

She undressed in silence, wishing she had brought them both up a brandy, but somehow now the moment had passed, could not be retrieved. She put out the light. The moon was just as bright as the night before but Ian had drawn the curtains over the windows. Only a long pale slit of light, where the curtains should have met, speared in across the room, falling across the middle of the bed, making a sharp clear division.

At least, she thought, Dickie was home.

Five

K atie was escorted home by her father. George had unexpectedly been at the bus stop when the last bus from town pulled into the lay-by. She had been as much startled by his presence as by the fact that Dickie was just passing the bus after having followed it all the way from town on his motorbike.

When she had refused to ride pillion again – 'Aren't you in enough trouble?' – he had told her to sit on the back seat of the bus. At every stop he too had stopped, waiting behind the bus for it to draw away again. She turned each time to watch him, and though he made no gesture of acknowledgement, she felt his gaze focused on her from under that dehumanizing helmet. It would have been scary, had she not known who her stalker was, but she could at will prise him out of his disguise, at will reach out to all she knew of him.

She had sat looking back at the headlight of the bike and remembered another time when the two of them together had stalked trouble.

They had been ten and twelve – she 'old enough to know better', he condemned as 'a disgrace' as the Philippses' old nannie had to be revived from what she called 'a replay of the pram incident'. The two of them had rushed from place to place among the shrubbery, calling to nannie to 'Come quickly. Come quickly!' She remembered herself and Dickie as hot, hysterical children, almost delirious as they crouched and ran beneath the laurels, the distressed questions and crashing progress of the old nurse following them. She had been more excited because Dickie held her hand so tightly and drew her along into his game, his world. She wondered if she had begun to really love him then, or whether it was before that.

The bus driver had been aware of the motorbike shadowing his vehicle, for when she had got up to alight he had asked, 'You going to be all right? Lonely spot this.' She had nodded, then seeing a figure emerge from the gloom near the hedge had added, 'Its all right, my dad's here to meet me.'

'I think he knows that too.' He had nodded in the direction of the motorcyclist as the machine roared past the bus and into the distance. She had not answered, just pleased her father had been too far away to hear the driver's comment.

'Your mum said you'd be on the last bus, so I thought I'd come and meet you.'

'I'll be all right, I do know the way!' She had tried to keep the irritation from her voice – she had desperately wanted a few more moments with Dickie.

'Aye, well, better safe than sorry. I never mind you know that.'

They crossed the road to the field path. 'Good film, was it?' he asked.

'Not very actually,' and from some corner she dug up the name of the film that they had paid to go in to see. '*Waterloo*.'

'So the company was better than the film then?' he asked.

'You could say that,' she replied carefully, then added a final-sounding 'yes', in case he was thinking of more gentle probing.

It seemed to her that her dad relaxed at this, as if satisfied she had enjoyed her evening.

Relaxed was the last way she felt. Alarmed, afraid, yet elated, was a better description, and as she and her father walked towards home, she thought the one thing she did not recall about the day was doing much in the way of actual office work.

She vividly remembered lunchtime and Dickie waiting for her. She had not recognized him until he spoke her name. He had stood half concealed in a doorway, his jacket revers pushed over, one inside the other like a down-and-out, as if he needed every ounce of warmth he could get over his chest.

She had been glad she was on her own, and not, as she might well have been, with Mary, the other office girl. Mary had gone to the dentist. He had pulled a hand from the front of his coat and reached out to her. His hand had been cold, hungry for her, clutching her warm fingers as if gripping a lifeline.

'But . . .' she had begun and then had got no further, aware of the curious glances of those passing by, secretaries, clerks, bosses from all the nearby offices.

He had been aware only of her, and his intensity as he smiled down at her had alarmed her.

'We could do with vehicle access this way.' Her dad's voice startled her.

'I suppose so,' she answered as she stepped through the gate he had opened for them.

'Folk go to the city now, more than to the old market town our main track leads on to. Life changes.'

'Yes,' she was able to agree to that wholeheartedly.

Dickie had told her that no one was sympathetic to his idea of leaving school, and when she had said she quite understood that, he had stopped trying to walk normally by her side and limped to a halt.

'I thought you were on my side.' He had sounded for a moment so like a child, she half expected him to add, 'It's not fair.'

'Its not a question of sides,' she told him, walking back to him, rounding him up with her disapproval. 'Its a question of what's right, what's best.'

'Best, who for? I know what's best for me, and I thought that meant what was best for you. What we both wanted.'

'Dickie?' His name came out like a puzzle. 'Dickie, the world doesn't always let us have what we want, when we want it – not the very minute.' Her father's words.

'Sometimes the world needs a push, then.'

It had been her turn to slow and stop, and his turn to hobble back, while the world, the office workers going off to lunch, and shoppers on the way to the market square, must part and circle them. 'If we push too hard we may lose everything.' There had been real fear in her heart. 'Everything.'

'What are you saying?' Though he suspected she was telling him the same thing her mother had when she had gone from the role of friend to farm employee with a clatter of pots and pans and a wielding of the broom.

He took her hand and stood stalwart by her side, ignoring

47

the growing flow of humanity they hindered. 'You can't change my mind, Katie, no matter what you say. I am not going back to school.'

She had become alarmed at his adamant refusal to listen to any idea of their having to be apart for yet more term times. She did not want to be held responsible for trouble in and between the families. 'It will only split *us* up, because we will begin to quarrel.'

'Never!' he had exclaimed and she had thought for a moment he was going to get down on his knees in the middle of the street – it would have been like him. She had taken him to the self-service restaurant in a big store, but they had reached no decisions, found no compromise.

'Look,' she had pleaded when she was already late returning for the afternoon's work, 'just go back home. We could meet in the village tonight, somewhere on the square near the telephone box, say.'

'I'll be outside your office when you finish, so we can talk some more,' he had insisted and she could not persuade him to do otherwise.

'But your ankle . . .'

'No,' he shrugged all thought of that aside. 'I'll wait,' he stated 'we'll have much more time together.'

She had given in at last and had telephoned her mother to say she would not he home until the last bus. He had crowded into the box with her. 'I'm going to the cinema,' she had said without planning the lie, but as she primly explained to him before she ran back to work, the last bus meant a visit to the cinema to her ma.

During the afternoon's work of taking dictation and typing she had wondered constantly how he was passing the time. She wondered with a sinking heart how they were ever going to manage to be together. There would be opposition on all sides. Her conclusion was that it would be far better if he did go back to school; when he left at eighteen he would legally be 'of age' thanks to the lowering of that age from twenty-one a few years before. Then they would have some clout, the two of them; then he could do as he liked, as she supposedly could now.

She had left the office to find him in the same place, but

he looked paler and as they set off his limp was much worse. She had wondered where they might go so he could rest and they could talk properly – and she could make him see sense.

'You can't walk around like that,' she had censured, 'you look terrible.'

'Thanks.' He grinned ruefully at her. 'I've been sitting in the Reference Library most of the afternoon, but it was worse when I got up again.'

'I expect you should have had it propped up,' she said shortly, then added, 'Look, the Savoy is just here. Why don't we go in, at least you can rest for a bit.'

She had later realized this had been the worst possible idea, for he led her to the back row, slipped his arm about her and leaned over her before she had more than glimpsed the screen. His lips, first tentative and tremulous, had become fierce, hot, astonishing. Rod Steiger and Christopher Plummer had fought old battles while all thoughts of being sensible and responsible were lost in their first real lovers' kisses. They had aroused in her passions that at another time, in another place, could have thrown every kind of caution to the wind.

She tried to raise the spectres of their families, her father, his stepfather, whispering what they might say and do – though beyond the fact that no one would be overjoyed she did not really know what the consequences might really be. She could imagine, *knew*, if she was honest, that the heir to the Philipps estates would be lined up for some-one from the county set, or some wealthy industrialist's daughter.

Between his growing thirst for her lips and his hand creeping down from her shoulder to beneath her arm, his fingers reaching the line of her bra, she had tried to tell him that this would not do, this could not be.

'I just want *us* to be happy,' he breathed in her ear, and when she had gone on trying to explain more forcibly, people had turned in their seats and shushed them.

In the end they had left the cinema and gone to sit on the seats circled around a fountain in the nearby Town Hall Square. The street lamps on the surrounding roads were softened by the trees which flanked the square's narrow lawns, rose beds and the walls of remembrance to the city's war dead.

When they had been able to talk without disturbing anyone, they had been silent, as if overwhelmed by the forces they had unleashed in each other. She glanced at Dickie, wondered what he was thinking.

'The facts are,' Dickie said at last, 'that I love you, always will, there will never be anyone else – and I'm not going away again.'

'The facts are,' Katie had taken up, trying to suppress the irreverent image of God reaching a forefinger out to Adam to give life, as a comparison for the charge of electricity which had flowed through her as Dickie touched the edge of her bra. 'The facts are that you are sixteen, I am eighteen, everyone is going to say we are much too young to know our own minds – you in particular,' she had added though she knew he would hate her to say it.

There had been a long pause, then he had said, 'You know my father committed suicide.'

It had felt like a threat: agree with me, or I might do something awful.

'Wasn't he in the war?' She pleaded the cause for the man she had never known. 'Wasn't that what made him?'

'I think my mother and stepfather know the full story, and I think it had something to do with Ian being my mother's first love.'

'If they talk of your family in my house, Mum always says that "justice was done in the end" and for once when she mentions the "big house" my dad grunts agreement, so . . .' She had shrugged, then demanded, 'So why are you mentioning it now?'

'Not sure. Not that I think I would ever commit suicide, but to be with you . . .' His laugh had wavered, died, and he went on, 'Bad luck's dogged the Philipps men for generations. My father dies in our lake, my grandfather dies in the Second World War, my great grandfather died from injuries received in the First World War. I've got to break the trend. I've got to take hold of my life, make it go the way I want, not be fed into some world mincing machine willy-nilly. If we're determined enough, Katie, nothing can stop us.'

She had suddenly felt quite enervated and leaned her head on his shoulder, consenting in an unspoken way, following his enthusiasms, as she always had. Then she had sat upright as an elderly tramp stood fidgeting before their bench as if a little put out that it was occupied.

'A pigeon pair!' he declared. 'G'on, mate, give 'er a big kiss.' He had chuntered a bit under his breath, then moved on to the next bench to set up his bed of coats and newspapers, chuckling and repeating his observation. 'G'on, mate, give 'er a big kiss.'

To Katie it seemed like the world already intruding, as she knew it would. 'I think the only way we can be together at all is if we keep how we feel a secret . . . for years . . . and years . . . two years at least until you're of age.' Her heart gave a sudden bound as she was convinced that he would meet someone else long before that time was over.

'My father, stepfather, has already guessed anyway,' he told her.

She was aghast. 'You mean, you and me?' she asked. 'But he doesn't *know*, he's only guessing. He can't know, can he? You haven't told him anything?'

'No.' His turn to shake his head.

'Then we must hide it and if they ask . . .' She had looked at him as if they were suddenly turning into different people, conspirators. 'We must tell lies if they ask direct like.' She felt it such an outrageous thing to say, to even contemplate. 'Is that awful?' she asked. She remembered her grandfather, who had been adept at sayings such as 'sins and lies sting the one they belong to sooner or later'.

Her mind had become a whirl of questions and worries and she heard herself lapsing more and more into old village phrases. 'Do it upset you that I should think such a thing?'

'Me, no, my education has been about learning not to blub or blab. Don't show your feelings and don't say what you really think.' His laugh had been ironic, almost bitter.

She stumbled on the footpath as she remembered the time he had first been sent away to school. He had cut off his hair with the scissors; everyone had said they did not understand him. She had been nine at the time – she had understood – but he had been taken to the barber's and tidied up and still had to go to school.

She was aware she must have made a cluck of reproach for the squashing of that rebellion, for walking by her side her dad asked her if she was all right. 'Not had much to say for yourself,' he commented, opening the last field gate before their back garden.

'Tired, I guess,' she said, suddenly ashamed of the way she had just trudged along in silence, lost in her own concerns. 'Thanks for meeting me, Dad, it can be a bit spooky sometimes.'

'So you've no problems, m'bonny Katie?' he asked.

She turned to him and smiled in the darkness at the use of his little girl name for her.

'Quite happy about this chap you've been out with tonight?'

'Oh yes, very,' she answered, her voice full of unguarded enthusiasm.

Six

'Julian!' Ian was startled to find his son sitting on one of the feed bins in the stables. 'What are you doing here?'

Julian was dressed in his jeans, after a week's wear broken in with scuffed patches on knees and well crusted with cement around the back where he had wiped his hands.

'I thought you'd gone to your grandpa's ages ago. I thought your mother said she had taken you?'

His son did not answer, pushed his hands under his thighs and swung his legs so his heels thudded back on the bin.

'Julian?'

The boy's scowl deepened and he did not look up.

'Your mother did take you.'

Julian nodded. 'I came back.'

'Hmm.' Ian swung his leg over a saddle on a stand, adding, 'You walked *all* the way back, that has to make it fairly serious.'

Julian tucked his chin in deeper.

'Grandpa has visitors,' he offered.

'Visitors,' Ian repeated and played for the laugh he could usually evoke. 'Building inspectors, then.'

Julian shook his head, keeping his chin down so as not to give in.

'A rival firm of builders?'

'No, *Dad*!' he exclaimed, trying not to grin, but adding, 'Lord Markham.'

'Ah! He of the shoot – quite soon, I believe.'

'I don't want to go in Dickie's place,' the boy asserted.

'No, of course not!' he exclaimed. His boy was too young – he tried to temper his indignation. He in turn had little sympathy for a 'sport' which needed beaters to crash and thrash around in the undergrowth to put the keeper-reared birds into the air. 'It's not been suggested, has it?'

'Sort of,' he frowned, looking to his father as if for enlightenment. 'It's just that Grandpa looks at me as if I'm an out-and-out failure if I don't want to do these things.'

'Oh! Julian!' The exclamation was heartfelt. He was at once annoyed, no, damn it, he was angry, appalled to think his son might be toiling along the same road of self-doubt and anguish Bess had done all her childhood, all her adolescence (all her married life too if he did not intervene from time to time), as she tried to keep Edgar Bennett's approval. 'Your grandfather really shouldn't make you feel like this.'

'It isn't him though, is it?' Julian tried to explain. 'It's me, I don't like the things he thinks I ought to. I know I'm never going to be like Dickie.'

It was on his tongue to say that at least they had that to be thankful for. 'We are all entitled to be different. I don't want to shoot, or hunt, I like to be a bit more *constructive* in my life.'

'Yes' – the word cheered the boy – 'but I did cut and run. I shouldn't have done that, Grandpa will wonder where I am.'

'I'll drive you back. Knowing m'lord's liking for a whisky in the middle of the morning, they probably won't have missed you.'

Julian laughed at the comic 'm'lord'. He took his father's hand, a gesture becoming rarer as the boy grew, without appearing to notice that Ian treasured the moment – the young hand gripping his so unself-consciously.

'You know the sooner you tell your grandpa that you never ever want to shoot birds or hunt animals, the better,' he said as he drove. 'It'll save a lot of misunderstandings.'

Glancing at the boy, he saw him pull down the corners of his mouth.

'Want me to say it?'

'No, he'll cross-question me anyway.'

It was Ian's turn to grin: the boy had the measure of the grandparent. 'Well, if you need an ally any time . . .' he said.

Lord Markham's car passed them in the farm drive – the men lifted hands; Julian slid down in his seat. When they arrived at the farm Edgar was still outside. The word that came to Ian's mind as he saw the old man was 'gloating'. Coming to greet them, he even rubbed his hands together with the satisfaction of one who has pulled off a good deal, and instead of questioning Julian's second appearance at the farm in one morning, brought once by his mother and once by his father, merely commented, 'Forget something, did you?'

'More a matter of standing back to see where he was,' Ian answered.

'Ah! Good, excellent, what we should all do from time to time.' Edgar dropped his hand on the boy's shoulder with approval, then nodded at Ian, who immediately felt dismissed. He also felt uneasy, as if he had missed some vital piece of information in this scenario, like coming from a meaningful dream and forgetting it on the instant of waking.

He drove home, realizing what he dreaded was that Edgar's smugness came from some interference to do with the step-brothers, some connivance that would cause trouble between himself and Bess. Whatever it was, the old man was not prepared to reveal anything to his son-in-law. 'Or not yet,' he said aloud, banging the steering wheel with the flat of his hands.

He found Bess in the office, her hand on the telephone receiver as if in the middle of contacting people. The diary of Pony Club events, which were gathering momentum for the twenty-fifth anniversary of the Queen's accession to the throne in '77, open on the desk.

'Where's Dickie?' he asked.

'Still in bed.' She hesitated, then added, 'I've rung Dr Michael to come and have a look at his ankle. It's terribly swollen.'

'Why doesn't that surprise me?' He went on to tell her of finding Julian, of the boy's dilemma and taking him back to the farm. He also reported Edgar's apparent satisfaction with life.

'He telephoned,' she said, lifting her hand from the receiver as if not wishing to be accused of complicity.

'Your father?'

'Just now.'

'While I was driving back, then?' She nodded.

He waited, saw her jaw slide to one side, watched her bite her lip. He wondered if it was her tongue she would prefer to bite, but there was obviously something that had to be told, something her father had proposed – or worse, *done*.

'Pa's been talking to Lord Markham . . .' she began.

'Julian does not want to shoot, *ever*, your father is not replacing one of our sons with another just to keep in good face with his county friends.'

'No.' She closed the appointment book and leaned her weight on it. 'It has nothing to do with Julian.'

He saw her struggle to find the right way to tell him what had passed between the aristocracy and her father. He despised himself for it, but not for the first time he felt a real pang of jealousy at the thought and attention she gave to her father's every idea, every word. He found he was clenching his teeth, preparing to keep control. 'Dickie has shown no remorse for what he's done,' he reminded her, 'never even apologized as far as *I* know, so I hope it's nothing to do with *him* going.'

'It's nothing to do with shooting, hunting or anything like that, it's about Dickie's education.'

'Don't tell me your father and Lord Markham are arranging our son's education now! Why didn't your father say something to me while I was there? Markham had only just left.'

'It's a bit complex, I suppose.'

'Though obviously not too complex to tell you on the telephone.' He tossed up his head and made to walk out of the office. 'Why bother to tell me at all?'

'You are Dickie's stepfather and legal guardian.'

'You'd never know, the way your father acts . . .'

Then they were distracted by the sound of a high-powered car coming up the drive, skidding to a halt in a shower of gravel, some of which hit the window.

'Who the hell . . . ?' Ian began. 'Another of your father's surprises?'

'No, of course not,' she snapped. 'I've no idea who it is.'

'Or even what it is?' Ian said, looking out of the window. 'Male or female.'

Bess came to his side and looked out at a figure clad in what looked like a jumble-sale assortment of clothes.

'King or queen of punk,' Ian said. 'It's coming to the door.'

For a moment the tensions between them lessened as they grimaced at each other, and both went to the front door, which they opened to an icon of anti-establishment seventies. A girl

56

dressed, it seemed, in everyone's clothes but her own. Her jacket, beige with an incongruous dark-blue velvet collar, looked as if it had been inexpertly laundered and never pressed back into shape, a crumpled man's white shirt with a tie at half mast on a level with a red badge bearing the message 'I don't care'.

Ian noted her jeans, although decoratively patched with red, were new, as were her boots and her red sports car.

Bess was fascinated by the girl's head and hair. The blonde hair was shaved off except for two upswept wings above her ears, like horns, the ends dyed bright red. She had to stop herself exclaiming, 'Oh! What a shame!' She also had a feeling of having seen the face before.

'Oh, hi! I'm Elizabeth Forsythe-Sutherland, I've come to see Dickie. Are you . . . ?'

'His parents, yes,' Ian supplied. 'Come in. He's still in bed.'

'Lazy blighter!' she exclaimed, looking up the stairs. 'Which room is it? I'll roust him out.'

'I've never heard him mention your name,' Ian said, 'Elizabeth . . .'

Bess suddenly remembered that she knew this girl's mother – the face, the petite features and figure were so alike, but in every other way . . . She wondered how the perfectly coiffured mother she remembered from the mid-fifties, with the beehive hairstyle, twin-set-and-pearls taste in clothes, coped with this offspring.

'Call me Lizzie, everyone does. My mother's a Markham, I understand Dickie and I'll be going to the same school next term.' She paused and laughed. 'Don't know what else to do with us, do you?' She started up the stairs. 'Which room did you say?'

'Third on the left,' Ian supplied, turned on his heel and went back into the office.

Bess followed him as Lizzie bounded up the stairs. 'Why did you tell her?'

Ian closed the door. 'Why? Perhaps because I am helping your father.'

'What d'you mean?'

'Lord Markham's granddaughter, going to the same school as Dickie. God! Yes!' he exclaimed. 'Just what the doctor ordered. Just what dear Pa wants. Marriage to a Lord's grand-daughter, ideal –' his tone fell from mock humour to flat heavy sarcasm – 'she might just as well go straight to his bedroom.'

'I don't know why she is here, or what's been said to her. All I know is her grandfather told Pa about this special school which has such marvellous results, and he told me.'

'But not me.'

'I suppose he thought we could discuss it.'

'It seems it's all arranged without discussion. Like the motorbike.'

'This isn't how it was meant to be. It was just a suggestion, that's all. They've had problems with this Lizzie and they've found a special college which takes this kind of youngster – apparently they have advanced liberal teaching methods.' She wanted to add, 'You know, like digging your heels into a horse trying to run away with you so it wonders what's happening and stops to think' – but Ian would not appreciate the analogy, particularly not if he knew it was how Lord Markham had explained the methods of Banford College to her father. 'Anyway,' she ended, 'we'll have to see what Dickie thinks.'

'Dickie's been perfectly content until Katie Wright came back into his life, and he began to think he was all grown-up.'

'You are quite, quite, wrong! I've told you Katie is going out with someone from her office, but *you* don't seem to want to listen to me.'

'Or you to me, and the evidence of my eyes, and of his housemaster.'

'His housemaster?' she queried, suddenly still.

'Yes, because I am his stepfather and legal guardian I spoke to his housemaster when this nonsense first began.'

'You didn't say.'

'He assured me that Dickie gives every indication that he is happy. He is involved in rugger and cricket, achieving excellent results. They have him down for a certain place at Oxford.'

'He told Pa he would have to be taken back in chains.'

'So be it if necessary,' Ian answered, 'but when he sees we are not falling for his stupidity I think he'll go back willingly enough.' He did not add that he thought it was something much stronger than the proverbial chains that was binding him to the idea of staying at home.

'I think I know my son better than—' she began but was interrupted by a shout of pain from upstairs. 'What's she doing to him?'

'Does he know this girl?' Ian asked.

'Not to my knowledge – the family live in Perthshire,' she answered as they both reached the curve halfway up the stairs. 'I knew her mother before she was married and moved away.' At the bedroom door, Bess knocked but did not pause before entering.

Lizzie was sitting on the end of the bed cross-legged. Dickie was sitting bolt upright, the bedclothes drawn up to his chin.

'She sat on my ankle,' he accused.

'Many apols,' Lizzie said and, looking at the two in the doorway, asked, 'Did you think I was raping him?'

Bess felt her mouth drop open, but Ian immediately retorted, 'Well, he does have the air of a frightened virgin.'

Dickie lowered the sheets to his knees.

Bess swallowed and asked, 'Would you both like some coffee?'

Dickie frowned, looked bemused. 'You're not a new kind of doctor or nurse, are you?' he asked Lizzie.

'No!' she exclaimed. 'I'm you're new school friend.'

He laughed uncertainly. 'You're not from any school I've ever been to . . .' He eyed the strange cross-legged thing on the end of his bed, Lizzie beamed at him, and he added, 'Unfortunately.'

'Well, we're going to be,' she enthused. 'Didn't you know?'

'New school!' Dickie exclaimed. 'I'm not going to a new school, in fact I'm not going to any school again.'

'That's just what I said!' Lizzie exclaimed delightedly and launched into a description of the differences of Banford College, ending, 'It supposedly treats its pupils like grown-ups, with trips to London shows as rewards for effort and good behaviour, generally more carrot than stick. I'm thinking about it because it means my grandfather will take me in for the rest of my schooling, so instead of going home to Perthshire, I shall just come here.'

59

'I'll go and make coffee for us all,' Bess said in a pause.

'I'll help,' Ian offered, thinking the girl was doing a better job than anyone else might in persuading his stepson that further education was the inevitable future for him.

In the kitchen Bess stacked crockery on a tray and wondered about Lizzie's mother, a woman to whom keeping up appearances was a way of life. What had happened to this offspring, and that household?

Ian noted the brooding frown of concentration as she watched over the kettle, waiting to pull the whistle from the spout as soon as it sounded.

'Don't know whether she's what you'd call a breath of fresh air, or an icy draught,' he said, trying to lighten the moment.

'You must at least now believe that Dickie knows nothing about this girl or this college,' she said.

'Yes, I do believe that,' he agreed, slipping back into the ruts of the dispute. 'What I don't understand is why you and your father think he is likely to want to attend a *new* college, when all the evidence is that he has been perfectly happy where he is, and all *he* wants to do is stay at home.'

She did not answer, just getting on with making coffee. When it was done, he picked up the tray and followed her back upstairs. They heard laughter coming from the bedroom. He wondered what Julian would make of this aristocratic punk who had landed in their midst with all the unexpected suddenness and novelty of the proverbial snow in harvest time. At least, he thought, Julian still seems to appreciate my humour; I can make *him* laugh.

He carried the tray to the bedside table and handed coffee to a jubilant Lizzie. 'I'm going to take Dickie to see Banford,' she said, 'then you two can give it the once-over if he likes the look of the place.'

Seven

George leaned back in his chair, replete with Colleen's steak-and-kidney pudding, mashed potatoes, the last of the peas from the garden, and bright-yellow custard made with eggs from the farm. He regarded his womenfolk and informed them both, 'Saw young Dickie Philipps today in a red sports car, with that granddaughter of Lord Markham's. Looked as if they were having a right old time.'

He accepted the cup of tea Colleen handed him.

'Don't know if they'd get wherever they were going,' he elaborated, 'taking the bends on two wheels, more or less. Dread to think what it costs to insure her car.'

Katie felt as if the world had stopped. Her world had frozen, come to an end, but hadn't she known all the time it was too good to be really true? Hadn't she agonized time and time again over her dad meeting the bus, preventing Dickie arranging their next meeting? Now her dad sat there, giving her more bad news, and grinning all over his face.

She had found comfort in the fact that her mum had said Dickie was being kept in bed until his ankle improved. Now her black-leathered suitor had swapped his motorbike for a red sports car – had met someone else, as she had feared he would – but not this soon.

Every waking moment she had pondered all he had said, weighing every word, and she had come to think she believed every one. She had dared to dream of a future together, of being not the daughter of a friend of the lady of the Hall but the wife of the heir.

How ludicrous, she thought, and shook her head. Looking up, she found her mother watching her as she stooped to put William's meal into the Aga to await his return from the cricket match. She was glad her brother was not there: he would have wanted every detail, about the car mostly of course; worse than an old washerwoman he was, pumping every situation dry.

'Tea?' her mother asked. She shook her head – from feeling merely full she now felt sick.

'So that's what's making Edgar Bennett look like the cat that's got the cream,' Colleen declared, stacking the dirty plates near the sink. 'I knew there was something.' She nodded to herself, then to Katie.

'What d'you mean?' Katie asked.

'W . . . ell, it's obvious. There's been all this trouble about that boy riding that motorbike without L-plates—'

'They're having a barrister, did you know,' her father put in, 'a barrister!'

'. . . then not wanting to go back to school. Now your dad sees him in a car with Lord Markham's granddaughter, and she's being sent to some private *mixed* college to finish her education, because no one can do anything with her. Stands to common sense, 'e's going to go there as well. Suit Mr Bennett very well, will that: money marrying money.'

'Marrying!' Katie exclaimed. 'One minute they're going to the same college, and you're only guessing about that, then they're marrying!'

'It's how things happen though. You go out with a young man from your office; Dickie gets involved with his own kind.' She turned and began to run water into the sink.

Katie threw a mental lifebelt towards the thought that if you wanted a thing badly enough you could make it happen. Dickie had said that. 'No, he doesn't want to go off to another college,' she said and her face flamed as she realized she was in danger of revealing more than she should know. 'You said he wanted to stay at home,' she added.

'Sounds like there'd be other attractions than reading and writing at this new place,' her dad chuckled, head nearly on chest, drowsy after a day in the open and a good meal, a sudden belch lifting his chin.

'Obvious we're not his kind.' She rose so quickly she had to stop her chair toppling over, more angry with the remark about this co-ed school than the burp.

'Do we want to be?' George was wide awake again now

and looking hard at his daughter. 'Something wrong?' he asked.

'You're going to sleep at the table,' she said.

'Isn't that done in polite society?' he asked.

'She'll never bring that boyfriend home to see us at this rate,' Colleen turned from the steaming sink to query, 'will you, love?'

'She'll bring him home when she's good and ready,' her dad said complacently.

Katie felt she must get out of the house, though the routine was that she dried the crockery for her mother. 'I think I'll walk down to the village, meet our William.'

'They could still be playing,' George said, looking wistful.

'You'll see him play Saturday, last match of the season, over at Packman,' Colleen told him, then turning, took the tea towel from Katie's hands. 'Go on, go and enjoy the evening, I'll dry up – stuck in an office all day. Pity your fellow can't come out and enjoy a bit of country air.'

Katie bit on her lower lip. It was all so easy: they had just jumped to conclusions about her dating Ken North, as if she ever would.

She left the two together, so cosy, so close, no worries for them about their future. She doubted there ever had been: her parents had always known each other, had married young, and she had appeared on the scene soon after, followed by William three years later.

She left the roadway and took the more direct footpaths, striding out, even running at times. She had no idea why she felt in such a hurry, except to put distance between home and the misunderstandings she was allowing to become outright lies by keeping silent – and for what? Perhaps she was running to try to forget the idea of Dickie in a red sports car, Dickie with another girl – having a good time.

She reached the cricket field too soon, still not ready for company, but her attention was caught by a sudden roar of raised voices, a mixture of howls of disappointment and triumphant hurrahs. She was just in time to see William walking back to the pavilion, out, but waving his bat to some enthusiastic applause. She glanced at the scoreboard. The match apparently still hung in the balance, though William had scored twenty-eight. The home side wanted seven with one wicket to fall.

She watched him reach the pavilion and was only then aware of the red sports car parked with several others next to the white wooden building. It was a coincidence of course, there must be lots of red sports cars in the area – belonged to one of the opposing team probably – but she scanned the small crowd of people standing, sitting and sprawling around the boundary. Someone waved at her from the far side. She recognized Joyce Bentum, an old classmate. Joyce Green now, for at eighteen she was married with a child, and her husband, Dave, would be playing for Counthorpe. She walked over to Joyce and realized Dave was going into bat in place of her brother.

'Seen what's in the pavilion?' Joyce greeted her with a grin, hooking a length of lank blondish hair behind one ear.

'No, what?'

Joyce laughed. 'Enough to put everyone off their tea, it was. Glad she didn't serve me. She must be a punk rocker or something: shaved head, clothes from the jumble sale, and –' she paused to throw a thumb back towards the cars – 'that's her car.'

'Who is she?' Katie asked though she was half afraid she might know the answer.

'She's only 'ere 'cos her own mother can't do anything with her. I said to my Dave we don't want the likes of her round here giving the village a bad name.' Joyce broke off as her husband tapped his bat into the crease ready to take his first ball. He missed by a mile, but she added loyally, 'Not got his eye in yet, and he is a bowler.'

Katie dutifully peeped into the pram at the tiny baby.

'Didn't plan to have one this soon,' Joyce said with a shrug. 'Here's your William coming, and that punk girl's with him.'

'What!' Katie straightened from the pram and could see William edging away from a figure that in the distance looked like a second boy dressed in his big brother's clothes. William reached them at a trot.

'See my innings, sis?' he asked.

'No, just saw you coming out, but you got a good clap. Who's the ...' She nodded back towards the girl, who she now realized had a tray and was collecting stray cups and saucers, plates and glasses for the ladies doing the washing-up in the pavilion.

'She's with Dickie Philipps,' he said as if she would not have been tolerated in the pavilion had she arrived with anyone else, and he added scornfully, 'laughing like they've got a secret every time they look at each other.'

His first words pierced Katie like a physical pain, his summing up twisted the knife. She had hurried here; now all she wanted to do was run back home.

'She's supposed to be helping, but she's just showing off,' he added. 'She's punk – or something, rebelling against fashion and society – that's what she's been telling everyone in the pavilion.'

'Bet that went down well,' Joyce commented dryly as the girl approached.

'Gloria West said she could afford to rebel with all that money behind her, no danger.'

Joyce made a low grunt of agreement with the sentiment of the second-generation village shopkeeper, who had just gone self-service at considerable expense and was not pros-pering even so. She also nodded a warning as the girl approached them.

'Any cups or glasses?' she asked.

'No.' Joyce and William offered together, flatly and bluntly, while Joyce added a tut at her hairstyle, or lack of hair.

'You just don't understand, do you?' The girl's accent was so upper-class Katie felt she might just as well have added, 'you hicks. You hicks just don't understand.'

Joyce looked her up and down and then at the tray of crockery she was holding. 'I don't know what you think you're doing here, or what you think you're proving.' She began rocking the pram with some force as her baby murmured.

Katie was amazed to see colour rise in the girl's face, and glimpsed a terrible vulnerability in her eyes, gone in a moment. It was certainly not seen by Joyce, who gestured the girl away at the sound of bat on ball, a loud resounding crack, as her Dave skied the ball. She swam the girl out of the way with a flailing arm, and William leapt to his feet. They held their breath as an outfielder on the far boundary tried to position himself under the ball, hands cupped skywards.

'Out!' The cry echoed around the ground.

'There!' Joyce turned to exclaim at the stranger as if it was her fault. 'We've lost now!'

The girl turned away – tail between her legs was the expression that came to Katie's mind, though she felt more threatened by this girl now she had seen her close to, seen she was vulnerable. Dickie was capable of very unwise gestures if he thought it would make someone pleased or happy. She remembered his stepfather saying that Dickie would promise the moon, and give it, if he could net it up out of a puddle. She wondered if he did know what was real, and what was just a reflection.

She agonized silently, while William bewailed the loss of the match, then left to go and drown his sorrows with the rest of the team with a Coke in the yard of the local pub. In the pram the baby stirred again, began to work up to a cry.

Joyce sniffed and rocked. 'Better take her home, soon want a feed.' She nodded at the girl's back. 'Suppose she'd breast-feed her baby in public.'

Katie laughed in spite of herself. 'Don't suppose she'll be around long enough for us to find out.'

'Oh, I don't know.' In the act of bearing her weight down on the pram handle to turn it homewards, Joyce nodded towards the pavilion.

Dickie had come down the steps and was taking the loaded tray from the girl.

'Coming?' Joyce asked. By the time they had pushed the pram half way to the field gate, Dickie and the girl had climbed into the sports car and zoomed noisily off.

'Parasites,' Joyce commented. 'Come back and have a cup of tea with me, you can make it while I feed and change little 'un.'

'OK.'

'You can see how it's done,' Joyce said.

'What d'you mean?'

'Well, babies and that, for when you have one.'

'Not very likely, the way things are going.'

'Heard you were going out with someone where you work.'

* * *

66

It was dusk before she began her walk home. She supposed her brother, like Dave, would have arrived home ages ago. The village was quiet – just the odd car – and once she climbed the stile on to the field footpath the only noise was the sound of her own footsteps. The air held the moistness of falling dew and the odour of the first leaves rotting under the hedgerows. It was the kind of time one walked slowly, mulled over events – the time to solve the problems of the world, her dad said. 'But not mine,' she whispered, unable to see any solution for herself. Caught out, game over, that's me, she thought.

The sudden flapping clatter of a wood pigeon disturbed from its roost in an ash tree set her heart beating, then before her irritation with this minor alarm had settled, her heart thumped again as she heard a man calling, shouting from a distance.

There was the sound of someone coming fast – after her? Then she realized it was her name that was being called, and with a sense of disbelief she recognized Dickie. It seemed too big a leap in too short a time, from sports car to field foot-path, from Lord Markham's granddaughter to Katie Wright.

She was not sure whether the colour flooding into her cheeks was anger or sheer joy. She both wished him there, and a million miles away at the same time, and kicked child-ishly at a tuft of grass. She noted that he ran with a kind of stiff-legged gait, keeping some of the weight off his injured ankle.

'What do you want?' she asked as he came panting up to her.

He stopped short, for a moment, then laughed. 'You're joking, aren't you? You know very well what I want.' His voice dropped suggestively and he reached forward as if to take her hand, but she stepped back, shrugged him off.

'No, not me,' she said, shaking her head at him. 'I'm not the joker, I think that's you.'

'I don't know what you mean.' His hands dropped to his sides and he leaned forward a little as if to see her face more clearly in the fading light.

'Where's your punk friend?' she asked. 'The girl from your set, the granddaughter of Lord Markham. I hear you're both going to the same college, that'll be cosy for you both, and won't your grandfather be pleased!'

Once she had started she could not stop, and she was appalled to find the tears were running down her cheeks. 'After all you said!' she exclaimed. '"I'm not going back to college. I'm staying here. Anything's possible if you want it enough."' She could hear the echo of her own ranting ringing in her ears, hated the coarse, rude, sound of it, finished with a sob and stepped back, stumbling towards the thorn hedge.

He caught her arm, saved her. 'Have you finished?' he asked quietly.

'Seems we've both finished,' she said, shaking herself free. 'Finished, finito, The End.'

'Katie,' he tried to take her hands again and she tried to pull away, but this time he would not let her. 'Katie, just listen to me.' He held on as she again tried to pull away. 'Please. You have got it wrong you know. Listen.' He bent over her and said softly, 'Listen, There's only one uncertainty in my life.'

'You're lucky then,' she snapped.

'It's my court case on Monday. I'm not quite sure what will happen. I'm hoping for just a fine, and if that's so, everything, our future, everything, will be fine – wonderful.'

'I don't know what you're talking about.'

'No, because you only know one quarter of what's happened. Yes, I have said I'll go to this Banford College place and, yes, Liz is being sent there as well.'

'Nice for you both.'

'She drove me over to look at the place, and my folks are going next week.'

'All arranged then.'

'Look –' he took her firmly by the shoulders and for a moment she thought he was going to shake her – 'will you stop behaving like some stupid prejudiced erk? I'm trying to tell you this solves all our problems. This place is only in Northamptonshire. When I'm back on my motorbike I could be home in a couple of hours – well, not home, but to see you. We could meet regularly, no one need know. Don't you see, I can please everyone. I can finish my education and yet we need not be parted for whole terms at a time. I'll do my two years there, then I'll be home on the estate for good and everyone will be happy.'

She felt he was right to call her an erk, that was just how she had been behaving, but she still shook her head at him. 'You know no one is ever going to be happy about the two of us.'

'They'll get used to the idea sooner or later.' His good humour, his persuasiveness, was irresistible. She went on shaking her head but at the same time she was laughing and allowing herself to be hugged, jumped and joggled about, as if they were still children. 'I'll have you as mistress of the old estates, and wife to the jolly old squire – that's me of course – before they know what's happened.'

'Even though I am an erk?'

'Perhaps because you are one.' He bent to put his cheek next to hers and kissed down into her neck, making her bend over at the warmth of his lips, and his breath whispering beneath her collar. 'And because you're my very own particular erk.'

'You make me feel a bit ashamed, I thought . . .' she remembered her jealousy, 'that girl at the cricket field?'

'Liz? I mustn't forget she's coming back to pick me up, running me home.'

'So she knows you're here, now?' Try as she might she could not prevent the dying fall at the end of her question.

'Sure,' he said with breezy abruptness.

So this was not a secret, not, as he said, one they must keep. This punk Liz girl knew. 'What will prevent her telling everyone you're seeing me, and if she's at this same college, she'll know when you're there and when you're not, won't she? She'll be able to tell anyone who asks.'

'But she won't,' he said with triumphant certainty.

'I don't know how you can be so sure. You can't be,' she concluded and pulled away, stepped in front of him, challenging. 'This may be just one of your games to you, Dickie. I thought it was serious.'

'No, it's deadly serious. Never doubt me, Katie, never.'

His utter conviction made her heart hammer.

'What's the matter?' he asked gently. 'What's made you feel like this, doubt everything, after all we said?'

'Nothing,' she said, 'nothing's the matter.'

'You really don't need to worry that poor old Liz will ever say anything. She's going to be my official alibi while we're at the college. We took ages coming back from Banford because we stopped and both unburdened our troubles.' He lapsed into what could only be described as a sympathetic silence for 'poor old Liz'.

'Poor?' Katie heard herself repeat, gauging the car, the expensive trousers and boots below the tat, even though she knew this was not Dickie's meaning.

'She's a poor, troubled, girl.'

'What exactly is her trouble, then? If she is sharing our secret I think I should know hers, and what makes you so sure you – we – can rely on her, and for what I'm not sure.'

'For alibis,' he said, 'if this college thing comes off, and I hope it does, she'll give me alibis for when I come to see you. She'll say I'm with her, or her friends, or wherever. She has lots of places she can go.'

'But why should she? Why should she risk getting herself into trouble?'

'Perhaps,' he said after a moment's thought, 'she feels two wrongs will make a right.'

She began to protest again.

'If I tell you her story, you'll understand.' He pulled Katie close under his arm. 'Liz has been in all kinds of trouble. She got herself pregnant by someone quite unsuitable.'

The words 'pregnant' and 'unsuitable' tossed about in Katie's brain, but it was 'Pregnant!' that came out of her lips. She felt incredulous: to think that a girl not just from that stratum of society, but looking as she did, could ever get herself compromised in such a way. She wondered who the 'unsuitable' chap was: the gardener, the butcher's boy, son of an employee?

'So when is the baby due, she doesn't look – and how can she go to college.' She stopped herself as the truth dawned. 'They've made her have an abortion, haven't they?'

She felt him nod.

'Was he a punk rocker too?' she asked.

'Liz has only just gone punk,' he said, 'since the op. It's a kind of rebellion, I expect.'

'So she wanted to keep the baby?'

He shrugged. 'She feels she's done something terribly wrong now. She writes poetry to . . .'

'. . . the baby? Oh dear, that's terrible.' Katie remembered Joyce's crack about breast-feeding and, now she knew the truth, guessed Liz would have been pleased to be able to do just that. Joyce and Dave were having a real financial struggle, but better than a lifelong moral battle. 'But if she was forced.'

'She thinks she should have run away.'

'Easier said than done,' Katie said, determined that she would never get herself in such a position. What on earth would her dad say for a start?

Eight

'I won't be made to come to this college, will I?' Julian asked for the umpteenth time, and was ignored. 'Not ever, I mean, not even when I'm older?' He banged the side of the car with the side of his fist.

Ian cleared his throat meaningfully, but drove on in silence.

'So anyway, why do I have to come today?' he persisted.

'Because,' Bess told him with weary patience, 'there's really no one around to keep an eye open for you.'

'I could have been at Grandpa's doing my wall.'

'That's the point, you know Grandpa's—'

'Shooting,' Julian provided, 'and Dickie, I know.'

'So there's no one there if you had a mishap.'

'I don't have mishaps when I'm just using a trowel, and *anyway* I could always have gone to Colleen.'

Ian tutted, this needlessly repeated and emphasized word, 'anyway', had recently slipped into Julian's speech pattern and was beginning to irritate.

Bess noted that, like Dickie, her younger son had dropped the 'Aunt': no longer were they Auntie Colleen and Auntie Bess to the children. She gazed out of the car window at the rolling Northamptonshire countryside: herds of black and white Freisans; some fields ploughed, some golden stubble, long and even 'not like a good old close shave'. Her pa had made that comment the first year he had used a combine harvester. Sign of the times too, she supposed, Julian dropping the 'Aunt', these children thinking of themselves as grown-ups, equals.

'Anyway,' Julian began again, 'why is he suddenly let off everything?'

Ian maintained a stony silence.

'We – I at least – think he's made reparation,' Bess told

72

him, not elaborating on Dickie's profound apology for everything after their visit to the barrister about his impending court appearance, and the way he had insisted he took his mother for lunch in the restaurant of the most prestigious shop in town, and buying Ian a green silk tie.

'Never noticed,' Julian said, 'and I still don't see why I had to come!'

'Julian, for goodness' sake, it's not going to be more than a few hours,' she said, then braced herself as Ian braked sharply.

'We're here!' he announced with great surprise, coming to a skidding halt on the 'B' road seemingly in the middle of nowhere. He swung the car hastily right into a drive. Jerked to the side of the car, Bess just had time to register that 'Banford College' was announced on large wooden signs, gold lettering on dark maroon background, either side of the large brick gateposts. She saw that the ornate wrought-iron gates were pushed right back, and, she thought, looked as if they were never closed.

'This is not far at all,' Ian said as if in condemnation, and appeared to be attempting to read the trip meter.

'Has Dickie got to be sent further away than this?' Julian asked.

'No, of course not,' Bess replied, 'just somewhere he'll be happy to complete his education.'

'Away from home?' Julian persisted. 'Anyway there's colleges, all sorts, in Leicester, he could go on the bus every day. Colleen's Katie goes every day to work in an office.'

Neither answered, though Ian itched to say he thought the boy had unwittingly hit all kinds of nails on the head. This college was within easy motorcycling distance of home, less than a couple of hours, an hour and a half on a fast bike. He was going to be asking some very searching questions about the supervision of leisure time at this college.

There were other expensive cars in the car park at the rear: Jaguars like their own, an expensive sports car or two, Bentleys, a Rolls. A lot of out-of-control children from wealthy homes, Ian reflected.

The grounds were pleasant, sloping down from a terrace – to the left were hard tennis courts and, beyond, an expanse of fields showing the effect of the long hot summer, though there were pitches that had obviously been kept watered, probably from the river, Ian surmised.

He looked up at the house, mansion really, well-proportioned Victorian Gothic. He turned to see Julian making a similar appraisal and looking as if his grievances at the enforced trip might be a touch mollified.

There was an atmosphere of calm and a smell of beeswax in the entrance hall, where floors and panelling glowed. Elbow grease, Bess thought. From a door marked 'Reception' came a smart, navy-suited, woman with grey hair waving most attractively up from a face which spoke of an outdoor, healthy lifestyle. 'The perfect antidote to misgivings' was Ian's summing up of Olga Hardy, receptionist and wife of the headmaster, as they shook hands and were then invited to 'wander around' if they wished until her husband was free, which would be about fifteen minutes.

'Anywhere?' Ian queried, looking towards the staircase.

'Please,' she said. 'We have nothing out of bounds here.' She was aware of Ian's sharp glance, and added, 'Our students behave like responsible adults and are treated so.'

'And if they don't?' he asked.

'The headmaster will answer all your questions,' she answered, smiling. 'Just be careful if you get as far as our swimming pool area, there is some retiling being done.'

Smug bitch, he thought.

'Could I wait outside?' Julian asked.

'You won't find too many people here at the moment,' Mrs Hardy told him, 'not until term starts.'

'If you get bored, come and find us,' Bess told him.

'I won't be,' he said patting his pocket. 'I might draw something.'

'Julian is interested in architecture,' Ian explained, making amends for his unworthy judgment of the woman.

'Oh! then I must show you the way to our folly.' Enthused with the idea, she threw down the notepad she was holding and, putting her arm around Julian's shoulder, took him back out into the sunlight to point out the path to take. 'We're very lucky here – we not only have a famous former pupil who is an international award-winning architect, but one of our masters is also an A.R.I.B.A.'

'I want to do building,' he volunteered, 'you know, laying bricks.'

'Like Winston Churchill then,' she answered as she pointed him towards a tower springing from the middle of an expansive mass of oak and ash trees. 'The trees,' she told him, 'were planted a hundred and ten years ago when the folly was built.' She turned him round to look back at the school, his parents on the top step. 'Look for the weathercock on the top of the old stables when you come back, it's a good landmark, no fear of you getting lost.'

'Thanks.' He walked on towards the spinney and wondered about coming to a school like this. He liked the feeling of walking through these spaced stately trees, of knowing he approached a folly. He often dreamed of buildings, of wonderful palaces with fantastic gardens, and when he woke could recall many rooms and pathways, much as if the places were in his memory rather than his dreams. It was one of the reasons he was so sure what he wanted to do with his life, even his sleeping self knew.

The folly came into view as the path twisted away into more trees to the left, but ahead in a large clear circle of well-mown lawn was a tall and totally noble stone tower. He stared and wondered at the castellated solitary fort. It was strange, for though it seemed complete as it was, at the same time he felt it was part of something bigger. With a frisson of excitement he knew it was like his dreams, and though this tower was real, in one's mind it could be part of many things: a castle; a great cathedral; of Camelot even.

At the thought, he scrabbled feverishly in his pocket, pulled out his pad and pencil.

He drew the outline, did careful foreshortening, then walked closer to appreciate how the mason had cut, fashioned, and laid his stones. He walked slowly around the mown area of grass, noting slit windows winding their way up and around the tower, suggesting they lit an inner stairway. He came to a door, stout and studded, and lifted his hand to grasp the iron ring.

'It's locked,' a voice said. 'I've already tried.'

For a moment he could not see who spoke, then in the deep shade he saw someone sitting on the grass, a coat flung down

75

nearby. He felt he must go over to speak, though really he wanted to explore and make a drawing he could study at home.

'So much for being allowed to wander where you like, eh!' the girl said, then asked, 'What are you doing here? You're a bit young for this school, unless you're a real special case.'

'No, I'm not,' he said. 'My parents are here about my elder brother.'

He strolled closer, taking in the pale crumpled jacket thrown on the grass, the large red button on the lapel – 'I Don't Care', but most of all it was her bald pate, the blonde wings of hair, that made him say, 'I know who you are. You brought Dickie to see this place last week, didn't you?'

'Dickie Philipps?' She sat up straighter. 'Yes. Are you his stepbrother?' She appraised him afresh as he nodded. 'He told me about you.'

He waited to hear what, but she went on, 'I've come back to have another look round. Sit down if you want to.' She nodded towards his pad. 'You can draw while we talk, I was told you were mad about buildings.'

She did not speak again until he had seated himself cross-legged and begun to mark in the slit windows.

'I feel right here,' she said quietly, 'right being here, sitting here, near this folly. Perhaps that's it, one a building and one a person, but still two weirdoes together. Do you think that's what it is?'

He struggled with his immediate reaction, which was to say yes. He studied the folly with great concentration, then looked back at Liz. 'You're both different, but . . .'

'But?'

'I think you're sad.'

She looked startled for a moment then scowled down at her feet, drummed her heels into the turf. 'A sad case,' she said.

'Unhappy,' he amended and was startled by the mixture of anger and anguish that crossed her face and apologized hurriedly, 'Sorry, sorry.'

'Your stepbrother said you were an intuitive little tyke,' she said and he could see she was controlling the threat of tears.

'That sounds like Dickie,' he said though he was not quite sure what was meant. 'Why are you sad?' he asked and when she did not answer he added, 'Has someone died?'

'Yes,' she said with such alacrity that it startled him. 'Yes, died . . . killed.' She jumped to her feet, thrusting her hands deep into the pockets of her jeans, shoulders hunched as if against an attack.

'Oh! I am sorry, so sorry, that's awful.' He too scrambled to his feet, feeling there was something else he ought to be able to say or do. He remembered something his mother had said and done for his grandpa after his brother, Uncle Ben, had died. She had taken his arm and walked him away into the fields, saying that they should walk and talk about it all.

He cleared his throat and asked, 'Do you want to talk about it?'

She swung violently away from him, and after a moment he realized she was crying, dabbing at her eyes. He felt he ought to put his arm around her shoulders or something. 'I wish I was older,' he said.

She made a sound like half sob, half laughter. 'You're a nice kid, but –' she paused, shaking her head, trying to master her emotion – 'I guess I should be making a move.' Her voice trailed to bitterness as she added, '*Moving on* is what they tell me it is all about.'

He retrieved his pad from the grass and they walked back to the house in a silence agreeable to both of them, until they came to the steps where Bess and Ian stood with the head-master, who greeted Liz by name. 'Hello, young Liz, getting acclimatized? Do you know Mr and Mrs Philipps?'

'Sinclair,' Ian corrected.

'Your son's Richard Philipps, that's right, of course, apologies.'

Mr Hardy shook hands with Julian, who assured him he was a Sinclair. The headmaster turned back to Liz. 'So what's the verdict?'

She gave Julian a wink the others did not see as she turned to answer, 'I think I shall feel quite at home here.'

'Excellent, that's how we want everyone to feel.'

She smiled, then turned to Ian and Bess, 'Dickie and I will be able to look out for each other. I feel we've a lot in common.'

She turned back to Julian. 'Give you a ride home if you like. I've a call to make but we would be home as soon as your parents – probably.'

Ian's lips parted in consternation as Julian accepted with a hearty 'Yes, *please.*'

Liz grinned at Ian and added, 'You trusted me with Dickie!'

A few minutes later it was a delighted Julian who waved goodbye from the open-topped red sports car, his fair hair blowing freely about, a strange contrast to the girl's stiff blonde horns.

'She's probably safer than many older drivers,' Mr Hardy comforted. 'You must remember how much quicker their reactions are at that age.'

Ian was unable to throw off his displeasure and with his tone of voice and manner overruled Bess's inclination to settle matters there and then for Dickie to join the college at the beginning of the Autumn term. He asked the headmaster to give them another day to decide. 'I'll ring you first thing in the morning,' Ian promised.

'What's to decide?' Bess asked in the car. 'Dickie wants to come, the standards seem remarkably high.'

'Considering he takes drop-outs from other educational establishments, you mean.'

'I felt by any standards. Why are you being so anti and pompous?'

'Because I am not easy about it all, about Dickie's motives.'

'You weren't even easy about Julian going home with Liz in that car, though you were perfectly happy for Dickie to go off with her.'

'What are you trying to say?'

'Double standards, Ian. One for Dickie, one for Julian.'

'No –' for a second his foot went to the brake then retracted – 'no, that's not fair. My concern's as great for one as for the other.'

Bess was silent, then said, 'You hardly treat them the same.'

'Do you?' He glanced at her. 'They are different, need different things, at different times.'

She reviewed Dickie's happy baby days, while Julian had been fretful until a toddler. Now Julian was so directed and contented, while Dickie was, what? Mercurial – heart-led – but a bit of an enigma to her. She would have preferred some explanation in the matter of the locket, but, when asked, her son had just lowered his eyes and shaken his head, saying he didn't know.

'It seems to me that at the moment Dickie needs this college,' she said.

Ian made a disapproving noise in his throat.

'Ian?' she questioned sharply.

'I'd just be happier if it were in the north of Scotland.'

'You are not still thinking of Katie Wright!'

He did not answer, remembering the feeling of foreboding he had experienced with Edgar Bennett at his back and Katie Wright fleeing in a flick of pale skirt.

'It seems to me he will have plenty of diversions at Banford,' Bess was saying. 'Liz seems well disposed towards him and to Julian, a nice girl underneath.'

'Of the kind your father would prefer,' he commented.

'That too is not fair,' she retorted. 'Why bring my father into this?'

'He has never been out of it – ever,' he said and could hear his own bitterness, his own resentment. It would be true to say that there had always been another man in their marriage – her father. Not the same kind of love, he knew that, but love all the same. A love which seemed to hold sway over her, made her include the old man in making every decision: with every holiday, every little thing, there was her father first in her mind to consider.

She sat silent, twisted he knew in the tangle of loyalties; he could see her knuckles white as she clenched her fists – and he was sorry. He knew her loyalties, her loves, included him; perhaps he should not want more. If only she would stop trying to do and be everything to everyone. She should – a word his printer had used came to his mind – prioritize; get her priorities sorted. He began a list for her, his list for her – himself at the top, then Dickie, Julian, Edgar – then he wondered about the Hall; the Philipps Trust, that would be in there somewhere.

'Bess,' he tried again, in what he hoped was a thoroughly reasonable tone, 'why should Dickie be any happier at Banford College than at his present school? Think about it. He has friends of long standing there. He's popular, good-natured, willing, doing well. What more as parents could we ask?'

She did not answer, somewhat ruffled by his condescending manner.

'Nothing,' he concluded. 'So why does Dickie want to leave?'

'He wants to be at home . . .'

'Precisely. Now tell me why he should prefer to come here?'

'Please don't talk to me as if I was an idiot child.'

'He only wants to come to this college because he can get home easily.'

'You are obsessed with just one idea, and you are *wrong*.'

'You *think* I am wrong,' he answered, noting that they were already nearing their home village, no distance at all.

'Ask Colleen about Katie if you don't believe *me*.'

'Will that be all right with your father?' he asked and knew as the words slipped from his lips that he had crossed some kind of Rubicon. He felt her start almost from her seat, and thought for a moment she was going to get out of the car as they were travelling along.

Julian was pleased when they took a turning away from home – he wanted this experience to last as long as possible. He wondered what Dickie would say. He glanced sideways at Liz as she drove, very fast, but she kept her eyes on the road and did not talk.

He soon noted the difference in the houses, half timbered, some with their first storeys overhanging their first floors, Elizabethan. He knew they must be heading into Warwickshire, Shakespeare country.

'We're going to call in on my old nanny,' Liz said. 'It's quite near really. Very convenient –' she looked over at him and laughed – 'or it will be when Dickie and I need excuses.'

'What do you mean?' But even as he asked he felt he knew. Dickie always seemed to need excuses. He'd heard Colleen said he was an expert on 'reasons and excuses' and 'ways and means' to get his own way.

'Oh! It always pays to have an escape route, or a bolt hole, I find,' Liz said.

Liz's old nanny lived in a black and white timbered cottage that delighted Julian. He spent a happy hour drawing it and being lavished with home-made lemonade and home-made brandy snaps. In the background he was aware of the old woman bending over to talk to her former charge and making comforting gestures, patting Liz's hands and her back as if she were still no more than a toddler, or a baby even.

When they arrived back at the Hall he was dropped off and went inside to find his mother alone and very preoccupied; of his father and brother no sign.

That night he included Liz in his prayers: after the 'Our Father', he added his personal pleading. 'God bless Ma and Pa, Dickie, grandpa, Colleen and family, all the uncle and auntie Tophams and all my other friends and relations, and Liz, who is sad. I suppose you and her nanny know why.'

Nine

'You said it was about her *sadness*, what did you mean?'
Dickie demanded through near-clenched teeth.

Julian scowled. 'Well, it was.'

Dickie had followed him up from the Sunday breakfast
table, and before he could close his bedroom door had put a
foot in it. 'You mean Liz was talking and you earwigged.'

'No, I was drawing.' He looked towards the pad on his
bedside table, defensive now they were alone. 'They just talked
and Swish patted her back a lot.'

'Swish?'

'She told me to call her that, and Liz said *she* called her
that because when she was a little girl she always heard her
clothes swishing when she—'

'We don't need chapter and verse.' He stomped on the
fulsome explanation, furious that Julian was privy to the place
that was to be his excuse should his absence from both home
and college ever be questioned. This place was supposed to
be secret, not sketched by this architectural anorak.

He swooped on the notebook and riffled through the pages:
a local bridge; the canal, locks; the folly at Banford College
and a thatched and beamed cottage.

'You should leave other people's property alone!' Julian
exclaimed. Their eyes met as they both remembered the locket
and the fight beneath the bedroom windows.

That and the fact that Julian had written the full address
below the drawing was the last straw. He wondered he hadn't
drawn a map with the explanation. 'If Dickie is not at home
or college this is where he says he'll be.'

'I think I'll keep this,' Dickie said and tugged at the page.
It tore diagonally across.

In the pause following the tearing sound they became

aware that they were not alone. Their mother stood in the doorway.

'What's going on?' she asked, her voice low in this Sunday-morning, preparing-to-go-to-church house. She came in and closed the door behind her.

'What's this?' she asked, holding out a hand for the note-book. 'Why are you tearing up Julian's drawings?'

'He's always butting in where he's not wanted.'

She took the notebook and the page, fitting it back to the other half, she read, '"Swish's home, 3 Arden Lane, Bottswell"'.

'Yes!' Dickie shouted. 'That's just what I mean. What business had he got to go off in Liz's car, cadging a ride, butting in?'

'He was asked. Liz *asked* him. Your father and I were there.' She stressed each point and did not miss the sharp look from Dickie, knew the thought of denial that shot into his mind when she called Ian his father. She held his gaze, defying him, and assuring him she would not tolerate this ridiculous denial of Julian as his brother, Ian as his father. Whatever her own feelings about the icy relationship that still lingered between herself and Ian, she would take her husband's part.

She looked from one son to the other and thought how wrong young couples were to think children could cement a relationship. She and Ian had barely spoken since the journey back from the college yesterday. Their quarrel had begun with the children, as it usually did these days, though ended, as it usually did, with her father.

'There was no need for this surely,' she displayed the torn book.

'I can draw it again, anyway,' Julian cut in, defiant but hurt, 'and, it's all about what Auntie Colleen used to called "reasons and excuses", "ways and means".'

'No!' Dickie exclaimed so loudly it made Bess start. 'It's about you being an interfering pest.'

'I'm not!' Julian denied, but sounding near to tears. 'I do *know* Liz is sad. She told me that someone had died, or been killed, or something – and when we went to her nan's she knew as well, and was . . .' he envisaged the pats on the back, the older woman bent low over the seated hunched figure of Liz, '. . . being really kind to her.'

'There's been no bereavement in her family, as far as I know,' Bess puzzled.

'We could do with a few in ours.'

'Dickie!' Bess snapped. 'That is a stupid, terrible thing to say.'

'He always wants me dead.' Julian's shout was high, broken and he turned to run from his room, only to canon into his father, who stood with a hand raised ready to tap the door.

'What's this?' he asked. 'Who wants you dead?'

'No one of course,' Bess stepped forward in front of Dickie.

'He said it!' Julian said, trying to negotiate his father and escape, but Ian held his shoulder.

'Why?' Ian turned on Dickie. 'Why do we always seem to come back to burying, or killing, your brother. Should I be taking this really seriously?'

'Have me put away privily, you mean?' Dickie asked.

'Ian, please leave it,' Bess pleaded, 'it's only talk.'

He glanced from her to Dickie who looked beside himself with emotion – certainly he was angry, but there was more too. 'I came to say I'll take you to court tomorrow.' He paused and looked the irate youth up and down, 'I trust it will be your only ever appearance.'

He turned and in silence they listened to him going back downstairs. Bess gave Julian a push after him. 'Go to church,' she said. 'We may not be coming.' He opened his mouth to protest, then changed his mind and, picking up his jacket, he followed his father.

Bess turned back to Dickie. 'You must not make these remarks. It's no longer a joke, it's upsetting for everyone. I'm having enough trouble convincing your father that Banford will be a good choice for you.'

Dickie reminded himself of the saying that when you're in a hole you should stop digging. 'I wouldn't be much good in the diplomatic corps, would I?' he said.

She did not return his smile, but went to sit on the bed, then gestured towards the basket chair in the window. 'Sit down.'

He slumped into the chair and bent his head forward,

combing his fingers rapidly through his hair as his father had done in moments of stress. Greville Philipps had drowned himself in his lake because he could not bear to think he might lose something, or someone, he needed and loved. His fears had been unfounded but the outcome had been the same. There was a verdict of suicide while the balance of his mind was disturbed. She studied her son, and worried whether this mercurial boy had inherited any of the same tendencies – always she had felt he must not be crossed too sternly. His reaction to criticism had always been extreme, and she acknowledged he had got away with more than perhaps he should. They had all doted on him as a small boy – Colleen, herself, his Grandmother Philipps – the fatherless child, poor little rich boy. He expected it still.

Dickie lifted his head as she reached over and replaced the notebook on the bedside table, the torn page marking his crime with a protruding corner. He wished he could say he had not meant to tear the drawing, which he hadn't. His thoughts slipped into the well-used rut that told him everything would have been different if his mother *and* his father had both been his blood relations. All his life, since the day he realized his surname was different to that of all the others in the household, he had yearned for that to be true. If he could have swapped his inheritance for Ian as a full blood father he would have done so without a second thought. His bravado, his stunts, had been for Ian's attention – look at me – look at me – you've got me as well as that baby, that younger half-brother. But now he had Katie, and Katie loved him with all her heart, and nothing and no one was ever going to come between them.

'It was stupid,' he said, 'I really thought he had forced himself on Liz.'

'You know that's not his way.'

'No, it's not,' he admitted. 'He's the paragon of all virtue.'

'Oh, Dickie! Don't!'

'Sorry.'

'Are you worried about court tomorrow?' Bess asked and in her mind's eye she saw him as an eight-year-old, being escorted back along a Norfolk beach by a uniformed policeman. He had become seriously lost in the dunes, a game of hide and seek becoming a lost-and-found trauma. Ian had carried him piggy-back up to the ice-cream van. They had come back laughing because Ian had bought '99s', cones with chocolate flakes, for all the party and then asked for two '33s' for their dogs. The woman in the van had not been amused, which had made it funnier.

'I should hate to lose my licence before I've even passed my test,' he said ruefully.

'You know what I told you Uncle Angus said: a repentant and respectful attitude can work wonders.'

'Ways and means, reasons and excuses, you mean,' he said and felt it was an inspired remark as his mother's face cleared.

'So that's what Julian was talking about!' She rose and went to the door. 'Come on, perhaps we'll make church after all. What d'you say, united family front?'

He sat next to Ian in church that morning and the following afternoon again sat next to him until called to take his turn before the magistrate.

Apologies featured very large in his case. His legal representative represented him as a model young man who had been tempted by a sudden urge to try his motorbike in town. After riding for some months on a bike belonging to one of his mother's employees on the estate land he had been bought his own motorcycle for his sixteenth birthday. 'So he was used to riding a bike without L-plates on private land.' The implication was that he had forgotten.

He had held his breath, waiting for the magistrate to question this assumption, to ask whether it was true. He swallowed hard and thought of Katie. He guessed he was prepared to lie on oath, but the question was never asked.

He was fined twenty pounds and the magistrate strongly recommended, with his eye on Ian, that he was immediately enrolled for professional motorcycle lessons.

Ian had nodded sagely. The magistrate had acknowledged the gesture with a lift of his chin, and dismissed Dickie with the hope that he would give his parents no further cause for concern. Ian had neither nodded nor looked at the magistrate at that point.

Outside the court building, which faced on to the same square where Dickie and Katie had sat and talked, they tacitly acknowledged that they had got away with things very well. The two local journalists in the press box had seemed totally uninterested during the proceedings, had not made a single note that Ian had seen; one in fact had left the court.

Ian eased back his shoulders and breathed in the fresh breezy afternoon air. 'I'd like just to look in on a couple of book-shops, see what kind of display my last book's been given in the horticultural section.'

Dickie looked across to the bench where he had sat with Katie, the leaves of the maples were taking on the red and oranges of autumn and some blew across the square, catching under the seats. 'I thought I might go and look around at these driving schools,' he said. 'I've seen a couple around the centre here. I could meet you back at the car.'

'All right, four o'clock now – half five OK?'

Katie's office had once been an old tailor's shop and the original window at street level, where men had sat cross-legged sewing, had been retained.

Inside, Ken North drew Katie's attention to the young man strolling by. 'Looks like young Lochinvar *has* come to pick you up tonight.'

She resented him for noticing the passing figure before she had, and for using that stupid name. She near hated him when he deliberately stood in the doorway to the photocopying room, forcing her to squeeze past him so she could finish her work and be away.

Ten

The brushing encounter on the way to the photocopying room, much closer than Katie intended in her hurry to be away, seemed to have made Ken North feel that if she was fair game for 'young Lochinvar' she was fair game for him.

He began to stand smiling at her at odd times during their working day. 'Is that creepy or what?' Mary grimaced as he left the general office. 'You're not encouraging him, are you?'

'No! What do you think?!'

'Well, you've certainly lit his fuse. First time ever, I should think. You'd better watch out.'

They had broken into an uncontrollable fit of giggles when the door suddenly reopened and he came back into their office.

He joined in their laughter, asking, 'What? What?' straightening the knot of his tie, pushing back his shoulders, posing.

'The doormat gets up and shakes itself,' Mary said scornfully when finally he left.

Katie, unlike Mary, had always tried to make allowances for him, thought of him as someone needing a friend, someone it did not hurt to give a kind word to. She had felt real sympathy for this man who had lived with his mother until she died and now lived alone in the same small town house where he had been born. He was a good accounts manager; she knew their employer thought a lot of him. Mr Benbrook treated him with an air of bonhomie, as one man of the world to another, and everyone in the office knew it was a kindness.

Ken's manner became a mixture of prospective suitor and paternal supervisor, and more and more he lingered in the front office instead of working quietly alone in his small office next to the photocopying room. He was, as Mary so forcibly said, fast becoming a very large pain in the butt – and it was not just confined to the office.

Mary had seen him loitering until he heard Katie leaving, then he would emerge with offers to walk her to her bus, or wherever she was going. He became a particular problem when Dickie began his motorcycle lessons twice a week. To try to divert him from the fact that she was not going straight home, she took to slipping off in the direction of the bus station, then doubling back to meet Dickie for a few precious moments before his lesson.

Dickie's mother had intervened on the matter of the timing of the lessons, insisting six o'clock was the latest they should be, because of riding home afterwards in the darker evenings. No argument was allowed and his return home was, he said, timed to the minute. 'Tuesdays and Thursdays I run to a stricter timetable than the railways,' he told her.

'You should be home by eight,' Katie calculated.

'Just what my stepfather said. He doesn't want me "hanging about town in the evenings". I told him I was a big boy now.'

'And he said?' Katie asked.

'He just snapped, "Quite", turned on his heel and that was the end of the discussion.'

'They suspect something,' she said.

'The thing is I can't afford to say too much at this point. We need my cycle licence desperately, term starts October eleventh.'

'Do you really think you're going to be able to sneak off from that college?' She shook her head, it was all the stuff of daydreams. Whenever it came to the practical, day-to-day things, she could not believe it possible, any of it.

'Yes, I do, I'm absolutely certain about that.' He squeezed her hand very tightly. 'Don't worry, Katie, we'll make out, no one will stop us. I've got so many plans, and I love you.'

His last three words were spoken as a statement of proof that all would be as they wished. *He* believed his dreams. 'And I love you,' she whispered back, warmed, astonished, humbled by his confidence.

'I'll try to meet you off your bus tomorrow night,' he said as they waited outside the building where his bike and several other motorcycles with bright-red 'learner' jackets draped over the saddles stood waiting.

'Great.' She felt her heart lift and she smiled up at him.

The more time she spent with him the more she could believe.

His voice was unsteady, gruff, as he said, 'I'd like to put you on one of those bikes and just ride off with you, now – just go. Shall we?'

She laughed unsteadily, half afraid he meant it, half afraid he did not. 'Some day perhaps.'

'No "perhaps". It'll happen, I'll make it happen.'

She believed he would, and left him to his lesson. She went to the bus station where she would dream into a cup of coffee until it was time to catch a later bus home. She had forty-five minutes to wait.

She became aware that someone was about to join her when a magazine was placed on the table, followed by a cup of tea. The magazine was the glossy county magazine, bought she suspected only by those who were liable to see their photographs in it. She glanced up at the person about to join her, then sat back in her chair, astounded. 'Ken?' She took a minute to recover, during which time he had sat down and stirred two packets of sugar into his tea and put several more into his pocket. 'What are you doing here?'

'I came to show you something,' he said and proceeded to finger through the magazine until he found a double-page spread headed 'Pony Club Party'. A party was held at the 'The Hall', Counthorpe, home of Mr & Mrs Ian Sinclair, opening the county's fundraising events for next year's Silver Jubilee celebrations. The special appeal for charity in 1977 would be to establish a trust fund as a permanent expression of the nation's affection for Her Majesty. Leicestershire had a minimum target of £100,000. Here followed a page of photographs with the names of each group of party-goers underneath.

She looked up at him and frowned.

'There!' He stabbed at a picture of Dickie with his parents and younger brother. 'It's your young Lochinvar! Do you see what it says? "Mr Richard Philipps, son of Mrs Sinclair and the late Greville Philipps of 'The Hall' Counthorpe.'" Ken paused for effect, then added, 'His father's family own half the county.'

'I do know who he is,' she said, biting back the information that everyone called him Dickie and she wished he would not use that stupid nickname.

90

'You know?' It was Ken's turn to look astonished. 'How long have you known?'

'I've always known.' She thought of explaining, but why should she, it was absolutely nothing to do with Ken North. She frowned as he sat staring at her, shaking his head.

'Then I would have thought you had more sense,' he said.

'More sense? Now what are you talking about?'

'You don't think anyone in his position is going to be interested in you, not seriously interested, not for any good to come out of anything?'

'What do you know about it? I think you should mind your own business.'

'I know this much about it,' he said earnestly and leaned across the table towards her. She caught the smell of him, a puzzling odour, like very old pepper. 'People from that class,' he went on, 'the wealthy classes, won't let their young men marry beneath them.'

'Oh, come on! This is the nineteen seventies, not the eighteen hundreds.'

'So you do think he's serious, that he has good intentions. My God,' he breathed and sat back as if he had received a personal blow. 'You say its not my business, but we've worked together ever since you came to Benbrook's from school. Mr Benbrook consults me about his staff. I don't want you to be hurt.' He hunched confidentially over the table. She automatically slid her hands into her lap, out of reach, as he went on. 'My mother worked for the aristocracy before she was married, she saw a lot of their goings-on. She used to say that they looked after their own and made sport of everyone else.'

She guessed he must still miss his mother, going back to an empty house after the office or his twice weekly visit to the billiard hall. 'That must have been a long time ago,' she said more gently. 'People mix far more these days.'

'Mix, maybe; take advantage of, certainly; but marry, that's a different kettle of fish altogether.'

'The Philippses are hardly aristocracy.'

'They're the next best thing, that's for sure. I've heard Mr Benbrook say more than once that he'd like the handling of their affairs.'

'Oh! That's just business.'

'I know it's just business, and I also know old Benbrook only butters me up because I'm a good bookkeeper. If I were to cast an eye in the direction of one of his daughters I'd be out on my ear in less time than it takes to say Lochinvar, or double-entry accounting, and that's a fact you can't deny.'

No, she thought, and it's a fact Mary and I didn't think you appreciated. 'Why are you here at the bus station?' she asked.

'When I saw who he was, I just wanted to make sure you knew what you're doing, or what *he's* doing is more to the point. Don't let him take you for a ride, Katie, you're too nice, too special. I'd hate to see you hurt.'

She thought two things: Mary would not have hesitated to tell him that she had no wish to be special to him and to mind his own business, and yet he sounded sincere.

'Remember money marries money,' he said.

'I suppose your mother said that too.'

'She did, she did indeed,' he acknowledged with some pride, then he asked, 'Do your parents know he comes to meet you from the office, and so on?' he asked.

'Our parents have been friends for years,' she told him.

'Oh yes!' he exclaimed, clearly not believing her. 'Be interesting to talk to them about you and young Lochinvar meeting twice a week.'

Her heart gave a great lurch of anxiety, as she realized her tactics had not outwitted him. 'What I do outside office hours is no concern of yours,' she snapped.

'But it is: everyone who cares for you would be concerned, your parents most of all.' He made it sound like a threat and he watched her closely. 'They don't know, do they?'

It was much worse than that. Her parents actually believed she was going out with *him*. Her mother had even defended her late homecomings. 'Stolen moments are the sweetest,' she had told her dad when he said her chap must be a better bookkeeper than timekeeper.

'I must go for my bus,' she said.

'You've got another twenty minutes to wait,' he said and caught her arm as she rose.

'I'm going outside to wait in the fresh air.' She tried to pull away but he held her tightly – he was much stronger than she would have thought.

'You OK?' a passing middle-aged woman with bulging shopping bag and mug of coffee asked. She paused to eye the restraining hand, which immediately fell from Katie's arm.

'I am now,' she said, nodding to this down-at-heel woman with the courage to speak out when she thought there was a need. 'Thanks, pity there are not more like you in the world.'

'Got one at 'ome don't think that.' She jerked her head towards Ken North. 'Bit heavy-handed like you,' adding to Katie, ''Night, take care.'

Mary commented on Ken's welcome absence from the general office the next day. 'Let's hope it lasts,' Katie echoed.

By evening, heavy rain clouds and a sudden downpour had everyone running across roads awash with reflections of head-lights, rear lights and the kaleidoscope of traffic signals.

Katie caught her usual bus home, but wondered whether the rain might stop Dickie meeting her. She turned to smile secretly at herself in the bus window, where lines of wind-driven drops streamed like tears over her reflection. She felt a thrill, half excitement, half fear, run up her spine. Would Dickie brave this weather? She imagined it a kind of labour of Hercules, a test. If he were there then nothing would ever stop him, or them, from achieving their hearts' desire. If he was not there, well then he was just the stuff of dreams.

The bus swerved and jolted from the main road to the begin-ning of its round of villages, Counthorpe first, with her stop the one well before any of the outlying houses were reached. The rain still poured down and a sudden fork of lightning split the gloom, lit the bus interior, followed within seconds by the thunder.

They approached the lay-by and she made her way along the aisle of the swaying bus.

'Night, Katie,' a man said as she passed.

'Oh! Hello, Dave. What a night,' she said as she recog-nized Joyce Green's husband. The last time she had seen him was when she stood with Joyce and their baby on the cricket field, and watched him caught out.

'Looks like you'll be all right.' He nodded towards the figure sheltering under a large elegant man's umbrella waiting at the stop.

She felt her colour rise but shrugged and pretended a non-chalance she certainly did not feel. She would have preferred Dickie to have waited across the road, along the path, or at least not so prominently. She wished so even more as he took her hand as she alighted, kissed it and drew her under the shelter of the umbrella. 'Thanks, old boy,' he called to the driver, and she winced inwardly, wondering what Dave Green was making of all this, and what he would tell Joyce.

'What are you doing?' she demanded as they crouched under the brolly and ran across the road. She wanted a champion, but not one this brazen. 'There are village people on the bus who know both of us.'

'Do I care?' He had to raise his voice above the drumming of the rain on the umbrella, and both instinctively crouched lower as another crack of lightning startled them, followed by an almost instantaneous roll of thunder.

'You may be made to,' she shouted. She stopped as they reached the edge of the spinney. 'Perhaps we shouldn't go any further into the trees until this storm's passed over.'

'We'll be all right,' he urged.

'Lightning has struck up here quite a few times.'

'And my umbrella has a metal tip.' He lifted it higher towards the sky.

You'm foolhardy. She remembered the words and the voice of a very old man, her father's grandfather, Noel Wright. 'Oh! Come on,' she gestured towards the footpath. He managed to keep the umbrella over her head as she climbed the stile, then passing it to her, put one hand on the top bar and vaulted over, nearly slipping as he landed. She shook her head at him but he grinned, tucked her arm under his. He stooped to her ear, the warmth of his breath on her cheek as he shouted above the rain. 'The trees are thicker near the pool, we'd find shelter and we wouldn't have to shout.'

Her common sense told her they should just hurry through the spinney and out of the trees as fast as possible.

They took the path down towards the beauty spot where huge tree trunks had been split to form the seat and backrests of benches and the Red Pool, which years ago had bubbled from a dangerous morass, appeared rust red amidst an arrangement of boulders and drained marsh.

They chose a stout oak tree and he drew her close into the trunk where the foliage was thick enough to keep off the rain that filtered through the outer canopy. She was glad of his warmth: the rain had chilled the air. He smelt of damp tweed and pine aftershave.

'This is nice,' he said, 'holding you, watching the weather do its worst.'

Another rumble of thunder came but much further away and the rain became less heavy. 'Its going to stop.'

'Oh, blow it!'

'Its definitely getting lighter,' she said. 'So now tell me?'

'Tell you?'

'Yes!' she asserted. 'I know that smile of yours, you can't keep it from the corners of your mouth. You've got something to tell. What have you done?'

'Now,' he added, 'to sound like a proper grown-up telling a child off you should add "now". What have you done *now*.'

She burrowed closer into his side. 'I think,' she said, 'you've done something awful at the driving school. Crashed! Run over the instructor? Gone the wrong way up a one-way street and run down a policeman? Go on – have you?'

'Not telling,' he said and, crouching down, he tugged at her sleeve just as if he were a naughty child. 'What a cross face,' he narrowed his eyes at her, then still holding her gaze, he raised himself up, very slowly, straight in front of her, leaning in closer and closer.

'Where do you learn such tricks,' she asked, breathless with the feeling, the desire, he aroused in her.

'Just being with you,' he breathed, 'thinking about you.' He stooped and kissed her lips, gently sipping at them as if he might draw nectar from them.

'There,' he said, scanning her face, 'that's a bit better, and you know I wondered if something, or someone, had upset you. When you got off the bus . . .'

She would have liked to tell him about North following her to the bus station the evening before, the grip of his hand as she tried to leave.

'It's just the office, you can't do anything without someone noticing. If I go a different way after work, or catch a later bus. Nosy lot!'

'I have all that at home. I feel I'm on probation; reckon if they could, they'd have me signing in and out.' Then he gave her an excited hug. 'But I've some really good news.'

'Oh! What? Come on, don't tease,' she urged.

'I am taking my test tomorrow.'

'Your motorbike test? I thought that would be months yet, well weeks.'

'One chap was put in for his test and now can't come, so there's a vacancy, and they've managed to put me in the slot. So our troubles will soon be over.'

'That's providing you pass,' she began, 'and—'

'I will,' he interrupted. 'I mean to, so tomorrow I shall meet you from the office, and we'll have a legal spin out some-where to celebrate.'

'Wouldn't it be better to wait until the next day?'

'I am sick of waiting,' he said, 'let's call an end to it.'

She shook her head. 'You know we can't, not yet.'

'We can to some of it, after tomorrow, we'll be freer. While I'm at home we can meet after you've finished at the office, and when I have to go to Banford there'll be weekends, and I mean *weekends*. You'll be able to get away, won't you?'

She wondered what he meant by 'weekends' and 'getting away'. She wondered about Ken North – and her dad.

'You will, won't you?' he persuaded.

She nodded uncertainly.

'Going to kiss the doubts away,' he told her and leaned over, kissing the tip of her nose, her lips, her cheeks. 'I love you, Katie, now, always, for ever and ever, Amen.'

She looked at him long and hard – he seemed to have no idea of the problems he was mounting up for himself, for her.

'For goodness' sake tell me you love me and you wish me luck for my test tomorrow.'

'Oh, of course I do!' She melted into his side, reached up to bring his head down to kiss his cheek and his lips.

'Which do you?'

'Both of course,' she said between kisses.

'Not good enough, you have to say both in full, or I won't believe you.'

'Look,' she said, 'the sun's coming out again.'

'So that's a good sign, and look at all the colours, like jewels.'

The lightest of breezes and the dancing of the raindrops on leaf ends made endless prisms in all hues from blue, mauve through red to orange yellow and diamond white.

'That's extra-special good, isn't it?' he asked.

'Yes, it's all a bit like you.'

'Because I'm too good to be true, you mean?'

'Of course,' she said with mock seriousness, 'that's what I mean.'

'Look,' he said, 'see the way the drops flash like diamonds. As soon as I am eighteen I shall buy you an engagement ring that catches the light like that.'

They dallied an hour near the Red Pool, kissing, whispering, laughing, promising and calculating the time when the next bus from town would be due and Katie should finally arrive home.

Eleven

When the time came for Dickie to go to Banford, Ian reluctantly agreed he should travel with Liz, just the two of them together.

'It still all seems a bit casual to me,' he murmured, coming to stand behind Bess. She had just given up trying to supervise and was watching as Dickie, Julian and Liz all helped toss cases and bags into the red sports car.

She was very aware of how close he stood. The night before they had made love: she had planned it, unable to bear the coolness between them any more. Ever since the drive back from Banford there had been nothing but tension. They had watched Dickie's comings and goings with anxiety, and every time her father appeared, or his name was mentioned, the gulf yawned. The abstinence in the bedroom had become like a dammed-up river, drowning not just sex and love but reason, everyday civilities, and she had determined there should be a release, a reconciliation. She had dug out the frilly white negligee he had bought for her last Christmas (never worn before because it was not at all to her taste) and bought a new perfume, 'Acqulina', which was both sharp and seductive, reminding her of the ocean, of the cliff-path cottage hung between sea and sky, where they had first made love.

He had appraised her as he entered the bedroom, and she had for a brief moment felt like a prostitute, but she had stood tall, challenged him with a toss of her head, how far was he prepared to come to keep their marriage secure.

There had been no mention of their differences – in fact neither of them had spoken. His response had been . . . She had struggled for a comparison ever since – and now watching the activity of the young people, it came to her. If his usual style was imaginative, innovative like his garden designs, last night had been workmanlike, a necessary chore, preparing the ground, digging the plot ready for better things.

She nearly laughed aloud, and she must have smiled for Liz beamed at her as she stacked yet another bag into the car. She leaned back a little, allowing her shoulders to contact Ian's chest; after a moment, his hand came on to her waist.

With Dickie safely away at Banford there would now surely be a more stable time for them. Day to day there would only be her father to keep an eye on, and she could rely on Colleen to let her know if anything was amiss at the home farm. She resolved to spend more time with Ian. He loved riding, though not alone. She would make time for just the two of them to ride regularly, though at the moment it would not be easy with the next hunting season upon them. Ian abhorred hunting and many of the more gung-ho types who patronized the Hunts. He always made himself scarce on days when the meet was either at the Hall or anywhere nearby.

Another and larger sports bag was hoisted into the front seat of the car. 'Leave room for the passenger,' Ian advised Liz.

'No, that's all right, and that's the last,' she said as she pushed a tape recorder into the well of the front seat. 'Dickie's going to follow me on his motorbike.' She paused and laughed. 'Well, perhaps I'll follow him, he's a bit of a speed merchant.'

Bess felt Ian's hand heavier on her waist then it was removed as he asked her, 'Did you know about this?'

'Well, no.' The term used to her had been 'travel with'. She suspected now that it had been clever wording, evasion of the whole truth, but she automatically tried to pour the old maternal oil on troubled family waters. 'But I suppose it makes sense. He'll be independent having his own transport.'

'He only has to make a phone call,' Ian retorted. 'We're always at his beck and call.'

'Actually he's going to take me over to see my old nan; she lives not far from the college, you know. Julian's met her. We'll probably go there a lot,' Liz said, opening the car door and climbing in. 'Cheaper running a motorbike than a car,' she added.

Bess could feel Ian seething with unspoken comments about this girl whose attire might be extreme punk but whose leather boots, luggage and sports car made mockery of any need for economy.

'Where is Dickie?' Ian asked, and turned as if to go into the house.

'Gone out the back way with Julian to fetch the bike. Julian was saying he's never ridden pillion.'

A full-throttled roar came from the direction of the garage and stables. Dickie, the bike, and Julian swept out from the arch under the huge stable clock. Julian attempted to wave as they approached but then had to grab at his brother as Dickie unexpectedly turned the bike away from the front of the house and roared off down the drive.

'He'll kill somebody,' Ian muttered, his voice rising as he went on. 'He's not the right temperament for a motorcycle. It's been nothing but trouble from Day One.' He turned to Bess. 'But of course your father once more overruled my opinion.'

Bess stepped away from him, from this sudden public outburst. She glanced at Liz, who shrugged and raised her eyebrows. 'Don't mind me, family arguments are my norm. I suppose it's the reason we're both going to this college.'

'It suits our son's hidden agenda, but I'm not supposed to talk about that,' Ian went on, then his attention was diverted by the sound of the bike backfiring violently. He stood and listened intently.

'He won't go far,' Bess said.

Ian shook his head at her as if she was a sad case, beyond recovery.

'He knows Liz is waiting,' she added.

The bike reappeared as on cue, and came speeding back along the drive swinging, swerving to delight Julian, skidding to a halt showering up pieces of gravel which hit the car.

'Be careful of the paintwork,' Bess said automatically.

'Don't worry, the car's just my sop for "being a sensible gel",' Liz said, 'I don't care about it, I'll probably sell it.'

Ian pondered the remark and remembered the headmaster at Banford saying *most* of his pupils had 'hidden agendas'. Then he stepped forward to steady Julian, who'd caught his foot on the bike's exhaust as he dismounted.

'It's OK,' Julian reassured him as he clutched his father's

outstretched arm. 'Dickie can take a pillion passenger now he's passed his test. It was fab! Can I have a motorbike when I'm old enough?'

'No,' Dickie ruled in tones exactly like Ian's, 'you can have a nice steady little dumper truck to carry your bricks about in.'

'What a good idea,' Julian enthused, 'I could have it at the farm, and—'

'We won't go down that road at the moment,' Ian put in, trying hard not to grin at Dickie's perfect mimicry.

'Are you going first, Liz?' Julian wanted to know. 'Or are you following Dickie, you know, like a motorcade?' He thought for two seconds then enthused, 'Yes, I think that's what you should do. You go first, Dickie.'

'Just a moment,' Ian said. 'I for one had no idea you were thinking of travelling on your bike, and does the headmaster know you'll both arrive with vehicles? If every pupil did that, parking would be—'

'No, its OK,' Liz cut in, 'there are a lot of bikes and cars, and there's an enormous barn-like place where anyone who wants can work on their bike or car in their spare time, plus there's a field for our vehicles if the parents and such are coming.'

With that ground cut from under his feet, Ian knew he had either to rant, rage and totally forbid, or he must wait until they were alone to try once more to make Bess understand why their elder son wanted to be at this college, with transport to hand. He had been totally convinced he was right even before he had met Katie in the village yesterday. She had behaved with such unusual formality towards him, over-polite, keeping her distance from enquiries about her family, her job, retreating from him, escaping as fast as ever she decently could – as fast as she had run along the hedgerow on the occasion of the dawn of all this trouble, the day he had come to think of as the 'day of the locket'. No one would ever have guessed that he had given her piggybacks on the beach at Wells-next-the-Sea, that their families had for years spent happy weeks together at their Norfolk bungalow, or Bess and her mother been bosom friends since childhood. He had been tempted to ask after her boyfriend at the office, and wondered now why he hadn't.

101

Dickie kicked the stand into place and left the bike leaning, but running, while he came to kiss his mother. Julian immediately cocked a leg over the seat again and took a businesslike grip of the handlebars. Bess called to him to 'be careful' and Ian for him to 'get off that thing'. Liz started her car.

Ian shook hands with him, looked him straight in the eye, wanted to tell him not to push his luck too hard, but instead said, 'I'll be ringing from time to time.' He did not specify that it would be to the headmaster.

'Sure,' Dickie replied, understanding.

In spite of all misgivings it was a relief to see them leave, Dickie leading, waving, as no motorcyclist ever should, before he disappeared out of the drive once more. Liz gave them a blast on her klaxon and also waved. Julian looked after them with the same expression Ian imagined Toad of Toad Hall had when he saw his first motor car, and if he had murmured a faint 'poop-poop' he would not have been surprised.

Bess stared fixedly, winging a prayer that Dickie would settle for these next two years. Once he was eighteen she'd really like him home, beginning to take the estate into his hands.

She turned towards Ian, but Julian was already asking after designs for a new fountain for a municipal park his father had a commission for. The two of them went off towards the office. She saw Ian's arm go around Julian's shoulders as they disappeared inside.

She turned, and on, round, full circle, like someone in a strange place getting their bearings. One moment surrounded by people, noise, talk – now she strained to hear even the sound of an engine above the sough of the wind in ancient trees. She felt solitary, no more than that: she felt a sense of real loneliness. She ached for Ian's company. She wondered bleakly if she would ever wear the white negligee again.

She walked away across the front of the house, on past the stable block, resisting the pull of the downward slope to the lake, or the upward pull of her duties in the house. She concentrated on a level course, cutting horizontally across the lawns and the mound on which the Hall stood.

At this moment of solitude she judged this was her life,

just trying to keep an even course – all things to all people, and how much did she mean to any of them? She knew exactly how much each meant to her, and she walked on, playing a game she had used since she was a child to try to assess her responsibilities and her affections.

She paired up the people in her life, then imagined a desperate situation with only time to snatch one of each pair from certain death. So by process of elimination she should arrive at her priorities. She stopped walking as, having saved Ian from her imaginary pit, she wondered if as he got older she would ever sacrifice him in place of either of her sons. She thought not, unless he became totally unreasonable.

She climbed a stile out of the gardens, walking on into her father's farmland. What she would really have liked to do was force Ian into a car and take him right away from this place, away to a Cornish cliff-side cottage. They could go away, surely they could, a week, perhaps two, now. Why not?! Julian could go to her father's – he'd love that, dear uncomplicated Julian. She quickened her pace, the idea giving new energy. If she worked out a few details, presented a proper plan . . . She wondered if she should ask her father about Julian first, or should she talk to Ian first?

She resolved to do neither – she would talk to Colleen. She'd go over to the farm now, tell her what she had in mind; ask Colleen to sound her father out at lunchtime. She would see Ian as soon as she got back, then Colleen could phone. She laughed aloud: scheming she was, scheming. She and Colleen hadn't had a good scheme for years! If her father brought out the anxious-to-please child in her, Colleen brought out the joyous moments of shared childhood and girlhood, the mysteries of growing up, boyfriends, first dates, schemes to pull the proverbial wool over the eyes of those who thought they knew what was best.

She was in sight of the farm, with the delight of her idea hurrying her along, when Colleen appeared in the orchard. She waved and Colleen lifted her arm, but not to wave, to beckon her, call her urgently on. Her friend seemed to hesitate between running to meet her and turning back to the house, but she came on, and Bess began to run. Something was desperately wrong.

103

'I telephoned, no one could find you,' she gasped, gripping her hand and turning back the way she had come.

'What's the matter? What's happened?'

'It's your father.' Colleen had no breath for explanations. 'I've only just found him –' she shook her head as they ran – 'I'd been in the house . . . He's upstairs, on the landing.'

Bess raced ahead. Colleen called after her, 'Ian's coming, and the ambulance.'

She noted the collie, curled in his basket, but uneasy, the white of his eyes showing, not coming to greet her as she ran through the kitchen, across the hall, up the stairs, the familiar warm woody smell of the old panelling enclosing her. There was total silence as she span round into the corridor to the bedrooms, and in her haste she nearly stumbled over the prostrate form of her father – he was so near the top of the stairs.

'Pa!' She knelt by him, moved back the quilt Colleen had thrown over him so she could see his face more clearly. He was like parchment. She stooped close to be sure he was breathing, so light, so shallow it seemed to her. Colleen came and knelt beside her.

'His leg's wrong,' she said and lifted the lower end of the quilt. Bess gasped as she saw his leg, though more because of the foot, at an impossible angle.

Colleen lifted the quilt higher. 'I can't see any blood anywhere.'

'No,' Bess breathed as they knelt close, childlike and useless.

'I think he's either bumped his head or passed out because of the pain,' she said. 'I wish Dr Michael would hurry up.'

'You phoned him.'

'First. He's out on his rounds but they were going to contact him.'

'Pa,' Bess called with urgent quietness. 'Can you hear me? It's Bess. Pa?' She put a hand under the cheek nearest the floor. He was very cold. 'Do you think he's been here long?'

'He's dressed, but he never fell while I've been here, that's for sure. I'd have heard. I only found him when I came upstairs to go round the bathroom.'

In the distance they both heard the wail of a siren. 'The ambulance,' Colleen said, 'thank goodness.'

There was a commotion downstairs: the dog barking, then

the doctor's voice in the hall. Colleen hurried down, hushing the dog, directing the doctor.

'Bess,' he greeted, moving in quickly by her side, a hand on her shoulder first. 'Let the dog see the rabbit, then.'

She moved aside for the doctor the community knew by his Christian name because his father, old Dr Hughes, had served the area for fifty years before him. He lifted and handed her the quilt, then kneeling, he bent low over his patient, looking, assessing, gently feeling.

'The ambulance is here,' Colleen called – more frantic barking, then heavy footsteps on the stairs, men's voices reassuring, their bulk and Colleen filling the space. Bess backed along the corridor to make room, but not too far, anxious to catch whatever they said. She caught the word 'splint' and one of the men brushed past Colleen, and was soon back with a complexity of blue straps attached to a special stretcher.

There were more voices downstairs, the barking different, and she recognized Ian and, she thought, Julian. Why had he brought Julian?

It was, however, only Ian who came upstairs, standing marooned, his way blocked by a concentration of men working over her father. They exchanged looks, hers of worry and fear, his of concern.

They watched the way Edgar was so carefully contained in the professional carers' arms: moved and strapped, swaddled; held taut, neck collar, head firm; his crooked foot, well, at a better angle than it had been. The doctor had slit his trouser leg to the hip and she could see the leg was much discoloured – blue, black – internal bleeding, she thought. Then with a stab of added alarm, realized that in all this her father had made no sound. He ought surely to have groaned, given out some low moan, during all this manipulation, however gently it had been done, however deeply unconscious he was.

'Doctor?' she appealed and stepped forward, only to see the enormous bump above her father's right temple. She gasped.

'Don't be alarmed by that – often it's better if the swelling is enormous, better out than in is usually the case. Will you go with your father?' he asked as the ambulance men prepared to lift.

'Yes, of course,' she said.

'I'll follow in the car,' Ian said.

'Julian?' she queried.

'He can stay with me,' Colleen said from the stairs. 'Ring me,' she said to Bess as they followed the stretcher down.

'Of course,' she answered as they gripped hands briefly.

'Ma?' Julian came to her outside. She must have passed him unseeing in the kitchen. 'Is grandpa going to be all right? Is he?'

'Trust us, young man,' one of the ambulance men put in, 'we're all doing our best.'

'You reassure that dog,' the man at the other end of the stretcher said, 'he's not liking us taking his master.'

Julian's eyes were on his grandfather, the bloody bump on his head, but he stooped and spoke to the collie, holding his collar as he grumbled uneasily, fixing the passing legs.

'I'll see you at the hospital, m'dear,' Dr Michael told Bess as she was helped into the back of the ambulance. I want to ask Colleen if she has any idea whether he's had breakfast, or how long he may have lain there.'

It was with a terrible shock of déjà vu that Bess realized she was being ushered along the same hospital corridor towards the same ward as the time her mother had died here.

Her father was pushed into a side room near the ward sister's office and Bess was allowed to sit by him. She didn't need the swift glance out of the window with the view of a huge central hospital chimney to confirm this room was where her mother had been.

She remembered her lying so straight, so neat; remembered wanting to hug her hard, hug her back to life. Now her father lay here, much longer in the bed, not so neat with a cage over the lower part of his body.

She heard Ian's voice outside, but it was the sister who came in, bonny, authoritative, immaculate in dark blue. She suggested she joined Ian in the day room. 'You can talk there, and Mr Chan will be along to see you after he's examined your father.'

Ian came quickly to her side, took her arm. 'You look . . .' he began. 'Are you all right?'

106

When they reached the day room she told him about her mother.

He gave a low groan of sympathy. 'But what have they said about Edgar?'

She shook her head. 'I think they're most concerned that he's unconscious, but I haven't been told anything definite.'

'We've obviously got to wait for Mr Chan.'

She smiled ruefully at him, thinking of the holiday plan she'd had.

Time dragged, twenty minutes, an age. Ian fetched tea in plastic beakers, which neither of them drank. 'Why did you bring Julian to the farm?' she asked.

'It was just quicker, he was in the car before I was,' he answered but she saw it had been taken as a criticism.

After fifty-five minutes, Bess was wondering whether the room where her father lay, and where her mother had been, was the place where they took people to die, like they used to say about the bed nearest the door in the old Nightingale wards.

'Do you think we should let Dickie know?' she asked.

'Certainly not at this point, he'll hardly have arrived.'

It seemed several ages since they had seen him and Liz off. The boys, she pondered, were close to their grandpa, both of them, certainly closer than Ian. She wondered if husbands saw fathers as rivals.

Both were startled as the door opened, and the sister came in again.

'I'm sorry it's been a long time, but your father came round while Mr Chan was with him, which is excellent.'

'Is he . . . ?' Bess began.

'Making sense?' Ian finished for her.

She nodded and smiled. 'Very much so, no worries on that score. You can come and see him when the surgeon has spoken to you, just for a few minutes mind – we intend to get him into theatre as soon as there is a slot. His leg is quite another matter, as serious break, near the hip.'

'Pa?' Bess hurried to take the raised hand when they were finally allowed into the room. 'What happened?'

'Slipped at the top of the stairs. Remember spinning round like a ballet dancer to save myself. That's all I remember.

Reckon I'd have been better to have just fallen down the stairs.' He looked at Ian. 'You'll see George for me, he'll know what needs doing.'

The operation, inserting a pin the length of his thigh bone, took place in the early afternoon. They visited daily, but it was as they were travelling home together two days later that Bess said, 'It's going to be when he comes home that will be the most difficult.'

'He could come to the Hall, surely that will be the simplest,' Ian replied, keeping his eyes firmly on the road.

Twelve

'Katie.'

She span round. 'Yes?' she questioned the tall figure, black in the doorway with the low autumn sun behind it. 'Dickie?' she breathed. 'You know, I wondered if you'd come, I was thinking about you.'

He moved into the kitchen, holding out his arms.

'Well, I'm always thinking about you,' she said, then teased, 'well off and on.'

'More on than off, I hope.'

She went to him, like a homing pigeon back to its roost, she thought. 'I didn't hear you coming.'

'Left the bike by the bus stop, knowing how your mother feels.'

'You've been to see your grandfather?'

'Yes, special request for home visit,' he said, holding her tight, twirling her round. 'Just back, I took a chance you might be here alone.'

You take a lot of chances, the thought came and went. 'How is Mr Bennett?'

'Pale, gasping for a breath of fresh air after being in "a hothouse" for nearly three weeks. Sister says he's becoming very irritating and she'll be glad to be rid of him.'

'As irritating as him refusing to go back to the Hall. My mum wants to offer for us all to move to the farm to look after him. Dad and William don't want to. They've had words, quite a few actually. Dad says your grandfather is just being difficult and shouldn't be given a choice.'

'And Ma as usual is trying to be all things to all people. She's talking of hiring a nurse.'

'Will she?'

He shrugged. 'I don't know, I'm just grateful to be here

today. Good old Grandpa, say I. He's always been on my side.'

'Not to the extent of trying to throw himself downstairs,' she said, laughing, but then felt ashamed to be making a joke of the accident. 'He must have been in terrible pain,' she added.

'But –' he raised a finger, quoting back at her one of the old adages she used from time to time – 'it's an ill wind that blows no one any good. I'd never have been allowed home this weekend, it's kind of compassionate leave.'

'Without much compassion, to hear us talk.'

'No –' he drew her to him and kissed her full on the lips – 'that's not true, but one must make the most of opportunities, it's how we are going to make things work for us for the next two years.'

'It just doesn't seem right to benefit from other people's misfortunes.'

'Huh! That's because you're not landed gentry, they've been doing that since time immemorial.'

'No, I'm not landed gentry,' Katie said, slowly reminded once more of her inadequacies.

'Well, thank heavens, one lot hanging round our necks is enough. So what do you say?'

'To what exactly?' Katie asked cautiously.

'To making the most of our opportunity. I'm expected at home this evening, but tomorrow I could pretend to leave for college first thing. We could go for a ride out, go early. I could drop you back by five and still be back at college before lockout.'

'How could we? Well, how could I?' But even as she questioned, she knew if she said she was going out for the day, her parents would assume it was with Ken North. She could go as if to catch a bus. She looked at him, speculating, calculating. 'Are you serious?'

'I am, of course I am. You could tell your folks you're meeting a friend in town – that would be true enough.'

'They'd assume I was going to meet the office bookkeeper.'

'OK,' he said as if it was no problem.

'They'll be expecting me to announce my engagement or something if I begin doing things like that, going into town on a Sunday. You know how old-fashioned they are.' She shook her head at him. 'They'll want me to invite him here for tea, they've already hinted.'

'It's just a matter of expectations, isn't it? Our parents' expectations are not ours. Why should we feel guilty for wanting what we want, instead of what they plan? As long as you don't up and marry this bookkeeper, I couldn't care less.'

She laughed, but shakily: she didn't want even a pretend relationship with Ken North. A shudder ran icily over her flesh as she thought how she was again the focus of his attention, though somehow it was quite different from before. There was a kind of calculating menace that reminded her of how weasels transfixed rabbits with a stare before leaping for their throats. This was how she felt in Ken North's presence. She looked at Dickie, thinking to explain, but he was planning the next day, and future weekends, and she pushed the feeling of apprehension, of peril even, to the back of her mind.

Only minutes later they heard a car, her father's recently acquired Triumph Herald, coming back from the weekly shopping trip.

Dickie was away before her parents drew up, but they had made their plans. She would leave home in time for the first Sunday bus into town, she'd go just three stops and get off, and he would pick her up on the bike. They would head for Derbyshire, for a day out at Buxton, or Castleton. Dickie had heard that there were more interesting caverns near Castleton, but it was quite a long way past Buxton. Katie, who had never been further than the city of Derby, had no idea how long it might take them to travel to either place.

Her announcement of a Sunday out had been greeted by her mother as a matter of great importance, with a comic pulling-down of her mouth to repress a great grin, and a nod of triumph to Katie's dad, who had raised his eyebrows at his daughter. 'She'll 'ave you in church if you don't watch it.' They had all laughed, but Katie had been privately appalled at the thought of yet more deceptions, of deception going on for years – and years. They'd surely never get away with it.

In answer to questions about where they were going she said, 'Tell you when I come back.' They accepted this with great goodwill – in fact they both seemed in much better

111

humour generally – so she asked, 'Has it been decided about Mr Bennett, when he comes home?'

'*He's* decided,' her father answered, 'as I always knew he would. He's going back to the farm on his own, and he doesn't want any strangers in and out, he says.'

'Which will mean Bess at his beck and call every five minutes,' Colleen answered.

'And you there all the time,' he added.

'Not all the time.'

'No,' he said decisively, 'at least we know that much.'

In spite of the more relaxed feelings at home, the next day Katie was on tenterhooks until they had got well away from Counthorpe and Leicestershire, only beginning to really enjoy herself when they were well beyond Derby, beyond any place she had ever been before.

They stopped mid-morning in Ashbourne. They walked along, holding hands as they looked up at the architecture of the old Queen Elizabeth Grammar School, the Georgian 'Grey House'. Dickie bought ice creams and a bag of Bluebird toffees, which he pushed into his pocket. They walked on, licking around the edges of the 'sandwiches', flat rectangles of ice cream between wafers. They passed beneath the gallows sign of 'The Green Man' public house, which straddled the road.

Katie glanced towards a cafe where people were sitting outside having coffee and cold drinks and thought how pleasant it looked. Dickie caught her glance and looked at the ice creams. 'Would you rather have sat down and had a coffee?' he asked. 'I didn't think really.'

'We've been sitting on the bike, it's nice to walk along and see things,' she said but she noted that he thrust a hand into his pocket, pushing the toffees well down. 'We can always have some lunch at a cafe if you like,' she added.

'In Buxton then,' he said, but she felt his free and easy style did not quite return until they were in Buxton and seated in the back garden of a pub. Here he was the perfect gentleman, finding the table in the shade, procuring the menu, solicitous to her every possible need. She was not deceived: here in Buxton he was playing the man, trying to make up for what he saw as his shortcomings in Ashbourne.

112

It endeared him to her, but they used up a lot of time drinking shandies and waiting to be served in the busy public-house gardens, pleasant though it was.

Afterwards they explored the spa town. There seemed many parks, far too many to visit in one afternoon, a miniature Crystal Palace with exhibitions and entertainments of all kinds, but Katie wanted to see the countryside, and only felt she was really beginning to see the Peak District when they rode out to a nearby dale.

'"Water-cum-Jolly Dale,"' she read from a sign as they left the bike and walked. Soon they were all alone beneath huge trees on one side of a lane and huge cliffs towering above them the other. The solitude and the silence were wonderful after the busy streets.

'You know it's four o'clock.' She was shocked to see the time as they rested on a bank overlooking the dale and a stream.

'We just find paradise when it's time to leave,' he said, 'but not quite yet.' He took off his jacket and laid it beneath her shoulders. 'Lie back,' he said. She did and he lay propped on one elbow looking at her.

'Kate, the prettiest Kate in Christendom,' he quoted, stooping to sip her lips. 'I love you.'

'And I love you,' she whispered, her breath catching as he leaned over and put his hand first on her waist, then ran it gently up, cupping her breast as he stooped to kiss her again. 'Oh! Katie,' he breathed.

She did not answer. His hand locked on her breast felt hot, burning. He might have bought ice cream and toffees earlier like a boy, but he was in command now, and she was not sure how she was going to deal with this, or what she was going to do, or allow him to do.

All she knew was that she would not allow him to go all the way. This was their first real outing together – and she must do something before she lost control. Her mother had quoted the saying 'It's a man's place to ask, and a woman's to refuse' so often she heard it now as a sombre warning.

She raised her head and kissed his lips. As she saw his pleasure at her advance she did want to abandon all caution, but there was that bred deep within her that was so wary of these things, of the consequences of abandonment, that she shook her head.

'What's the matter?' he asked.

'I think I am not ready for, well not ready to . . .'

'I wouldn't do anything you didn't want . . .' he said.

'Mary, at work, says that's all right until your emotions take over, then you don't know what you're doing.'

'But you're with me, so it will be all right, I would know,' he said, but released her and sat up, cradling his knees with his arms. 'Mary an expert on these matters, is she?'

'She's just older.' She felt bereft now, aching for his hand to be back on her breast, his sudden release making her want to say wild things like, all right, all right, let's do it, let's get it over with. She had read books where the heroine had deliberately planned to be rid of her virginity. She had been astounded at their audacity; now she understood, or thought she did. 'You're not cross are you?' she asked, and knew the word she should have used was 'disappointed'.

'Cross –' he turned his head to her – 'of course not. Crossed in love, but never cross with you, my love, never.' He threw himself down by her side again and put his arm across her waist. After a few moments she took his hand and put it back on her breast.

He lay for a long time quite still, then his hand moulded more closely and she felt his fingers entrap her nipple. She swallowed hard and he groaned. 'We're going to be terribly late back,' she breathed.

He groaned again.

There was one long last passionate kiss before they walked back beneath the escarpments of rock where deep shade and the smell of dew falling reminded them how late they really were.

They had one stop south of Derby to buy petrol, and it was by this time nearly eight o'clock.

Before they set off again she suggested that Dickie should stay on the main road into Leicester and she would catch the last bus home. It'll save going across country, that must be quicker for you.'

'It would save me about ten miles, I suppose, but what time is the last bus?'

'Ten thirty, I should catch that easily. Then if there's anyone on it who knows me, and that's more than likely, it would sort of . . .'

'Corroborate our story,' he finished for her, then before they replaced their helmets he smiled and kissed her cheek. 'Katie, the telephone kiosk in the village, opposite the church, I've made a note of the number. If I rang you, say at seven thirty on a Wednesday, could you be there?'

She nodded, then thought about it. She could say she was going into the village to see Joyce Green and baby Crystal – and she could do that afterwards.

'Great!' Dickie enthused. 'Then as soon as I've completed various pieces of work, "achieved a certain standard, shown a real commitment", I shall be allowed out for weekends and we can plan more outings, more time together.'

'So you'll be working hard?' she asked, a hint of promise, even of seduction, creeping into her voice.

'You bet,' he grinned.

They sped back to Leicester at a good speed and it was still a little before ten when Dickie dropped her some four hundred yards from the bus terminus. They lingered, promising, kissing, and she watched him go, turning back on himself for a short way, then out of the city by the ring road which led him towards Northamptonshire.

It was ten minutes past ten when she reached the terminus, she went into the ladies' cloakroom and spent some time tidying her hair and powdering her cheeks. She wondered if her cheeks were not glowing too much to suggest she had spent the day in town.

Then she went to the stand for the Counthorpe bus. There was no one else waiting, though neighbouring stands had several prospective passengers looking at the buses' numbers as they turned into the bus station, swung round the stand and came to rest at their appropriate places.

When twenty past ten came and there was still no one else joining her she suddenly wondered whether the Sunday bus service was the same as in the week. She saw the late-duty bus inspector talking to people across the road and went across. A jovial-faced man, looking near to retirement age, confirmed the last bus to Counthorpe on Sunday was ten o'clock.

'What will you do?' he asked.

'I'll have to phone my dad,' she said.

'Good old dads, we have our uses. Got the change for the phone?'

He sorted through his pockets to help find her the right coins.

'You're very kind,' she said, 'thanks.'

'Don't do it too often, us dads and grandads need our rest.'

She dialled the number and heard it ringing for a long time. She hoped they were not asleep in bed – unlikely, she knew, when she was still out. At last her mother answered, cautiously, anxiously when she heard Katie's voice.

'Where are you? Your dad's gone across the fields to meet you off the bus.'

'I missed it, sorry.'

'So . . .'

'I'm still at the bus station in town.'

The tut said it all, and Katie felt very aware that had she even thought about Sunday bus services, she could have caught the ten o'clock bus.

'Do you think he'd come and fetch me?'

There was a heavy sigh. 'We've had a long day,' her mother began then broke off. There was the sound of muffled talking, her mother with her hand over the mouthpiece, then she came back. 'William'll go and tell your dad where you are.'

Nearly an hour later she sat silently by her father's side. He had opened the Triumph's door and she had got in. 'Sorry, dad.'

'This chap,' he said testily, ' – would have thought he would have seen a young lady safely on to her bus before he left her.'

'It was my fault,' she said, 'I told him to go.'

The noise he made was derogatory. 'What is his name again?' he asked, and when she did not answer he turned to look at her as they travelled out through the deserted suburban streets.

'North,' she said, the lie dragged from her once more. 'Ken North.'

At twenty minutes past seven on Wednesday evening she

116

hovered self-consciously between bus stop and telephone box. It was not a bad time to be in the village: most workers were home eating, most young people not yet ready for the evening out, only children playing out last games lingering when they knew they should be home.

Then as the church clock began to chime the half hour, one of these boys, about ten, came scuffing along the gutter and at the last moment, as on a whim, he diverted into the kiosk. She opened her mouth to protest, then went forward author-itatively to stand just outside, looking at her wristwatch as if the call she wanted to make was urgent. The boy scowled at her under his eyebrows, then gave button 'B' a savage thump to see if any money would fall out; none did. He came out, grinned, and held the door open for her just as the church clock finished sounding the half hour.

She shook her head at him, took the door out of his hand and went to stand in the box, pretending to sort out change from her purse while glancing anxiously up and down the street, fearful someone would arrive who really wanted to make a call.

An age seemed to pass. She glanced at her watch again. Thirty-five minutes past seven, nearly thirty-six minutes past. The telephone rang and she dropped her purse; ignoring it, she snatched up the receiver.

'Hello,' she said urgently.

'Katie.' His voice sounded just as urgent.

There was a moment's silence as each tried to assess the reason for the low quick tones of the other.

'Katie,' he said then broke off as someone else spoke to him and he answered. 'Yes, thanks, I'm through. I'm in the secretary's office,' he explained, 'so I mustn't take up too much time. I just wondered how Grandpa was.'

'They think you're ringing home?' Katie said in a low voice.

'Yes. That's right. So how are things?'

'Fine, and you?'

'Just to send my love,' he said. 'And tell Grandpa it will be four weeks before I'll make it home again.'

'Four weeks! A month?'

'Yes, sorry,' he apologized and someone close to him made

117

a comment. 'Mrs Hardy says I mustn't try to cheat the system, and you were right I was very late back. I have to earn my home privileges back again now.'

'Someone's listening?'

'Yes. I do know Grandpa may be disappointed, but hopefully you understand.'

'Of course I do, but shall I be here again next Wednesday?' she asked.

'Yes, that's fine. I'd better go now, Mrs Hardy is waiting to use her telephone. Love to you,' he said. 'Bye for now.'

'Goodbye, Dickie,' she said, and was overwhelmed by a desire to just stand and cry. She looked up to find an elderly man looking at her impatiently through the small red-framed panes of the box. She went to leave and kicked her purse, she had forgotten all about it.

She picked up the stray coins, then walked home, slowly, feeling desolate. She was greeted by her mother. 'You're soon back, thought you were going to see Joyce.

'I forgot,' she said.

'You must be in love,' Colleen said with a laugh.

The man waiting outside the kiosk had said the same thing as she nearly walked away without her purse.

Thirteen

The Wednesday evening waits by the central village telephone box were never comfortable: people noted her presence; occasionally there'd be someone using the telephone at just her time. Then, when she did finally go to see Joyce, her husband, Dave, had winked at her and said, 'He's not meeting you off the bus these days, then.'

She had decided at that point that she would tell as much of the truth as possible – and no more. If asked, she would just say she was waiting for a call from a friend, and if anyone wanted to know more she would tell them to mind their own business.

One evening the following spring she was leaving the box in a state of great excitement when she heard her name called.

'Hello! Katie!'

She looked up and down the street, then a further cry focused her attention on the churchyard. It was Dickie's mother, who waved as she pulled the churchyard gate closed behind her.

'How nice to see you, it's been ages.'

Katie struggled to appear delighted rather than guilt-stricken. She had just been talking covertly with this woman's son, planning not just a secret liaison for an evening, or even a day out, but for a whole weekend away – 'together quite alone' had been the exact words. She had left the kiosk on a high of anticipation, certain that this weekend was going to be one of the most momentous, if not *the* most momentous time of her life.

Bess waited for her to cross the road towards the church, put an arm round her and kissed her on the cheek. 'It is good to see you,' she said, 'really good. Where are you off to?'

'Home,' Katie answered, 'I'm just walking home.'

'How is everything in your life, then?'

119

'Oh! Fine.' She hesitated to ask how Bess's affairs were for she knew from talk at home that things were certainly not all fine for Bess. She had heard her mother say Ian Sinclair had accused his wife of 'collusion in her son's deceptions'. She felt sick with guilt, but as Bess gave no sign of leaving her, felt forced to ask, 'Are you keeping well?'

Bess laughed at the rather formal enquiry. 'Better in health than in temper some days, I must admit,' she said as they turned to walk together. 'I've just been to put flowers on my mother's grave for my pa, it's their wedding anniversay, eighteenth March. He always remembers.'

'That's nice,' she answered. 'I don't remember Mrs Bennett.'

'No. She died when *I* was a young woman, before my first marriage, to Dickie's father, but you know I still miss her.'

'Really,' Katie felt she knew how it was. She missed Dickie all the time, and after end of term, or the weekends, when he managed to come home it was worse when he went away again.

'Dickie's doing very well at his college, did you know?'

'Working hard, is he?' Oh, Katie Wright! she thought, what a tangled web of lies and half truths. She knew exactly how hard he was working for his privileges.

'He is,' Bess enthused, then she added resignedly, 'the one thing that is going right really.'

Katie did not answer, stopping uncertainly as they reached the end of Church Street. She looked around for one of the vehicles from the Hall.

'I've walked,' Bess said as if sensing her hesitancy, 'from the farm that is, not the Hall of course. I'm at the farm for a while,' she added, 'so we can walk back together. You said you were walking home.'

'Yes,' she agreed, trapped.

'I'd be glad of company,' Bess added.

For some reason Katie felt she meant sympathetic company. 'Is it because of Mr Bennett? I mean that you're staying at the farm. It's not still his leg, is it?'

'Not really. I think it's more about me.' She sighed deeply. 'How do you feel about your father, Katie? Is his word your bondage, that's what my husband says about my father.'

Katie was totally surprised by this line of conversation, but grateful, for it steered away from Dickie. 'I think a lot of my dad,' she replied, 'I love him of course, but . . .'

'But?' Bess questioned the pause.

'Well, they can put a lot of pressure on you, can't they, and without saying very much really.'

'You mean, it's trying to live up to their expectations of you.'

'Yes, that's it, all the time, even when they're not around, they seem to stand in the corner of your mind wagging a finger at you,' Katie said, 'that's how it is.' She could truthfully have added, particularly when I'm with your son.

'Oh, Katie! I do wish I had a daughter, one like you.'

'Well, you will have one day,' she responded impulsively to a squeeze of her arm, then found herself gabbling on, 'I mean . . . I mean I was thinking you'll have daughters-in-law, won't you . . .'

'Looking ahead quite a time I suppose, yes. I mean, I do hope so, and grandchildren. Gosh, can't imagine that, can you, children of my children. We used to have an old family Bible, the Bennetts that is,' she began with enthusiasm, then broke off as if now *she* was saying too much. 'I wonder what happened to it?' she tossed the question in so lightly it was meant not to matter but it hovered.

They walked on in silence, leaving the lights of the village street behind, but their eyes had become well used to the twilight. Somewhere in the darkening fields a lamb bleated as if lost, but as they both listened the appeal was not repeated, there was only the sound of their footsteps and in the distance the sound of a car negotiating the village square.

'Bet it's still at the farm,' Katie said, 'the Bible. Those sort of things don't get thrown away, do they?'

'That's usually true.'

So was there something not usual about it, Katie wondered, then concluded there was nothing usual about anything that evening. When they parted, Katie to take the short field route to her home and Bess the track to the farm, Bess said, 'You could tell your mother I'm at the farm, so there's no need for her to come over quite so early.'

It was only when she reached home and relayed the message that she realized it was of any great significance.

'Oh! my God!' Colleen gasped, her hand over her mouth. 'She can't do this, surely she can't. I took it all as just talk, letting off steam.'

'Do what?' George demanded.

'Leave Ian.'

George lowered the evening newspaper to his knees, but before he could comment further Colleen sat down at the table and pounded it with clenched fists. 'I'll tell you when this all started, the day Mr Bennett bought that blooming motorbike for her Dickie.'

'Now you have lost me,' George replied, but Katie bit her lip, feeling it likely her mother had it about right.

On Friday night Katie was to meet Dickie at the far side of the bus station from the office – buoyed up by this, she had given Ken North a particularly bad time all day.

He had been called into the senior partner's room, where she was taking notes. She had found the leer he had directed her way to be particularly objectionable, patronizing and disturbingly possessive. She had risen and left abruptly as he was motioned to the other chair. She pretended not to hear Mr Benbrook's call that he wanted her to stay. She had gone hurriedly to the lavatory and stayed there until she gauged North was back in his own office. Later Mr Benbrook had asked her if anyone had upset her. She had hesitated, then said no, of course not.

Ken had shot her such a hangdog look of hurt before he slouched off towards home, she wondered if their boss had also questioned him.

Making her way to the bus station and the left luggage office, she could *almost* have found it in her heart to feel sorry for him. She was heading for a secret weekend full of excitement – and love proper, or improper, (which she felt she knew both all and nothing about) – while he, she presumed, was going home to an empty house, a solitary tea, then out to his usual Friday-night snooker. She wondered if anyone at the snooker hall had any particular liking for him. Feeling magnanimous, she hoped there might just be someone, some companion perhaps much like himself, who would be pleased to see him.

She retrieved her bag, went to the public lavatories, changed her skirt for slacks in one of the compartments, and from there hurried through the bus station to the far side opposite the huge City Technical College.

She immediately saw Dickie at the bottom of the main steps, looking as if he too had just arrived, and was perfectly at ease in a throng of students going up and down, in and out, of the college. He saw her coming, shelled off his helmet and pulled the bike on to its stand before she reached him. The chattering, milling crowd parted round them, some commenting, laughing, but inhibiting neither of them as, arms thrown wide, he greeted her.

'We made it,' he said, kissing her cheek, repeating the words against her lips before pressing a firm full kiss which held such certainty and so many expectations.

'So far,' she said, laughing, feeling shaky yet happy-go-lucky at the same time as one or two students whistled approval, 'but where are we going?'

'It's a surprise, but it's quite a long way.' He took her bag and strapped it on to the back pannier. 'On you get.' Obediently she pulled on the matching helmet he had bought her, together with a Derbyshire Blue John pendant, for last Christmas. 'But I'll tell you that you've been before . . .' he said as he remounted.

With that, he started off, and she was not sure whether she heard or imagined the 'many times'.

They took the road eastwards out of the city, towards Peterborough. She certainly knew the direction they were heading in, towards Lincolnshire, Skegness, Mablethorpe, or perhaps further to Norfolk, and she *had* certainly been that way many times before with him, his family, her family.

She held on and, unable to see over his shoulder, at first it was just house tops and street lamps she glimpsed; then on through countryside, the moon appearing steadily brighter as the night darkened. Soon the sky was like midnight-blue velvet pierced with brilliant stars. He rode the machine with skill now, no hesitation, no missed gear or over-hasty braking. She also realized he knew exactly where he was going. She envied men this skill of direction most of them seemed to have, including her father, William. She was more like her mother, who, her father said, taken through just a couple of field gates, could be lost.

He picked up speed as they came to the long straight roads of Lincolnshire, through the flat fenland, where now the moon picked out in bright straight lines the dykes and rivers going, like them, ever towards the sea. They were passing through Wisbeach, the road by the river, when she remembered a journey in the Sinclairs' car when Julian was quite a little boy, and had been entranced by such a moon as this, convinced it was following them, going with them on their holiday.

Wisbeach, King's Lynn, Norfolk, the coast road to . . . If her helmet had allowed, her jaw would have dropped, at the outrageous idea, no more than an idea, then a certainty, that came to her. They were on the way to Dickie Philipps's family holiday home.

She was still arguing with herself that she could not be right, that their destination would be a campsite or a caravan park, that there was no way even Dickie could arrange for them to be together – alone – at his family bungalow. She found herself shaking her head inside the cumbersome helmet and she must have clutched Dickie tighter for he pressed his elbows on to her encircling arms in response.

She would question him properly as soon as they stopped, but they did not stop. The North Sea lay on their left as they travelled south now, towards Wells-next-the-Sea. She thought of his mother, whom she had walked and talked with only two days before. Could she possibly have known Dickie was intending to come to the bungalow? And if so, who with? No, she could not have given permission, she could not believe that. His father – stepfather, as Dickie always corrected – would certainly not. He was suspicious enough already.

She wondered what deceptions Dickie had practised? She had told her mother she was going on a rambling weekend and, when pressed, had agreed with her mother's suggestion that they were all from the office. 'Oh, lovely! Don't do anything I wouldn't do,' she had pretended to joke, but Katie had caught the look of anxiety in her mother's eyes. Perhaps what she had wanted to say was don't get yourself into trouble and have to get married. She had never heard it discussed, but Katie knew from her calculations of wedding day, birthday and her own birth weight that added to her mother's anxiety was the anxiety for her daughter not to do as she had done. Katie smiled, it had turned out all right for them in the end: they were happy in their way, happier together than many. Today of course marriage was no longer regarded quite so much as a woman's natural 'comeuppance' as Mary called it.

It was dark now, late, gone nine thirty – she had glimpsed the lighted face of a clock on a cobbled Norfolk tower before they approached Wells. It felt most oddly strange and familiar all at the same time. She had explored this place with Dickie when they had both been clad in shorts, T-shirts and flip-flops and hardly large enough to peer into the shop windows, and secretly put pennies into machines for balls of lurid bubblegum.

At last he stopped his bike on the road near a small post office, where she knew keys to the Philippses' bungalow were kept.

He tipped off his helmet. 'Won't be a moment,' he said and was gone across the road through a side gate by the post office and out of sight. She tried to imagine the conversation with the businesslike Mrs Coombs, the postmistress, who augmented her income by supervising holiday homes. She ranged from Annie Coombs refusing to let him have the keys – or coming out expecting to see a carload of people from the Hall – then refusing to let them have the keys.

Too early for proper holidaymakers, and too late for locals to be abroad, Katie looked up to the moon for company, and willed Dickie back quickly. She shivered, more with nervous anticipation than cold.

So this was what a 'weekend away' felt like – and had she prepared herself, been sensible, thought about precautions – because no man could surely expect less than everything if you agreed to spend two nights away with him? The short answer was no, she had not; she had even been too embarrassed to ask Mary's advice, and goodness knows, Mary talked freely enough on the subject – perhaps that was the trouble – she did not want asking for some kind of progress report after the weekend.

He startled her when he came rattling back through the side gate. 'Right, the last bit,' he said.

'She gave you the keys?' She felt and sounded astonished.

'Of course!' he exclaimed. 'What did you expect?'

'But how?'

'Wait until we get there.'

The bungalow was on the cliffs, alone, its ground enclosed by a stout fence dating from the time the children had been small, but with its own private scramble path down to the beach. The memories and her sudden anticipation of being alone with him were shattered as he swung the bike around to the front and she saw there was a light on inside.

'Who's here?' she asked as they dismounted.

'No one. Annie said she'd left the light and the night-storage heaters on for us. We told her we should be late.'

'We?' she queried.

'Well, Liz really,' he said, pulling a ring of keys from his pocket and giving them to her. 'I'll bring the bags.'

'Liz?' she questioned. 'Liz spoke to your mother.'

'No,' he said with a grin, 'she pretended to be my mother. She rang Annie.' He stood, holding their bags, outlined by the yellow light from the kitchen window, while the bungalow, a nearby group of pines and the land were etched in silver and greys by the moon.

'So no one knows we're here, I mean no one from either of our families.'

'No.' He let the bags fall to the ground, and reached forward to her hand, still holding the keys, but he led her around the bungalow to the sea side. 'Listen,' he said 'and smell.'

The sea was a moving carpet of silver with the moon making a brilliant rippled path across the calm waters. The only sound was the shushing of waves rolling pebbles gently in each rise and fall. The air was replete with the smell of the sea, the ozone, laced through with the resins of pines.

The one time her father had come here he had said that it did his Midland heart good to smell the sea, but he had never come again.

'It is lovely,' she said.

'No regrets then?'

'Not so far.'

'You'll never have any regrets, I won't let you have, ever,' he said.

A million questions crowded her mind as he took her into

126

his arms. 'Are you cold?' he asked. 'Out here, I mean.'

She looked up into a sky and saw a shooting star travel up over his shoulder and head, then disappear. She shook her head against his chest and controlled the shivering.

'Katie, I love you, need you, you do believe that don't you? I wouldn't want to live without you.'

'I do believe you,' she breathed, 'and don't say such things as not living,' she told him as he unbuttoned her coat and slid his hands inside, over her back, her buttocks, and pressed her to him. She was both startled and awed as she felt his erection, and she knew that this first time proper was going to be here on these cliffs, beneath this moon. She pushed her arms up around his neck and hung there, looking at the moon that seemed to have come with them, spreading its enchantment, just as Julian had thought so many years before.

'Katie, you are sure?' he whispered. 'I mean, I've come prepared but . . .'

'I am sure,' she said, feeling suddenly so for the first time since they had begun this intrigue of secret meetings, and because she was sure she said, 'so let's not make it a hole-and-corner thing.'

He laughed. 'I do love your sayings, they're just part of what makes you you.'

He put her coat and his on the ground and they lay down together.

He undressed her slowly, reminding her of someone uncovering a great treasure (an Egyptologist on television, layer by layer), and he paused between each garment as if to give her time to object. Then he stood up in one swift movement and pulled of all his own clothes, and she in turned treasured the sight of his athletic body before he came to cover her mouth with his, her body with his. It was swift, surprising, painless. His gratitude sweet as he lay kissing her over and over, everywhere. 'That was not fair to you. It will be better next time,' he said, 'or so they say.'

'We'll find that out,' she said, keeping her astonishment at the brevity of the whole affair to herself.

'I wonder how many times,' he said. 'How many times will we make love? Hundreds, thousands, millions.'

'This weekend, you mean?'

He laughed and, lying on his side, pulled her to him, tight, so their fronts were warm, locked tight, with no gap for the night air that chilled their backs, and she felt his erection coming again. She thought they would make love again there and then, but as he moved his hands over her back he said, 'I think we should go inside – your back feels icy.'

'And yours.'

He was on his feet, scooping up an armful of their clothes.

'You've got the keys.'

'I must have put them down on the grass somewhere.'

They first stooped, then got down on hands and knees to run their hands over the grass, and were soon both hysterical with laughter as he searched doing a variety of farmyard impressions – cows, sheep, pigs – but no keys.

'Clothes on, I think. Never thought I'd say that this weekend.'

She giggled as they pulled on their outer clothes and coats. 'What will we do?' she asked.

'Break a window,' he said, then as he resumed the search in a much wider circle almost immediately gave a whoop of triumph. 'No, got them.' He sat back on his haunches. 'I shan't have to blame you for breaking a window after all,' he said.

She threw herself at him, upending both of them.

'Oh Katie, Katie!' he exclaimed, then was silent, and they both lay on their backs quite still, looking up into the stars and infinite distances.

'What are you thinking?' she asked.

He laughed.

'No, truly, what are you thinking?'

'That I could fuck you for ever.'

'Dickie!' she reprimanded, not used to hearing the word at all, even poshly spoken.

'Do you think we'll laugh about this when we're an old married couple – on a distant wedding anniversary, say.'

'You mean when we've made love millions of times,' she said.

Fourteen

In spite of her niggling concern for Bess, when she had rung to say there was no need for her to go to the farm early the next morning, and that she could take a break if she wanted, Colleen had immediately thought of George's wish to visit an elderly aunt in Rutland – and with Katie going away for the weekend it had seemed an ideal opportunity.

George had arranged with Mr Bennett to spread his work between the other men and a part-timer, and they had left Thursday evening, returning just before Katie arrived home on the Sunday night.

It had been a happy evening at the Wrights' home – they had all had such a fulfilling weekend. George's Aunt Gladys had been overwhelmingly pleased to see them, joyful when George and William had dug over and planted much of her garden, and Colleen had put a coat of emulsion on her kitchen. They had achieved a lot, and Katie had obviously had a good time, positively glowing and seeming very content to listen to all they had done.

Colleen was eager to catch up with Bess on the Monday, and so deferred her usual Monday wash day so she could be there bright and early. She was in sight of the orchard when she saw Bess walking to meet her. They greeted each other with a long hug, a sure sign these days that one or the other had real trouble.

'I wanted to have a word where Pa couldn't hear,' Bess said.

'What's happened? You look . . .' She was suddenly struck with the idea that what Bess looked was bereaved. 'Your pa?'

Bess shook her head at the idea. 'He's fine.'

'So?'

'It's Ian –' she stopped and looked earnestly at her friend – 'and me. It's all gone terribly wrong.'

'Is this why you're still here at the farm?' Colleen took both her hands and wrung them between her own.

'Part of the reason,' Bess admitted.

'You can't do this, you and Ian, you can't think of . . . It's not possible. I can't think of you two apart. You've loved each other since, well, since you were children. You can't have changed.'

'No – that, according to Ian, is the problem. I've not changed. I'm still the father-dominated woman who can't say "get stuffed" to her father.' She sounded close to tears.

'He doesn't seriously mean that – or even say it, I know him better than that,' Colleen said, turning her friend resolutely away from the farm and walking back along the path. This was going to take too long to walk straight back to the farm.

'What happened last Wednesday night didn't help,' Bess said.

'The first night you stayed at the farm?'

Bess nodded. 'We'd had yet another row about Dickie, and this college, a big row. Ian is forever telephoning them. The headmaster rang me to say he could understand my husband's concerns, but thought we should give Dickie more space, more "elbow room" as he put it "to be himself". I only intended to go out for a walk, clear the air, and my head, but I carried on to see Pa. I found him all upset because the florist had delivered the special flowers for Ma's grave on the wrong day. You know how he's always so particular about remembering their wedding anniversary. He felt they would fade before they were put in place, so I said I'd walk over to the churchyard with them, there and then. I was worried about him – just the flowers coming on the wrong day seemed to have really thrown him. Then I remembered him taking his gun up to the spinney after Ma died. I couldn't get it out of my mind, so I decided to stay over. When I got back to the farm I telephoned Julian. He said he'd tell his father, and I also asked him to walk the dogs.'

'Go on,' Colleen urged as Bess seemed to come to a halt.

'So Julian did his homework, walked the dogs and when Ian was not back left him a note to say where I was, and went to bed. He just went to sleep, woke up Thursday morning, Mrs West was there. He was having his breakfast when I rang

130

to check everything was OK and told him he'd better remind Ian that he had to drive him to school.'

Bess stood shaking her head, then sighed with some exasperation. 'He rang me back to say he couldn't find his father, and only his own bed had been slept in.'

'Oh!' Colleen exclaimed. 'So where was Ian?'

She gave a tut of exasperation then went on. 'I was getting really worried. I took Julian to school, then went back and finally read through Ian's diary. The only appointment was with a Mr Springer the afternoon before. There was a number by the name, so I rang, and Ian was still there. He said he'd telephoned several times the night before to let me know he wasn't coming back. The first time must have been while Julian was walking the dogs, later Julian would have been asleep. Ian assumed we were both at the farm.'

'But why had he stayed?'

'Mr Springer wanted him to see exactly how his garden looked in the early morning light.'

People with time to worry and consider such niceties were quite beyond Colleen's comprehension, and she was prompted to say what she instinctively felt. 'Say what you like, all this trouble has been caused by that motorbike just like it was the first time, giving young men wild ideas.'

Bess turned to her and saw she was reliving the old torment, the past overwhelming her. 'Colleen, don't!' she implored. 'It's not the same thing.'

'I've never forgiven our Roy for what he did to you, even though he was my brother, even though it makes me shudder to speak ill of the dead, I say he was wicked.'

'You still can't blame a motorbike.' She tried to make the idea sound ludicrous, at the same time placing a calming hand on Colleen's shoulder.

'Why can't I?' She shrugged off the hand. 'If my brother had not had that bike, he'd never have made such a "friend" of that pansy postman, and they could not have schemed together to keep Ian's letters from you.' She paused to draw breath, then turned to face Bess as if to accuse her. 'You wouldn't have married into the Philipps family, you would not have had Dickie, and we wouldn't all be involved with another machine of death.'

She was left speechless by the dramatic harangue.

'You can't deny it's caused a lot of trouble already?' Colleen added.

'No, I can't deny that –' she spoke quietly but felt quite battered by Colleen's blunt summary of her life – 'but I don't regret marrying Greville and having Dickie.'

'You regret his suicide, all the trauma you went through before you found Ian again. None of that would have happened if it had not been for my brother flying off on his motorbike, killing himself and his postman "friend".'

Bess did not think she had ever hear Colleen sound so hard, so bitter. She thought of reminding her that no one would have known about the letters unless Roy had been killed, they would never have been found in his belongings.

'There's no point in this discussion, is there?' she said as her mind began willy-nilly to reconstruct her own life as if circumstances had been different, as if Greville Philipps had not drowned himself, then seeing Colleen looking ready to launch on a new tirade any moment, added firmly, 'No point at all.'

'There is if you come to your senses and get back where you belong.'

Bess felt let down, she had wanted to tell Colleen how unreasonable Ian was being, how he was fixated by the idea that Dickie was cheating on them somehow. Now she didn't feel able. Instead of sympathy she found Colleen locked back into what had happened twenty years ago.

They both stood, becoming aware of the chill March wind cooling their faces, tumbling their hair, emphasizing perhaps the sudden lack of warmth between them. Colleen had compressed her mouth into a tight line, as if she had resolved to say no more on the subject.

After a time she straightened from the gate. 'I might as well go back and do my washing.'

Bess let her go, trying to push the past into its place, in the past. Colleen had advised her to go back where she belonged, or did she mean who she belonged to? Perhaps she was just tired of belonging to anyone.

When she arrived back at the farm, Ian's car was outside and her first instinct was to turn on her heel. Walking into the ever-cosy kitchen she realized how cold she had become.

'I've come to sort out what we are doing.' Ian greeted her.

'Ian tells me Dickie's spent the weekend with Liz,' her father put in.

Bess shot a look at her husband: the only way he could know this was because he had telephoned the college again. She had laughingly remarked that if she didn't know better she would think he was having an affair with the headmaster's wife, Olga Hardy. He had not been amused – he was not amused these days by anything anyone said, except perhaps Julian. She felt a pang of – what – jealousy? Surely she couldn't resent her own son, their mutually achieved son. Things were coming to a pretty pass.

'I thought it would please your father to know that,' he said poker-faced.

'Keeping the right company,' Edgar put in. 'Of course I'm pleased to hear it, wouldn't any sensible grandfather be.'

It was not a question, it was, as so often with Edgar, an assumption he presumed they all fell in with.

'I wondered how long you'd be staying here?' Ian asked bluntly.

She glanced at her father and as he dropped his head and frowned she wanted to say 'indefinitely'. 'I'm not sure,' she compromised. 'Perhaps Julian should come here too, that might make your life simpler.'

'Julian's spring break starts in just over a week, if you're . . .' he hesitated as if to find the right words, but failed. 'I thought I'd take him down to see his other grandpa in Cornwall. He's keen to go and perhaps by the time we come home you will have sorted things out here.'

Both instinctively looked at Edgar.

'It's nothing to do with me,' Edgar stated, 'don't consider me, I'm fine.'

There was just the slightest hint of pique in her father's voice, and neither of them missed it.

Bess felt she could match the feeling. She had a great affection for Ian's father and the artist he had married some years after he had moved to Cornwall. 'I've some prints for Barbara,' she said. 'I'll come over tomorrow and dig them out.'

Ian looked from her to her father and she expected more

verbal infighting, but instead Ian nodded and walked out. She followed him to the car.

He got into the Jaguar and rolled the window down. 'So you think it fit to leave me, a Sinclair, in charge at the Hall, the Philipps inheritance. Bit ironic, isn't it?'

'It's your home as well as mine.'

'It's my home only because it is yours, and it's yours, "your sacred trust", because your first son will inherit. Bess, if this thing is to go on for any length of time I shall move out.' He started the engine. 'For God's sake, look beyond the end of your nose, beyond your father, beyond what Dickie wants you to believe. Question Colleen, question Katie.'

'As you're questioning Mrs Hardy?'

'Yes.' His face darkened.

'So you really think Katie has a boyfriend at the office and Dickie on the side then!'

He started off, taking the car from under her hand on the window frame. It was the second time she had been brushed off that day – and it wasn't yet nine o'clock.

She saw no one else all day, had no phone calls, and the way she and Colleen had parted weighed heavily. Her father still slept a little after lunch, an unheard of thing before his fall. She went out to speak to George when he arrived in the yard to supervise the afternoon milking. He looked grim as she approached. 'If you think anything of our Colleen, you'd best get over there before the day's gone. She came back in a right state this morning, thinks she's upset you so much you'll never speak to her again.' He paused, looking down at her and though he was much taller he reminded her so much of his grandfather, Noel Wright, who had been both her father's waggoner and her childhood guru. The same wise blue eyes looked at her as he added, 'Though from what she tells me she gave you nothing but good advice.' He turned and walked away before she could answer.

She went immediately to tell her father where she was going. Waking him with a cup of tea, 'I've got steak for later, so I'll grill that when I come back.'

'You worry too much about other people,' he said, watching her as she bustled about, 'rushing off just to see Colleen, is it necessary?'

'It is,' she answered, ignoring the humph and not explaining. 'You'll wear yourself out.'

It was on the tip of her tongue to retort that it would also help if *he* agreed to have someone live in, but knew from experience that the less she argued with her father the better, because in the end she always let him win so as not to upset him. Her mother would have understood, though she doubted anyone else ever would. Her mother had known that the burden they both carried in life was that they loved Edgar Bennett too much.

As soon as she reached the open door she knew what Colleen had been doing all day: not only was there a line full of sheets, pillowcases, overalls, shirts, blowing in the wind, but the kitchen shone in every corner. 'Cleaning,' she said aloud, and as if in answer Colleen came from her pantry, cloth in hand, her face blotchy and her eyes red with crying.

She began again as she saw Bess, then held out her arms and the two hugged each other. 'You silly thing,' Bess told her, 'did you really think I could ever really fall out with you – well, not for long anyway.'

Colleen rested her forehead on her friend's shoulder. 'I shouldn't have raked up the past,' she said, 'I was sorry I'd done that.' She straightened and threw the cloth into the sink. 'But the rest of it . . . Cup of tea?

'I need to spell everything out to you,' Bess began, 'exactly what Ian believes.'

Over the tea she told of his conviction that their Katie and Dickie were involved with each other.

Colleen laughed. 'They were close as children, but our Katie's two years older and has this man-friend, off this last weekend the pair of them, with two others from the office.' Another thought seemed to strike her. 'But would you have minded if, say they were older, your Dickie was to go out with such as our Katie?'

'No, I'd be delighted. In fact –' she recollected her conversation with Katie – 'I told Katie I'd love a daughter like her.' She remembered Katie saying that she would have daughters-in-law some day, then becoming a bit shy as if she had said too much.

'Though I always think of them as more like brother and

sister,' Colleen mused, then went on more forcibly, 'but those two are not really the cause of the trouble between you and Ian. It's your dad! It's always been your dad.'

Bess felt the energy go out of her and she shook her head. 'I can't abandon him, drop out of his life, can I?'

'I don't know whether he does it on purpose or not, but he knows that you run to his every beck and call, stand on your head to please him – and *always have*.'

'I know,' she admitted, 'habit of a lifetime.'

'Even if it breaks up your marriage? Come on, Bess. You and Ian not together, I don't want to live to see the day.'

Bess frowned at her. 'Don't say things like that.'

'I mean it,' she stressed. 'I really mean it, and there's one thing we can do about all this and that's clear up this business Ian's got in his head about our Katie. You can stay and see her, she'll be home by a quarter to six.'

'Pa will . . .'

'Never mind Pa anything!' she exclaimed. 'Let's try and settle this nonsense. What if you ring Ian and tell him to come over, let's have it all in the open.'

Bess made a grimace. 'What about George and William, you've got their meal, and they won't want to be involved?'

'They are involved, aren't they? If I'm upset, it rubs off on them.' For a moment she looked apologetic but added, 'Don't suppose I'm any different to anyone else in that respect. When did you last see Ian?'

She told her that Ian had been there that morning and of what he had said.

'So why don't you make that your deadline for staying at the farm? Go with them to Cornwall.'

'I don't honestly think Ian wants me. He's talking of a cooling-off period. He seems to be relishing the idea of taking Julian away on his own.'

Colleen tutted. 'All right then, make it when they come back, be back at the Hall for when they come back.'

Bess pushed out her bottom lip but knew it was a positive idea, a kind of not too imminent deadline for herself and Ian. 'But then there's Katie.'

Colleen took the remark as an acceptance of her advice, and seized the next moment triumphantly. 'Ring Ian, leave a message if he's not around, then our Katie can tell him all about her chap. He's the accountant, you know.'

William came home first, trailing his school satchel bulging with homework asking, 'What's to eat, Mum, keep me going till dinner,' before he saw Bess. They talked as he ate an enormous slab of saucepan cake, one of Colleen's specialities. Twice a week she threw everything into a saucepan, boiled it and then baked the fruity mixture – she vowed it kept George and William going between meals.

Shortly after George arrived, he looked at Bess a little sheepishly. 'You made it then,' he said.

'Of course,' she answered with a nod.

'Everything OK now then between you two?'

'We're going to have a family conference,' Colleen announced.

'Oh no!' William said. 'Not about motorbikes.'

'No!' Colleen said. 'But you know where you stand on the subject.'

'Yes,' William replied, 'Dad's going to teach me how to drive the car as soon as I'm old enough.'

George cleared his throat.

'That's what you said,' William accused.

'That's what I said,' George repeated heavily, 'and I don't suppose I shall be allowed to forget it.'

'No.' William grinned at his dad, helped himself to another wedge of cake and as his mother protested said, 'I really need it to help me through my homework, I've got masses.' She waved him away.

'He does his homework in his bedroom, we've got it cosy for him up there, with a heater and a desk and everything,' Colleen explained.

'So what's this pow-wow about?' George asked.

'Basically Bess has two problems,' Colleen began.

'My father and my husband.'

'Your father needn't be a problem. The trouble is you, and your mother before you, spoilt him, you both heeded his every whim, every need, that's why he missed your mother so much. You've tried too hard to be there in her place.'

'I have been told,' she nodded at Colleen, 'but there was no one else,' she said. She reflected that it was all very well

137

for Colleen to make judgments. George's grandparents, who had brought him up, were long gone, and Colleen's parents were a comfortable self-sufficient old couple, living in the village right next door to one of Colleen's sisters.

'No, but if and when it does come to the stage when he really needs someone, he's got the money, he can afford a live-in housekeeper,' Colleen put in. 'Good gracious *his* mother had one for years enough. Do you remember Miss Seaton?'

They all grinned at the memories of Grandmama Bennett's housekeeper. She had been the bane of their young lives on many an occasion.

Reminiscences overtook the agenda and they were laughing with each remembered incident, until Colleen heard the click of the gate between path and garden. 'Here's our Katie,' she announced and they all fell silent.

'Ian's not here,' Bess commented, feeling she had known all along he would not be.

All eyes turned to Katie as she entered the kitchen, glowing from her walk, a smile on her lips. When she saw the waiting group she stopped in her tracks, one hand clasping her shoulder bag to her side, the other going to her mouth. 'What's happened?' she asked.

'No, no, nothing,' her mother reassured.

'Yes,' she denied, 'something must have.' She looked from her mother, to father, to Bess and saw smiles, of a kind. Smiles like those of a Spanish inquisition, she thought, before the interrogation began. Had they somehow found out about the weekend? Had something happened to Dickie? The motorbike, had he had another accident? She scanned the faces again, as her mother poured her a cup of tea and placed it on the table before an empty chair. 'Come on, sit down. What kind of day have you had?'

'Fine,' she said cautiously, 'fine.'

'I was telling Bess about you going off for the weekend,' her mum said.

Katie nodded. She'd worked in a solicitor's office long enough to know a little about court work: leading questions; policemen told to say just yes or no wherever possible in answer to barristers' questions.

'We went over to Rutland, Manton, to see my aunt,' George

put in as if to fill the gap left by his daughter, whom he treated to a look which said, come on girl, speak up.

'Colleen told me, sounded as if you all worked hard.'

'We did,' William said, reappearing from upstairs.

'There's no more cake,' Colleen said, 'you'll not want your dinner.'

'No, just wanted to see what was going on.' He looked at Bess. 'Mr Sinclair's coming, could see his car from my bedroom.'

Katie was pleased no one was looking at her as her teacup wobbled violently, spilling a fair amount in her saucer. This *was* something to do with her and Dickie, she had no shadow of doubt now. She had felt Ian Sinclair had been on the point of questioning her when she'd met him in the village some time ago. She found Bess's gaze on her, but there was no accusation there, more as if she was apologizing.

'Ian thinks Dickie is using his motorbike and the nearness of his new college, to . . .' Bess paused and shrugged, 'to come home to meet you.'

'Thinks,' was the word she picked up and repeated.

'He just needs convincing that he's wrong.'

'I told Bess how you spent last weekend with your office friends. I thought you could tell him all about that.'

A car door closed and George rose to open the door. The two men greeted each other. Ian greeted them all as he came in, and said to Bess, 'I went to the farm, I thought that's where you were.'

'I said—' She broke off. 'Well, it doesn't matter – you're here now.'

'Yes,' he said and looked around, grinned at William. 'Great to see you all – but why am I here? Why am I specially summoned?'

'They all think your Dickie's trying to abduct our Katie on his motorbike,' William said with a laugh.

'If you can't say anything sensible keep quiet,' his father told him.

'Go and get on with that homework,' Colleen said and pushed another wedge of cake into his hand.

There was an awkward silence and with everyone looking at him William shrugged and obviously felt obliged to go, cake in hand.

'I don't think Katie minds telling how she spent last weekend, or about her office friends, if it helps.' Again he looked at his daughter as if urging her to speak out.

'It is to help our oldest friends,' her mother prompted.

Katie's fears were fast turning to anger, which in turn could easily have brought tears. She got up from the table and turned her back on them all.

'Katie,' Bess began but Katie span round.

'No,' she said, 'it's not about friends at all. The truth is you want to make sure that a son of the landed gentry is not going out with the daughter of a farm labourer.'

'It would certainly be inappropriate,' Ian said ponderously, 'for a sixteen-year-old public schoolboy to think he can take advantage of a—'

'An ignorant village girl,' Katie again put in. She could not escape the feeling that she was giving evidence, in the dock, and that she was about to lie on oath.

'Don't be silly,' her mother put in, 'it's nothing like that, but there's no point in anyone even thinking such a thing when you're going out with someone else, is there? Tell Mr Sinclair.'

She ached to tell them all that she and Dickie really truly loved each other, that they would go through hell and high water, and more, to be together, that no one, least of all their families, was ever going to stop them being together at every possible opportunity.

'Tell Ian about . . .' Colleen urged with a forceful lunge of her head, 'Ken . . .'

'You were away for the weekend with him,' George supplied.

'Yes, yes,' she almost shouted, 'Ken North, he works at our office. We all went for a dirty weekend. Now are you all satisfied?'

'He's a professional man,' her mother added, the words there in her mouth for speaking before she quite realized what Katie had said, 'an accountant.'

'Right, so that's OK then. If everyone is now happy, I'll go and change and get on with *my* life.'

They all listened to her run upstairs and to her bedroom door bang.

'Well, I hope you all think that was worth it,' George said.

Fifteen

'We went to see where they'd been filming all the Poldark books,' Julian enthused, 'and Barbara's done me a watercolour of the farm they used, Botallack Manor Farm. She stood near the wall and sketched it from there, then she made a note of the colours and painted it at home. It only took her a few hours. It would take me days! But she said it's only a matter of practice, and that she knows I could do it.'

'I'm sure . . .' Bess began, her heart lifting at her younger son's enthusiasm for all things Cornish. She sat enjoying the pleasure of just looking at his glowing young face as much as hearing that the 'Nampara' of the film was really two houses, the back of one at Pendeen and the front of Botallack Farm.

She watched him, a smile on her lips, as he went on about how amazing it was that Barbara looked quite an old lady ordinarily but when she was painting, 'or telling me about it, she becomes young and all . . .' He looked at his father for the word and he supplied it. 'Yes, "animated", that's it.'

'*And*,' Julian added and this was obviously going to be the biggest plus of all, 'Dad's bought me a proper set of water-colours – tubes, you know –' he nodded the importance of this difference at her – 'not a paintbox.' He turned to his father with such a look of glowing gratitude she felt excluded.

'I wish I'd been there.'

'We could go again, couldn't we, Dad? Barbara and Grandpa Sinclair said we must, and soon.'

'Be nothing to stop us, if—' Ian began.

'Is Grandpa Bennett OK now?' Julian asked. 'And what have you been doing?'

'Yes, he's fine, and we've had the Jubilee Show and Gymkhana, that's kept me busy.'

'So you are back home?' Ian asked, holding her gaze.

'Yes.'

'Good,' he said and for a moment made her remember the day they had re-found each other after years of misunderstandings not of their making, of the way he had reached across a milk-bar table, gripped her forearm and said, 'Thank God.' She lifted her eyebrows at him, an infinitesimal invitation that she saw him register but not respond to. Obviously it was not quite enough to be there with a greeting and a meal ready for the second they arrived. He made her feel like goods taken 'on approval', not decided on, as yet. She was not sure she was going to make the grade, not sure she had the energy to keep trying.

Julian ran back to the bags they had just unloaded from the car. 'This is for you,' he said, pulling a solid square parcel from his sports bag. 'Hope you like it? I chose, but Grandpa helped me pay for it.'

It was a handsome set of all the Poldark novels.

'I've been wanting to read these. Thanks, Julian, very much.'

'And Grandpa,' he added.

'You couldn't have chosen anything nicer. I shall have them on my bedside table, and start reading tonight.'

In normal times there would have been some shift in the room, some sign that meant Ian was thinking that after weeks apart there'd be no reading tonight. She kissed Julian and hugged him hard, and he filled her heart as he said, 'It's good to be home, Ma, to see you.'

'Good to have you back,' she said, 'both of you.'

Looking back on that first day when they arrived home from Cornwall, Bess felt she could honestly say she really had tried to placate Ian. She felt a curious feeling of having wooed back his body but not his heart, she felt he was holding that in reserve, her prize for when she really got it right. She had certainly not won his mind.

One evening in August they rode out together, an unplanned coincidence of being in the stable block at the same time. They stopped to give the horses a breather at the end of a wooded bridle path. He dismounted first and pulled her down from her saddle into his arms. There was a fresh determined urgency about him, and she instinctively checked over his shoulder that the horses would be fine just left to wander. She felt elated by the hope that this moment would turn their relationship round, make them friends as well as lovers again, two people with mutual aims, mutual interests, mutual feelings about their loved ones.

'You know,' he whispered in her neck, 'you give a whole new meaning to the phrase "Daddie's girl".'

She felt her patience snap, any wish to try to bring back the past evaporate. She pushed him violently away. 'Won't you ever let it rest?' she shouted. 'I've tried all ways to please you, to show you that as my husband you're first in my life. But no, you can't accept that. You've been like a bloody stand-in for a husband, it's been like living and sleeping with someone who didn't really want the job. Well, I'm sorry, Ian, but that's it, that's as far as I go. I'm pussyfooting around you no more – like it or lump it, my father is part of my life, I'm part of him, and I won't let you pull me in two over this any more.'

'It was a joke,' he said, spreading his hands.

'It's no joke from where I'm standing, it's just sheer bloody unrewarding, hard work.'

'Really,' he said mildly. 'I'm sorry you see our marriage in those terms.'

'I do these days,' she said, shaking her head at him. 'We've lost something.'

'Spontaneity,' he suggested.

She didn't answer as words rushed about her head, all to do with his old-style, wonderful, love-making, words she could not say in anger, even perhaps in daylight.

'Do you want me to move out?' he asked.

'No!' she exclaimed, but her anger was overlaid now by a dreadful feeling of losing something so precious, so central to her life. 'No,' she repeated, 'for Julian's sake I want you to stay. Whatever more you do or don't want to do is up to you. I shall be carrying on as usual.'

'That's is what I've come to expect. The only thing that puzzles me is whether you put the Philipps estate, Dickie's trust, Dickie, or your father first – it must be quite difficult for you.'

'That's unforgivable,' she told him, shaking and shocked

by having all her efforts on all those other scores thrown in her face. She felt an urgent wish to cry. Instead she retaliated. 'You're like a little boy who always wants to be first.'

He opened his mouth as if to speak but she snatched at her horse's reins, making it start, toss its head, regard her with white-ringed eyes, circling nervously as she remounted.

'Yes, that's right!' he shouted after her. 'Sometimes that would be really nice.'

They kept up appearances for Julian's sake – and Mrs West or, in other words, for the village and the outside world. Sometimes she saw Julian looking at them in a strange way but he never put his questions into words. Ian threw himself into his work and was soon amassing more and more clients further and further away.

'I know your fame is spreading, but aren't you in danger of overstretching yourself, with so much work, so far away?' she had commented.

'So do you want me to feel like a kept man as well as everything else?'

'Everything else?' she had queried but he had not answered. She supposed she would eventually stop throwing lifelines, stop trying, stop talking even.

Shortly after this he began to sleep in what, in more gracious Edwardian days, had been the dressing-room adjoining their bedroom. She was grateful that the rooms went from one to the other, so that Julian never saw their separation, they came and went from their bedroom by the same door, and she made very sure the state of the other room never revealed anything to Mrs West.

While she and Ian kept up a pretence of 'all's well', Dickie and Julian really did seem rather content. Julian also noted how much happier his Grandpa Bennett was. 'Well, you go more, don't you, Ma. I think he likes that, and Dickie goes with Liz in the car, he *really* likes to see *them*. Liz took him for a ride the other evening, did you know?' She could have wished he had said all this without Ian listening, eyes down, at the other end of the dining table.

During the second summer of their estrangement, and the second year of Dickie's sojourn at Banford, she proposed to her father that she might take him, the boys 'and Liz if she wants to come' to the Norfolk cottage. 'If we don't soon use it again we might as well sell it.'

'You shouldn't think of doing that,' Edgar said, 'there's years and years ahead. You might be taking grandchildren to it before long.'

'Dickie's still not quite eighteen,' she reminded him.

'That Liz comes over to see me quite a lot, even when Dickie is busy doing other things,' he added, then ruminated wickedly, 'Wonder if her little ones will have her clothes sense.'

'Or worse, the Markham nose!' Bess was glad to laugh with him. 'Poor things, hope they're not girls.'

When Liz came over to see Dickie the following day she looked at her with a new interest. Could it possibly be that this girl might be her daughter-in-law? Her clothes were now more hippie than punk – surely that must be a good sign. She would arrive in something that looked like curtains with frills, and no shoes – heaven knew how she managed to drive – or a high-necked blouse, long black skirt and boots, looking like a Victorian flower seller. Fashion rules had apparently gone out of the window. Her hair was longer but her eyes were sometimes so sad it twisted Bess's heart. Most times she was the outrageous extrovert, but occasionally she looked like a little girl who would slip down some emotional well if no one was there to hold her hand. She resisted any effort Bess made to know her better and flatly refused to talk about her own mother. She was, however, a great mate of Julian's, who worshipped her and her car.

Bess felt drawn to this girl who obviously had problems, seemed not able to settle in her mind either who she really was, or who she wanted to be. She wondered if the fellow feeling was because of her own hung role between father and husband. She felt a change, a trip to the sea, to their Norfolk cottage might really help; long walks, particularly along beaches, were good for talk, for airing problems and confidences.

When she went over to the farm the next time she made a firmer proposition for a week away. Her father's immediate response was how very few weeks there were left before cubbing and the first shoots of the season. Even though he was negative, she laid the idea very gently on the table at the

145

Hall that evening. The enthusiastic 'yes' from Julian came at the same time as an emphatic 'no' and 'kids' stuff' from Dickie.

She had felt stubbornly determined to carry on with the idea – until the next day – when out of the blue Liz drove over with an invitation for Dickie to join her, and several others from the college, at a house party on the Welsh borders. 'Sorry it's short notice,' she said to Bess and Ian, 'but I didn't know until yesterday. You don't mind, do you?'

Of course, they all said no they didn't mind, when she had gone Dickie said he would probably go on his motorbike so if he wanted to come away before the week was up he could. Then, as these things do happen, some kind of Sod's Law, a friend telephoned Julian with a chance of a holiday in the Scillies sailing, a cousin having gone down with mumps.

'There's a big artistic community on the Scillies,' he told his mother. 'Barbara said so. I shall send you all cards.'

'Oh, so you're going,' his father said.

'Well, no one here ever does anything! When Ma wants to go somewhere no one else does. I get fed up with—'

'Us all,' Ian finished for him.

'Sometimes.' He tried to scowl at his father but it turned into a grin and he ran to put his arm around him. 'Not really.'

'Look, when you come back perhaps you'll take me to Cornwall,' Bess said, 'I'd really like that.'

'Great!' Julian said. 'Two holidays. Great.' He took his father's hand and pulled him over to where she stood so he could link her with his free hand. 'Now we are one,' he said.

'Where on earth do you pick up such sayings?' Ian wanted to know.

'From church,' he replied. 'You know, "God the Father, God the Son, God the Holy Ghost" – three in one – all of us together.'

Bess wanted to weep.

The following Saturday night Dickie and Katie were walking along the deserted stretch of beach below the cottage, the smell of the sea and damp sand laced by the scent of the pines.

'Don't you love the evenings and the early morning here?' he asked as they paddled hand in hand at the sea's edge. 'Just us.'

'I can't believe we've got a whole week,' she said – there was still wonder and doubt in her voice. 'I can't believe we've got away with this for so long. It's all too good to be true. Do you feel that?' When he did not answer she added, 'We must have been a dozen times at least, that's dozens and dozens of times I've held my breath expecting to be caught out.'

'We've just had the narrowest squeak of all. A letter came from Norfolk, from Mrs Coombs at the Post Office, but all it said was that the annual fee for key-holding was due and she was sorry not to have seen Ma in person for so long.'

'No mention of you going, or anything?'

'Not a word.'

'And this week, Liz covering for us . . .' she added.

'And your friends at the office.'

'Yes, but they don't know they are.'

'It was all so serendipitous,' he said and looped his arms around her. She leaned back, spread her arms in the breeze as if she thought to fly.

'All so what?'

'Happy chance, everything is going right for us, so "who shall stand against us."' He span her round and round, until they both toppled to the sand. 'Though when Ma proposed coming for a week *I* nearly gave us away.'

They lay side by side looking up to the stars and way to the left to the thinnest crescent of a new moon. 'We're going public the moment I'm eighteen,' he said with sudden decision. 'No one can stop us when we're both of age.'

She was extraordinarily still by his side, only after some long silent moments saying, 'It's going to be an awful shock. I believe everyone is expecting you to marry Liz, you know that, don't you?'

'And everyone is expecting you to marry the man from the office.'

'Oh no!' she exclaimed. 'Don't say that, even in jest. Don't talk about him.'

'On my eighteenth birthday there'll be a party of course, you'll be there and I'll announce it to everyone all at the same time: your family; my family. I'll have the ring, slip it on there and then. I mean, what can they do?'

147

'Cut you off without a shilling.'

'No, no one can quite do that. I have a small allowance from my grandmother coming when I'm eighteen, and anyway I wouldn't care if they did, as long as I have you.' He rolled over and kissed her ear. 'I love you, love you, love you.'

She stretched her hands above her head, pushing her fingers through the sand, and knew with complete certainty that this was one of the most precious moments of her life. She felt secure in his promises, intoxicated by his love. She never wanted this evening, beneath these stars, with the sound of the ocean, the smell of the sea and the firs, the feel of him near her, the excitement in her very soul ever, ever, to end.

The next moment he startled her as he leapt to his feet and threw his sandals down.

'Race you to the rocks,' he shouted, 'then we'll swim.' And as he ran he pulled off his shirt and threw that down, then paused to strip off his shorts. She sat up laughing at his latest madness, then followed. She threw her sandals to his, her T-shirt and shorts in random patterns between his clothes already strewn along the beach. She had her bra in her hand and, as he reached the rocks and turned, she whirled it over her head then threw it inadvertently into the sea.

He ran, laughing, to retrieve it. 'Allow me, madam,' he said and laid it ceremoniously over a smooth rock, then he turned and seized her. 'You're a wanted woman,' he breathed in her neck and pulled her down on to the sand once more.

She kissed his neck and his chest as he lay half over her, and remembered a novel; she thought it had been called *The Blue Lagoon* – a brother and sister had grown up together shipwrecked on a desert island, then became lovers. It had seemed no crime when she had read the novel, and now she had gone from feeling like a sister to Dickie, an older sister, to now lover and wife to be.

She was tender until their mutual passion mounted, then all else in the world fell away. She felt they reached new heights, that they had made a new, more mystic union, and brought back part of the magic with them, some reality or memory she would never lose. She wanted to lie quietly and listen – no one should move or speak – then unexpected tears flooded her eyes, ran over her cheeks, as the waves and wind resumed their courses.

Sixteen

October brought a hot Indian Summer, sunny days following heavy morning mists. For Katie, anticipating Dickie's coming eighteenth birthday in the spring, it was an enchanting time. She had begun writing to him every evening when he was at college, then kept the letters zipped up in a pocket in her handbag and gave them to him each time they met. He said they were his lifeline, the treat he promised himself after each day's study. There was going to be quite a bundle when next she saw him. The college had arranged an extended course on land and property management. They had both agreed he must take it, even though it meant three weeks without seeing each other, but April was almost on their horizons.

She had heard his mother say that Dickie had grown in manly stature, kind of filled out mentally and physically, become really responsible. She gave all the credit to Banford College.

It was not until the last weekend of the month, when official summer time ended and the clocks were put back an hour, that the weather turned colder and the mists became day-long fogs. It was still thick when Katie was due to set off to catch her bus on the Monday.

She had carried her breakfast crockery to the draining board and was peering through the window for any chance of sun, when sudden nausea overcame her. So sudden and unexpected was the feeling that she lurched sideways to the sink, and was swiftly and violently sick.

Wiping her mouth, she turned to find her mother watching her, a shocked expression on her face. 'Don't know what brought that on,' she said. 'I wasn't feeling ill or anything, it just happened.'

'Do you feel all right now?' her mother asked.

'I do,' she said, and was surprised. She had just been violently sick but immediately felt fine – it was really strange.

She glanced at her mother, who stood looking stunned, disbelieving. 'Our Katie,' she began, then stopped as the sound of George coming back to the house from early milking reached them. Colleen immediately came to the sink and turned both taps full on, rinsing away all sign of the incident. Her father came in and, seeing them both at the sink, strode over and made a show of pushing and bundling his way in between them.

'Come on,' he said, pushing out his hips first one side then the other to make room. 'Let the dog see the rabbit, let's get in to wash my hands.'

The censure in her mother's two words, 'Our Katie', the swift washing of the sink, and now her stunned silence, brought an idea that surely could not be true, but suddenly all Katie wanted to do was get out of the kitchen, out of the house.

'I'll be late,' she said, 'I must go.'

'See you, love,' her father said. Her mother did not speak: in itself a condemnation.

She picked up her shoulder bag and hurried from the house, from the garden, ran along the field path, the fog swirling, parting and reforming. She glanced over her shoulder: her home had disappeared. She shuddered as if someone had walked over her grave, then went on and did not stop until she was in the spinney.

In the trees she stood irresolute, felt like a hunted creature, like a fox-cub frightened back into the woods by the huntspeople, the folk with country pretensions, so there should be no escape, so their rapacious hounds could tear her to pieces. If she were expecting, disgraced, this would be the treatment she could expect. Even one of their own mated with the wrong person, they had forced into having an abortion – poor Liz, who wrote poems to her dead baby.

She turned off the main track that led to the road. The thought that she would miss her bus flickered briefly at the back of her mind. But surely this could not be happening to her. Surely she could not be pregnant, could not be expecting a child. Be calm, she told herself. She had been sick, once – like no other time she had ever been sick, but even so – just once.

Even as she tried to squash the idea, she acknowledged that her breasts had been painful, which often happened when her period was due, but the September period had not come and this next one was late. She had not worried, she had always been slightly irregular with her monthly cycle.

She went on towards the Red Pool, then as if looking for something familiar homed in on the massive oak she and Dickie had used to shelter from the thunderstorm. It was a weird place, alone in the fog; above and all around it was as if atmosphere and foliage had interwoven and created some new entity, a natural enmeshment she could not escape.

How could it have happened? When? Where? She had felt so secure after nearly two years of a relationship with Dickie.

Standing in this place where he had first made her feel the real thrill of physical desire, she remembered exactly when, where and how it had happened.

It had been the evening they had run along the beach, shedding their clothes as they went, and they had swum naked with the moon dancing over the sea. They had swum together in the broad light-rippled path of the moon, and Dickie had wondered what would happen if they just went on swimming, ever on, into the beam.

'We'll reach Never-Never Land, of course,' she had told him.

She turned, pressed, then drummed her forehead on the rough solid tree. She had reached some other kind of land now, the Land of Regrets, of remorse and shame.

After the swim they had made love again on the sands, and reached heights of love and passion they had never touched before. She had shushed him afterwards when he had wanted to talk, she had needed a listening silence afterwards – for there had been some mystical enchantment she had needed to take note of. Had that been so she could listen to this child, this baby, come into being? It was absurd, her practical self said, but deep in the roots of her being she knew it was true. She had known the moment of conception, even though at the time she had not recognized it for what it was.

'What am I going to do?' she appealed, looked up into the dense mysterious interweave. The fog was thicker, seemed to press closer, assume a quality of weight.

'All right,' she breathed. So this was something she was going to have to deal with herself, by herself; she didn't know how, but until she knew without any doubts, and until she saw Dickie in person she would tell no one.

She walked from the tree towards the pool itself, then sat down on one of the log benches, head gripped in her hands. There was a clinic you could go to – she had seen a kind of advertisement in the ladies' lavatories.

Of course, if it were true, it would ruin everything. There would be no announcement at Dickie's birthday, that was for sure, because by next April she . . . By next April, if she were pregnant, the child could be born. She had a wild picture of standing in the Hall in the long gallery holding her baby as Dickie stood up to make his surprise announcements.

What would her father say? And her mother? She remembered her conclusion about her own birth, the playful way her mother had so often said she was to do as her mother said, not as she had done. They would be so hurt, so disappointed in her. This might well be the worst thing, disappointing them, letting them down.

But what to do, now, this moment, today? She must act as normally as possible. She should keep her own counsel, go immediately, catch her bus to work. She peered at her watch: she had already missed her usual bus.

Arriving in town already an hour late, she went straight into the ladies. She paid her penny and locked herself in the cubicle, disregarding the poster until she had found that, as Mr Benbrook was so fond of saying 'status was indeed quo'. Then she stood, the smell of the bleach used in this place strong in her nostrils, and read the message pasted on the back of the door. 'Pregnant?' it queried. She made a mental note of the address of a clinic attached to a local hospital.

When she entered the general office, an hour and a half late, Mary immediately berated her for coming at all. 'You should have stayed at home and got over it properly. Hope it's not catching.'

Katie bit back any kind of smart aleck reply she could have made, and was pushing her handbag into her desk drawer when Ken North came into the office. 'You've only just arrived in time,' he said. 'Mr Benbrook would like you in his office with your notebook.'

'She's not well,' Mary retorted on her behalf.

'I'm fine.' She picked up her notebook, brushed past Ken, and left to take the day's instructions and letters. She was straight-faced, businesslike and industrious, and very quiet, for the rest of the day. Mary said she hoped she would feel better tomorrow.

She did not; in fact, worse when the morning sickness came quicker, so she only just reached the bathroom. She had to force herself to the routines of the morning, felt like an automaton, just doing the things she was programmed to do, her ritual duties.

In her lunch hour she went back to the public lavatories in the bus terminus and with a biro made a note of the phone number of the clinic on the back of her hand and went from there to the line of telephone kiosks.

She had felt hard, detached, in control, until the softly spoken Irish woman who answered her call was so kind to her. Her eyes immediately filled with tears as she heard that she could come to the clinic anytime – it was manned twenty-four hours, day and night, by volunteers, 'such as myself, and we are mostly retired nurses, so we know a lot about a girl's needs. Anything you tell us is in strictest confidence, and if you don't wish to tell us a thing that's fine too.'

She made an appointment for the following evening and rubbed the number from the back of her hand. She was aware that Ken North was alert to something different happening and was once more watching her every move. She was also aware that he knew exactly who Dickie was. She worried about this. Ken North was also one of the few people who knew she was not going out with *him*. Sitting waiting her turn in the clinic, she gave a short ironic laugh as she thought he might even get the blame for her condition. Several girls sitting nearby moved uncomfortably at the sound that burst from her lips.

When her turn came she was surprised to find herself sitting opposite an elderly bonny, pink-faced nun. 'I was the one spoke to you on the telephone,' she said and introduced herself as Sister Bridget.

Sister Bridget obviously wanted her to talk, but Katie could not – all she wanted was to be told how and when the test would be done. 'Bring in a sample of your urine, my dear, and you can ring for the result, but remember we're here to help with far more than just the knowledge of how you are. Will you remember that?' She nodded the importance of this to Katie. 'And,' she said, 'I'd like you to come back and see me personally, tell me how things are with you. I hope you will.'

She had swallowed hard, looked up at the sincere-seeming woman, and nodded, yes, she would.

On Wednesday night she was at the telephone box as usual to receive Dickie's call, this time not from Banford, but from a conference centre in Derbyshire. He sounded eagar, more himself, able to speak more freely in the security of a private phone booth at the centre.

'I've learnt some really good things I can put into practice when I take over,' he enthused.

She wished she could tell him she had learnt good things too, but a positive pregnancy test at this time must be the worst news of all. 'Good,' she replied.

'Katie?' he queried. 'Are you all right, you sound . . . kind of distant. Nothing's the matter, is it? I hate these weeks apart as much as you do.' He paused, then repeated her name when she did not reply immediately. 'Katie?'

'I'm fine,' she said and knew it was not convincing. 'I'm finding it difficult to hear you, it's a terrible line.'

'I can hear you all right.'

'It's just my end, then.'

'But you are all right?' he asked again.

'Tired, I guess, that's all. I've had a few very busy days at the office.'

'You'll soon be able to give it up,' he told her. 'You can work for me in the estate office, like Ma did for my real father.'

She ached to say, yes, that was what she had always wanted, it had been a secret dream, but now – now.

'Dickie,' she said, looking up and down the empty street, 'I'll have to go: there are a couple of people waiting to use the phone, one looks like it might be urgent.'

'Look, the other thing I wanted to say was that you could write to me here, send the letters you usually keep, that would be marvellous. If you posted them right up to, say the last Wednesday I'm here, I'd be sure to get them.'

'Yes, I could do that.' She wondered whether writing and hiding things might not be just as difficult as trying to talk normally to him. Her letters might be just as stilted as this conversation.

'So you will do,' he prompted.

'I will,' she said.

'Love you,' he said and she heard the eagerness and the desire in his voice.

'Love you,' she said very softly.

'You're right, it's not a very good line – shout it at me, Katie.'

She swallowed and put down the receiver.

By the end of the week Katie began to feel she could hardly bare to talk to anyone. She tried to control her mood, but knew she was not fooling anyone at the office. Mary had asked her what she had on her mind, Ken North regarded her with what she could only think of as watchful speculation, and Mr Benbrook said as she left his office on the Friday night that he hoped she would feel quite recovered after the weekend.

Part of the torment at home was hiding her morning sickness. She thought what a weird thing it was. If she lay quite still in bed she felt perfectly all right, but as soon as she began to move she had to rush to the bathroom without delay.

On the Saturday morning she was awake early, heard her father come back from milking, then her parents talking downstairs; the radio was on quietly. Dad liked to hear at least one news bulletin in the mornings. William got up and shortly afterwards left, so she guessed he must be playing in a football match.

It was all so normal, so everyday. The only thing wrong in this house was her: she was going to be the spanner in everyone's works. How could she avoid it? How could she avoid hurting her parents?

She turned away from the window, face to the dark; she had nothing to get up for, nothing pleasant, that was for sure. Then she heard her mother coming up the stairs. The door

155

was knocked and her mum came in with a cup of tea, the smell of which was in danger of turning her stomach before she even lifted her head from the pillow.

'I'll put it here, love,' her mother said, placing the tea on her bedside table. Katie did not dare to look up and meet her mother's eyes for fear of reading that she had guessed the truth.

Her mum turned to go, but at the door turned and said, 'Then me and your dad want to have a talk with you when you get up, before you go out anywhere.'

Seventeen

'We've tried to talk to her,' Colleen said, looking round as if afraid of being overheard, her voice no more than a despairing whisper. 'But she refuses to say anything, anything at all.'

'But are you really sure?' Bess asked, adding, 'Mrs West is not here by the way, and Ian's in the office.'

'Oh good, don't know as I want it making *News of the World*. But she's pregnant,' Colleen said with certainty, 'and more than a couple of months if the sickness is anything to go by.'

'And you think?'

'It has to be this chap at the office. She's been off for the weekend with him often enough.'

'But she's still not brought him home.' It was more statement than question. 'I wonder why,' Bess mused.

'He's older of course,' Colleen began, then went on with some annoyance, 'but then I don't really know that with any certainty. It's more the impression she gives.'

'So what do you know for certain, for absolute certain?' It distressed Bess to see her friend so distraught, hands plucking continually and unconsciously at her skirt as if trying to rid herself of something unwanted and unpleasant.

'That he works for the same solicitors, Benbrook & Co.' Colleen shrugged. 'And that's about it.'

'But there's something I know,' Bess spoke slowly, feeling her way into an idea that had just occurred to her, 'or rather there's someone I know. I've met Mr Philip Benbrook personally, in fact I know him quite well through the County Show. He has a son who showjumps. I could . . .' she paused, bit her lip, and looked speculatively at Colleen before going on, 'I could go and see him.'

'You mean *ask* him what he thinks?'

'Katie won't be able to keep her condition secret very long. He seems a very wise old bird – I could *tell* him our suspicions in the first place, then watch his reactions, take his advice perhaps. I might at least get a look at this Ken North.'

'Would you? It seems a bit underhand to our Katie . . .'

'But if she refuses to say, what are you going to do?'

'She'll always have a home with us. God knows I don't want another baby to look after, but we'd make the best of it.'

'George knows?' Bess queried.

'You know what I'm like, not very good at hiding problems. He was wondering if he should mention it to your father. We hoped he wouldn't mind if we did finish up with a baby in our house.'

'I don't see why he should.'

'Well, you know if our Katie doesn't get any support from the father she'd have to work, I'd be landed with the baby, and if I'm going to carry on working for your father I might have to take the mite to the farm with me.'

'He should be made to pay,' Bess declared. 'It's as much his fault as Katie's.'

'Not what the world thinks, I know that.'

'Come on,' Bess said sharply, hearing the hint of self-pity and defeat in her friend's voice, 'we won't go down that lane again, and times are changing, girls are not sent to Coventry for it these days.'

'You wouldn't say that if it was your daughter.'

'No, perhaps not,' she admitted, touching her friend's arm in acknowledgment. 'So shall I go to see Philip Benbrook? Do you want to come with me?'

'No!' Colleen exclaimed immediately. 'Our Katie'd never forgive me turning up at the office. At least if you go it will seem a bit more discreet, you could be just a client or something.'

'I'm not sure about that, but I'll certainly be as careful as I can. I suppose I could go in with a handful of County Show brochures and forms that might send the curious off on the wrong tack, that is if his staff know he's into horses.'

'Oh, his staff know that all right. Katie says there's always phone calls from his wife about driving a horsebox somewhere or other, or some such. He's even changed into his full hunting kit in the office once and his wife picked him up. Blocked the street outside with the horsebox on that occasion.'

'So I'll do it then, I'll go in tomorrow.'

'So we say nothing to our Katie,' Colleen checked.

'No, we don't want her staying away from work. These things do have to be faced, and really the sooner the better. She can't hide the facts, she has to deal with them, and so does this North.'

'Funny when you think about it,' Colleen mused, 'I know more about the Benbrooks' hunting habits than I do about this Ken North.'

Philip Benbrook received Bess courteously and just as Katie and the other young lady in the front office had done, took in the County Show material she had in her hand. Katie looked both pale and stressed, as well she might, but she smiled as she showed Bess through to the senior partner's office.

Philip Benbrook rose from his desk looking the epitome of the English country solicitor, or should she think 'county solicitor', Bess wondered, for it was almost as if he dressed and played both roles. Open-air complexion, spotted silk handkerchief flapping from his top pocket, a multi-colour dicky bow plus an open, frank and welcoming manner.

'Bess Bennett, well, well.'

The greeting by her unmarried name broke any awkwardness there might have been.

'Still astonishing everyone with your riding?' he asked.

'Well, I try not to astonish myself too much these days: a little more decorum, shall we say.'

They shook hands and she placed the leaflets on his desk. 'These,' she said, 'are a blind for my real purpose in being here.'

'Really.' He leaned back in his chair, interlaced his fingers over his stomach and looked at her with great interest. 'So the floor is yours, m'dear.'

She spoke quietly, succinctly and without hesitation; before she had finished, he was leaning forward on his desk, regarding her with unblinking attention.

159

'But North has no ties,' he mused, 'and she's an intelligent, attractive girl. I don't understand the man.'

'She will not admit who the father is,' Bess reminded him, 'but she has been going away for weekends with friends from the office, and has frequently mentioned Ken North's name.'

'And he lives on his own since his mother died,' the solicitor followed on his own train of thought.

Bess was silent now, the story told; she watched this man of the law ponder the best way to deal with this. He laughed briefly once as he pondered. 'Don't want to lose two good members of staff,' he said before placing his elbows on the desk and carefully matching up his fingertips; as the thumbs met, he seemed to reach his decision.

'I'll ask North to stay after everyone else has gone tonight. There will be no chance of anyone overhearing, he and I can talk freely, and I'll be in touch with you. In fact I'll ring you later tonight at the Hall.'

'You're very understanding,' she thanked him, talked of her Uncles Topham and their families for a time, then left the office, waving to Katie in the general office as she went. She thought the girl noted the absence of Show brochures and felt a pang of guilt that she should set up such a successful deceit, but argued it was for Colleen, and ultimately for her daughter's good.

When office closing time came, Katie was relieved, if a little surprised when Mr Benbrook came through to the general office as they were leaving, then waylaid Ken on his way out and asked him to go back into his office with him. At least, she thought, I haven't got to worry about him following me.

Ken took his raincoat off again and went with it over his arm into his employer's office. Mr Benbrook was already seated behind his desk, fingertips together and regarding him through them. He did not as usual immediately wave him to a chair. Ken wondered for a moment if he was going to be sacked, though why such a thought should come into his mind he had no idea – perhaps just the look of disapproval on his employer's face. Had he done something wrong? His book-keeping was a matter of immense pride to him: he took real pleasure in the neat appearance of his ledgers and accounts.

He felt more than a little uncomfortable as Mr Benbrook

seemed to study him, look him up and down almost as if he had never seen him before, or he was seeing him in a new light.

'Sit down,' he said belatedly.

North sat on the edge of the chair – for one thing it was office closing time – and as if the same thought occurred to his employer, Mr Benbrook got up and left his office, saying, 'I'll just check everyone else has gone, then I'll drop the catch, so we can be sure of not being disturbed.'

Ken was puzzled *and* disturbed. He looked all around the comfortable, highly polished, old-fashioned, office: the mahogany partner's desk; the antique wooden office cabinets; wondering if he had missed something new, something he should have remarked upon. Then he ran through in his mind all the clients whose accounts he ran, some lending large sums on private mortgages, others entrusting Benbrooks with large intestate estates, or probate monies pending distribution. There were one or two estates hanging fire a little, but nothing he would have judged serious or urgent enough to warrant this amount of secrecy.

'You'll be wondering what this is all about,' Philip Benbrook said as he came back, closing the door behind him, 'but we can talk freely – there is no one else in the building now.'

'Has something new come up?' Ken asked.

'Yes,' Philip Benbrook's answer was uncompromising.

Ken sat further back on his chair. 'It must be very confidential,' he said.

Mr Benbrook did not answer, just regarded him steadily. 'Confidential at the moment, yes, but not for too much longer, as is the manner of these things.'

Ken frowned and waited.

'You will, I hope, appreciate that I do take a real interest in my staff. We're a small office, it's important we all get on, work well together.'

Ken was silent: he wondered if Katie had complained about him following her, taking her wrist in the bus station, watching her every move whenever he could. Stalking? Could he be accused of that? He felt his colour rising from beneath his collar.

'You understand that?'

161

'Of course, Mr Benbrook, I've always . . .'

'What?'

'Appreciated your interest.' North was well prepared to grovel if it would help his case.

'Does everyone appreciate *your* interest, that is what we've stayed behind to find out.'

He lowered his head, let his lids mask his eyes. So it was Katie Wright. She had complained about him – that was not fair. He was just interested, no more than that, he was fascinated by her. His forehead prickled with a sudden rash of perspiration, but he made no move to draw attention to it by wiping it away.

The silence went on for some minutes, then Mr Benbrook said, 'You will understand that it is Katie we are talking about.'

'Are we?' He was careful to keep his voice cautious, questioning without being rude, but his heart was beginning to pound. He was surely not going to lose his job because of . . . well, he'd not go easily. He'd take his case to an industrial tribunal, take old Benbrook to court for unfair dismissal.

'We are talking about her pregnancy.' Philip Benbrook laid the words before his bookkeeper like an official indictment.

'Pregnancy.' Ken felt his mouth drop open and remain so.

Philip Benbrook knew the look of astonishment when he saw it. 'You didn't know?'

Ken shook his head.

'She hasn't told you?'

Ken shook his head more slowly, opened his mouth to ask why should she, then, heart thumping more heavily, held his peace. There was something in this situation which he had not yet fully understood, and he had learned over the years that it was not wise to admit ignorance, or appear dim-witted when by just listening the situation often became perfectly clear.

'You will not, I presume, deny that it is yours, and that you will be prepared to do the decent thing.'

'The decent thing?' In spite of his resolve this was all going a bit fast for him.

'Marry her, man. Marry her!'

'But . . .' The idea of marrying Katie left him with something

162

like a great white light shining in some region of his brain. Marry Katie? He'd do that in almost any situation, even carrying another man's child. Lochinvar's child. His lips began to twist into something like a malicious grin, but in time he pushed them outwards into a concerned pout. 'I had no idea,' he said in as repentant a tone as he could muster. 'Absolutely no idea.'

'So?'

'So, if that's what she wants . . .' he began.

'What she wants?' Philip Benbrook got up from his desk and paced up and down behind it, looking over his half reading glasses to observe this creature whom he'd always known was a bit of a creep, and whom, in spite of his very best intentions, in spite of the man's excellent work, he could not help thoroughly despising. 'Good God, man, you've been going out with her, going off for weekends with her, what did you think she had in mind? What did you have in mind?'

Is this what she said, were the first words that came into his mind, but instead he asked, 'So who did she tell?'

'Her family certainly, and Mrs Sinclair from the Hall came on behalf of Katie's mother. Everyone seems to know about it.'

'She should have told me,' he said humbly, 'she must know I would never let her down.'

'Ah! That's more the spirit, that's more what I wanted to hear. Knew you wouldn't let any one of us down.' He walked rapidly across to the man and held out his hand. 'Now we can make it a matter of celebration. Well done! Congratulations.'

'I'd better ask Katie before we—'

'Quite! Quite! Status will never be quo again for you dear boy.' He thumped him on the back, helped him back into his raincoat and saw him out of the door with the instruction, 'Don't be long in the asking, never had an office wedding before, we'll do you both proud.'

Back in his own office he immediately telephoned Bess. Her son Julian answered and in a most efficient manner referred him to his grandfather's farm and gave him the number.

Eighteen

Edgar had listened carefully to both the incoming call from Philip Benbrook and the outgoing call to Colleen, and had only then been made party to the 'goings-on' as he called it, adding the comment, 'Like mother, like daughter then – and like you rushing in to take Colleen's part.'

'Not at all.' Bess was short with him. 'Neither Colleen, nor George, deserved this worry.'

He was aware there was as usual much more she would have liked to say but *as usual* his daughter held her tongue. He sometimes wished she'd stand up to his nonsense more. He sometimes felt he'd really like to be taken more firmly in hand. He'd resist of course, but would have enjoyed the battle, the attention. A permanent loose cannon, Fay, his late wife, had once called him.

Perhaps because Bess left him rather quickly after their exchange and in less than good humour he could not relax. He realized she had detoured from town to call on him before she went home; in return he had criticized her beloved Colleen – and Katie.

Bess had asked if George had mentioned the subject of Katie's pregnancy to him, and the possibility of there being a baby in the Wrights' household again. His, as he thought, witty reply had been that there was no stipulation in the tenancy that said grandchildren were prohibited. It had been a flippant 'for effect' answer, which had fallen flat, and he was now ashamed of it. Fay would have been outraged, she would never have been facetious in such circumstances. She would have gone to the heart of the matter, would undoubtedly have been over at the Wrights seeing if there was anything practical she could do.

The idea grew in his mind as he stood looking out of his

164

kitchen window, watching the moon grow in brilliance, reluctant to draw the curtains and shut himself in for the night. With a sudden grunt of decision he picked up his stick and jerked his head towards the door, the ever watchful dog there before him.

His mood made it a sentimental journey. So much of his life was tied up with this land. He loved the place too well and could, he thought, well be a candidate for being tied here after death. He felt like a ghost now, walking in this spectral light. Every field, stile, brook, spinney, held memories, claimed him momentarily as he passed.

He came to what had been the boundary between Old Paget's land and his own. He recalled Old Paget escorting ten-year-old Bess and Ian Sinclair out of his spinney at the end of a shotgun. When the irascible old man had died Edgar had gone into considerable debt to acquire the adjoining farm. He had divided the old Paget farmhouse into two separate dwellings for his head stockman, and head herdsman, George Wright.

He walked on, reliving events, and was already in George's kitchen garden before he stopped, aware he could hear someone crying. He took a step or two nearer, then thought to retreat: his arrival might well be a crass intrusion. But this was no ordinary crying – this was a wild sobbing, the kind of weeping one felt should be curbed or the person might well do themselves some injury.

He felt he could not just leave, though if this was Colleen, George would surely be there comforting her, or trying to. He reached the back door and knocked, but the sounds came from somewhere deep in the house, or perhaps upstairs. He knocked again and when there was still no answer he tried the door; it gave to his touch. He gestured his dog to stay outside on the mat, then stepped into the kitchen and shouted, 'Hello! Hello! Anybody there?' He acknowledged it was a pretty stupid thing to shout, someone was obviously there but so distraught as still not to hear him. He also realized that he could hear no one else, no voice, no pleas for the end to this paroxysm of grief.

He went to the bottom of the stairs. Whoever it was had shut herself in one of the bedrooms and obviously thought she had the house to herself. To let go so completely one needed privacy.

'Hello!' he shouted again and jiggled his walking stick on the bottom bannister. The cries faltered as the woman listened. He called again. The sobs lessened to a semblance of control.

'Who is it?' a woman's voice called.

'Edgar Bennett,' he called back. 'Is that you, Katie?'

There was a smothered sound, then a complete shocked silence, but after a few moments the door at the top of the stairs slowly opened, and Katie came out.

'Dad's out,' she said, 'and Mum, and William. There's only me.'

'It might be you I should talk to,' he said. 'Will you come down?' He tried to keep Fay very much in the fore of his mind, think exactly what she might have said or done. Be gentle, she told him.

She reached behind herself, firmly closing the bedroom door, as if shutting off from this unexpected visitor anything that had taken place in the privacy of her room. She began to come very slowly down the stairs, her breath occasionally coming in great double intakes like the aftermath of a young child's distress, but gaining control, he thought, and was not unaware of the effort this must be costing her.

'It's Dad's darts night and Mum's gone with him. William's at a friend's for the night, birthday party,' she explained, then added with a toss of her head, 'but you're not here because of them, are you?'

He shook his head. 'I'm here because I thought it would be exactly what my late wife might have done, come to see if there's anything that can be done to help. I know Bess has—'

She interrupted with a brief bitter laugh. 'Yes, she has, she *really* has – and I wish she had not. I wish she, and everyone else would mind their own business.'

'Perhaps we all care about you and your family too much to let you suffer like this on your own.' He leaned heavily on his walking stick, noticing how this girl, like Bess, wrestled with things she wanted to say to him, but in the end remained silent. 'Could we go into the kitchen?' he asked. 'I could use a sit down.'

She led the way somewhat ungraciously, but, without asking, poured a small brandy and placed it on the table, pulling out a chair for him.

166

'Take one yourself,' he advised, but she shook her head, stepped further away from the table. This was not going to be easy: there were going to be no compromises, no voluntary revelations.

He cleared his throat. 'I understand the man has offered to do the right thing,' he said.

She turned away, pushed the brandy bottle back into the cupboard so violently he heard glasses fall over, possibly break, but Katie closed the door on everything.

'The man,' he began again, 'at the office, the one you have been going out with, I understand . . .' He finished somewhat lamely, so furious was her glance at him.

'You understand!' She snatched the word from his lips and stood shaking her head, shaking it just as violently, as uncontrollably as she had been weeping.

He half rose from his chair in alarm.

Immediately she stopped, raised both hands as if to fend him off, as if the last thing she wanted was him any nearer to her, then with the utmost bitterness in her voice judged, 'You! Understand? I don't think so.'

'He's offered to stand by you –' he felt he must justify his remark, make the situation as he understood it, perfectly clear – 'to marry you.'

She laughed then, such a bitter laugh it made him sit back from her. This young pretty girl seemed changed to a mortified but unbending creature.

'So do I gather you do not want to marry him, is that it?'

She lifted her face to look at him. So ravaged was her expression, he would hardly have recognized her in different circumstances. 'Perhaps,' she said, 'to marry him is what I deserve.'

He registered that the girl must obviously have just been playing around, and had slipped up. The crude expression demonstrating that she had taken seriously what had been poked at her in fun came to his mind. 'So you don't love this man, who is the father of your child?' he asked.

'No, I didn't say—' She broke off, but for a moment her voice, her whole manner had been softer, more sincere.

'So what do you say to this proposal of marriage?'

'From Ken North!' she exclaimed. 'I've had no proposal of marriage from him, nor do I want it. He's . . .'

He waited but the contemptuous curl of her lips told it all.

'Do your parents know how you feel?'

'I know how *they* feel,' she answered, in her voice a bitter echo of all that had passed between them before her parents went out.

'Whatever was said, in the heat of the moment, I know you can always stay here, I'm sure of that option. Your parents will never see you or your baby without a home. It's been talked of I think.' He stopped there, wondering if he had gone too far, assumed too much on her behalf.

'There's other things I can do,' she said defiantly.

'Abortion, you mean – well, I suppose so.' He never in his life thought he would ever seriously utter such a word, but this girl had sobbed as if indeed her heart was broken, looked as if she had a terrible desperation simmering not far from the surface – and if she did not want to marry the father of the child. He studied her closely; she was aware but made no move.

He put his hand into his jacket pocket to where he always carried ready money – he often paid cash in the cattle markets if the amount was not too great. 'I don't know about such things, but I know such times are expensive whatever you choose to do.' He laid a small pile of notes on the table.

'No, I couldn't take anything from you,' she said, and it seemed to him there was a strange emphasis on the 'from you'.

'Of course you can,' he told her, 'and if you do need more . . . I'm not sure if these things have to be done privately.'

He judged she was now certainly a great deal calmer than when he first arrived, seemed to be actually weighing up what she should do – perhaps she had even decided. He felt he had done all he could. 'Will you be all right until your parents get back? Though if you'd rather I stay, I'll ask your father to run me home in his car. Perhaps that might be best, don't want to risk another fall, I'd never hear the last of it.'

'No, I'll be fine, and I'll lend you a torch. You can't always rely on the moon.'

Her tone also left him in no doubt she wanted rid of him. He finished the brandy and stood up.

She gestured towards the money on the table, making him

feel she had definitely decided to make use of it. 'And thanks for that, but I'll repay you one day.' She walked him to the door.

He shook his head, but as she watched him go she was resolved she would do so. In the meantime she was going to use his money – use it to get away from her parents, from the office, from everyone who so completely misjudged the situation.

She wondered if Edgar Bennett would have suggested a termination had he known it was his own great-grandchild he was proposing to abort.

She had wanted Dickie to be the first person she told. That was surely right, though there was no way of telling such a thing that could soften the shock. She wondered how he would react? He could just behave like himself, launch them into wild joyous celebrations – then think of the problems it caused afterwards. She smiled: this was most likely to be his way – how she ached for him to come home.

But now who would tell him, how would he hear – and what would he hear? She had deliberately not gone to the village that night for their telephone call, because she knew she could not convince him all was well. She had needed to tell him in person, but now his mother and her mother had between them managed to disgrace her in everyone's eyes, and it seemed, most horrific of all, got a proposal of marriage for her from Ken North. What were *his* motives, she wondered?

She had to get away. She could neither go back to the office, nor stay here at home. She picked up the notes and went upstairs, pushed clothes into her suitcase and the small rucksack she usually took for weekends away, added a few personal pieces of jewellery, her Blue John pendant, the signet ring her parents had given her when she left school and a steel ring William had made in metalwork at school.

Downstairs, she found another torch and put it by her handbag, then wrote a hurried note to say they should not worry, that she felt it best if she went away for a time, but she would be in touch.

She left the house, walked to her usual bus stop and caught the eight o'clock bus into town. She was gratified to see there were only two youths on the back seat of the bus, neither of whom she knew. She wanted no one to be able to trace her steps, trusted only Dickie would realize where she would be. They had made pretence of it being their home so many times she felt in no doubt he would realize.

She hauled her case from bus station to railway station. She was a little uncertain about railway lines out to the east, and was reluctant to seek advice from any official. If anyone did come looking for her, her dad or anyone, she did not intend to leave clues.

She scrutinized the departure boards and made guesses about train connections. There was a train leaving for Cambridge in less than ten minutes; she bought a ticket and ran to catch it. She heaved her case and rucksack on to the rack, picked up a discarded newspaper and sat in a corner seat with the broadsheet obscuring her from the world.

She reckoned that with the £25 in five and one pound notes from Mr Bennett she had more than enough to cover her fares, a night's lodging in Cambridge and get herself to the cottage, *and* buy anything she might need until Dickie came after her. She probably would not have to spend too much of it at all. She was grateful Mr Bennett had seen fit to come over to see her: it had helped push her into action, had given her the means to make her escape. Her mother did not always speak well of him, she'd heard her say he used his money instead of his brain – but that she guessed had been about the motorbike.

When she reached Cambridge it was well past the time any normal lodging house and hotel took in guests and it looked as if the whole station would soon be deserted of passengers and staff. She was wondering where she might spend the night, whether the waiting rooms were open or not, when a porter saw her looking round uncertainly and asked if he could help. 'I'm going on to the coast tomorrow,' she told him. 'I need a place to stay, but—'

'Not too expensive. Right.' He took her to the first corner outside the station and directed her by the lines of street lamps. 'First right, number nine,' he said, 'Mrs O'Neill, she'll see you right, she's my landlady, heart as big as a bucket, she'll find room for you. Tell her Gordon sent you, and he'll be home in half an hour after his last train.'

Mrs O'Neill lived up to all he said of her, and after breakfast the next morning she felt reluctant to leave the hearty Irish woman who knew nothing at all about her problems, so treated her normal.

At the railway station she bought a ticket on to King's Lynn and waited patiently for her train. She boarded this second train, feeling like a stranger even to herself. The countryside was familiar enough, the flat fields, groups of trees cultivated around farmhouses, and all interspersed with the dykes and drains of the fens. She had ridden pillion this way, come so happily with Dickie, but now alone – yet not quite alone – it was not just November that darkened the landscape she saw. It was a terrible secret gift he'd put in her charge.

In King's Lynn she reversed the steps she had made in Leicester: now she went from train station to bus station, bought her ticket for Wells and waited out the time before the bus left.

She waited on a slatted wooden seat in a kind of wind pocket where discarded food cartons, sweets wrappers and other debris had collected. She wondered if Gordon, the porter, and his landlady would ever realize what their unquestioning kindness had meant to her.

The afternoon was already waning into early evening when she finally arrived in Wells. November was not the time for visitors and everywhere was closed. It was a trek to the cottage carrying her luggage. Dickie had always said it would be a good idea to leave a spare key under a flowerpot in case he ever forgot the one he'd had cut, so they need not keep bothering Mrs Coombs. He never had forgotten the key, and she had never seen him hide another anywhere. She wondered which window she would break to get in; one of the sea side, she thought; it was lower and the panes not so large.

A wind was rising and, while she had the torch, her eyes were used to the gloom and a certain amount of light still seemed to be reflected up from the wide expanse of water. The suitcase weighed heavier every step, and she stopped to change hands often, feeling as if she had been journeying for weeks rather than just over one day. She wondered how quickly Dickie would come. Tomorrow night?

She concentrated on walking, just getting to the cottage,

and breaking in, finding a stone large enough – or perhaps if she rammed the edge of her case into the glass?

She remembered losing the key the first time they had come here. It seemed several light years ago. It was a relief to come in sight of the familiar clump of pine trees and shortly after that, to the left and nearer the cliff edge, the cottage.

Purely because Dickie had just once mentioned doing it, she felt beneath the flowerpots either side of the cottage door. Under the second was a key. She felt her knees go weak with relief, and she found herself kneeling on the doorstep.

She struggled inside, her hand falling on the exact spot of the light switch. She held her breath as she pressed down, expecting somehow the place would be changed, strange even, just as she felt different, strange. But all was in order: the colourful throws over the easy chairs, the woven rugs. She hurried to draw the curtains and find the matches left near the Calor gas cylinder. She lit the small heater, then put some of the dry driftwood they had left in the hearth on a bed of screwed-up newspaper and lit the fire.

She knelt before it, reminding herself that the happiest days of her life she had spent here with Dickie, yet alone, it felt empty, dead. She jumped to her feet in a panic and rushed all around, drawing all the curtains, thinking with the blackness shut out it would be better.

Hadn't Dickie wanted them to live here for ever, hadn't he wanted them to leave everything and everyone else behind? Well, she had, but how soon would he think to come?

She put her hand on her stomach and just for a moment it seemed as if Dickie were there, with her, with their baby. She knew one thing for absolute certainty, there would be no abortion. This child of hers and Dickie's would survive and go on, no matter what, no matter what pressures were put on her, she would ensure its future – that she did have in her power.

Nineteen

The hooter blared and the driver shook his fist as Dickie
swept out and past the vehicle at the last moment. He
apologized with a lift of his arm. He had not seen the furni-
ture van until he was almost on top of it. The man must have
thought he was trying to hitch a ride in the back. He had just
lost concentration, his mind a mixture of jubilation and fretful
anxiety about Katie.

The success and usefulness of the estate management course
he was just leaving was beyond price for him. He had learned
so much about tenant/landlord relations, and not just the law,
but more importantly he had such news for Katie.

So well had he participated, so obviously relevant was it
all to his circumstances, his life to come, that he was going
to be given leave of absence from Banford until after Christmas,
providing his parents were agreeable. This was so that he
could put into immediate practice what he had learned, being
required to write a thesis about it for his last term in the New
Year.

He raced an MG sports car as the stretch of dual carriageway
was signed to shrink to single lanes again. All he could think
of now was seeing Katie, finding out why she had not answered
his telephone call on Wednesday evening. There had been a
blip once before when a line was out of order he reminded
himself, and she *had* written to him as she had promised. He
twisted the accelerator to its fullest extent and finally slipped
ahead of the speeding MG.

When he reached Leicester he was early, three-quarters of
an hour before Katie would be leaving her office.

He walked the narrow streets round about, where several
small family businesses were surviving into third and fourth
generations. There was a jeweller, a small black-painted shop

173

with a black grille, 'Palfreyman's, established 1824' the white gothic script on the fascia announced. He paused and studied the trays of good-quality jewellery, old and new. There was a particular ring that struck him immediately. It was a solitaire diamond, beautifully set – the golden shoulders, so gracefully curving up in Art Nouveau style, seemed to lap the stone, like the sea laps a rock, rather than secure it with solid claws. He moved and the spotlights at either side of the window made prisms, glinting in the stone with astonishing clarity and brilliance. The sun on raindrops after a thunderstorm, he remembered, and as he was about to take over his estate's office, and had his coming-of-age birthday so near, he strode into the shop.

There was a thin elderly aesthetic-looking man behind the counter, his grey hair a frizzled abundance – like an orchestral conductor was Dickie's impression. He placed his helmet on the counter and looked across into wary grey eyes, though the man's eyes first followed the hefty head-gear, and only slowly came up to meet those of the young man.

'The tray of rings in the window,' Dickie prompted. 'There's a solitaire diamond . . .'

'There is,' the man confirmed, chewing at his bottom lip.

The awful thought came to Dickie that the man thought he was a thief, coming in black leathers, towering over the old boy, putting his helmet in the middle of the glass counter. He had taken all these signs as threats.

'I am a genuine customer,' he said in a more gentle tone and, seeing a bent-wood chair his side of the counter, he sat down. 'The ring is so right for my young lady. I knew the moment I saw it. I want to know if you will take a deposit from me. I come of age next April and will be able to pay for it fully then, but I can give you a cheque now if you'll hold it for me.'

He gave his full name and address, at which point Mr Palfreyman began to relax. 'The only thing is,' Dickie said, 'how will I know it will fit?'

'That would be no problem, a size or two either way can easily be done.' Mr Palfreyman smiled, felt in his waistcoat pocket and produced a key, with which he unlocked the back of the window, and drew out the tray. 'This will be the one,' he said, taking the solitaire from the centre of the display.

'It is.' Dickie took the ring almost reverently, turning it and examining the inside, then slipping it so far on his little finger and turning it to catch the light, displaying again the kaleidoscope of colours.

He looked up at the jeweller with such a look of enchantment in his face, Mr Palfreyman shook his head at such young rapture, but he said, 'It is the one for you, I see that, but . . .' He reached forward and caught the tiny price ticket hanging from the golden circle so that Dickie might see it.

'Three hundred and fifty pounds,' he read, but this he knew was Katie's ring. 'Will you take a deposit? I'll guarantee to come back and buy it outright before next April?'

Mr Palfreyman raised a hand. 'Sorry I misjudged you.'

'Took me for a—'

'Hold-up man.'

'Really!' Dickie was both astonished and diverted, looking down at himself, his biking gear. 'Is that the impression I give?'

'There's been a lot of trouble in the town this last summer, ever since some of the local Rockers became Hell's Angels.'

'Really.' He looked at Mr Palfreyman with an added respect: he knew his youth cults. 'I'm sorry I startled you.'

He made a few calculations and insisted on giving the jeweller a cheque for £85, all the money he had in his account, in the world, at that moment except for loose change in his pocket. He obtained a receipt and left to meet Katie, resolved not to mention the ring – when he gave it to her he wanted it to be a complete surprise. He could barely contain his excitement as he anticipated that future moment. He never doubted for one moment that she would do anything but utterly love it, fall for it as he had done.

He found he had now overrun office closing by a few minutes, but he approached from the bus station side so Katie was sure to come his way. By the light from the doorway he saw Mary come out with Mr Benbrook. They walked to the first corner together then separated, Mr Benbrook towards the car park, Mary towards the town centre and the city bus routes.

He walked slowly on, his breathing more rapid as he anticipated the moment Katie would come stepping out, seeing him, running perhaps when she did, but as he neared the entrance to the office the lights went out in the general office. He stepped forward, waiting to greet her, but a man backed out of the door, pulling it to behind himself, checking the lock was dropped and the door secured. It was North.

He was so surprised, he let the man walk away in the direction Mary had gone, only belatedly hurrying forward and calling after him. 'Hello! Hello there.'

North's step faltered for a moment. He half turned, and when he saw who called him he missed a stride, stumbled. He stopped beneath one of the old street lamps, and looked to Dickie like some Victorian villain in flickering gaslight as the man's face twisted and distorted with a range of emotions, none of them pleasurable.

'Young Lochinvar,' he snarled, 'what do you want?'

'What did you call me?'

North laughed. 'What d'you want, there's nothing and no one here for you – any more.'

Dickie wondered if he were drunk, but he had only just come from the office. He stepped nearer to show he was not to be put off by the man's strange manner. 'I am only here to meet Katie as you have probably guessed. I know you've *seen* us meet before.'

North laughed. 'You're wasting your time.'

'What do you mean?'

'I mean Katie Wright's not for you, and –' he pushed his head forward like a man delivering a blow that gave him enormous satisfaction – 'she's not here.'

He went to walk on but Dickie caught his arm. 'Just a minute,' he said. 'I think you'd better explain exactly what you mean.'

'Clear enough, isn't it? Not only is Katie not at the office, but she is now nothing to do with you. So . . .'

'So?'

'Take your hand off me,' North forcibly shook him off, adding, 'and get lost.'

'I've no intention of getting lost,' Dickie's informed him. 'I need to know what you're talking about, and I don't know

176

who you think you're talking to, Mr Bookkeeper, but you'd better explain yourself pretty damn quick.'

'Oh, I know exactly who I'm talking to, Mr Richard Philipps of "The Hall" and other landed estates.' He tried to push by but Dickie prevented him.

'And?'

'And?' North repeated irritatingly.

'Where is Katie?' He stepped forward, nearly touching the man.

'I don't know.'

'You'd better know, you'd better think rather rapidly, Mr Kenneth North, or I'm going to forget I'm Richard Philipps of "The Hall", I'm going to just remember I'm beginning to hate your guts as much as Katie does.' He pushed the man out of the light of the lamp and up against the wall. 'Where's Katie?' he asked very quietly, quite ready to smash a fist into the man's sneering face if that's what it took to get a satisfactory answer.

'She's . . .' he began but as a forceful hand crashed and pinned his shoulder against the wall he seemed to capitulate, answered in a rush, 'She's off sick as far as I know, she's not been into the office since Wednesday.'

'Sick?' Dickie released the man.

'Yes, sick, now do you mind if I go about my business?'

Dickie did not answer and North took his opportunity to be off, looking back from time to time, to see if he was being pursued.

Dickie was not sure how to deal with this situation – all North's stupid remarks and insinuations meant nothing now. He had not thought that Katie might be ill. So did he ring her home? Or did he go to his own home? His mother would be sure to know what was wrong – that seemed to be the best option. He could hardly just turn up at Colleen's house, and if he arrived on his motorbike, she probably wouldn't let him in anyway.

He reached home in record time, put his motorcycle in the end stable and looked up to where the light from Tommy's flat streamed out across the yard. Tommy, he thought, did not go far these days, though he missed little and was at the window taking in who it was in his yard at that time. Dickie stood in the square of light from the window and gave him a salute, a hand lifted and the curtain dropped back into place.

As he let himself in the back door and walked from the kitchen along the passage to the hall he heard Julian call out.

'Ma? Everything all right?'

'No, it's me,' he replied. 'Where is everybody?'

Julian came running down stairs, ever surprising Dickie how tall and robust the fourteen-year-old was becoming. 'Hi! All right?'

'Fine,' he answered automatically. 'So where is everyone?'

Julian made a grimace. 'Gone over to the Wrights, big trouble there. Katie's gone missing, they're wondering whether to involve the police.'

'I thought she was sick.' He saw the question in his half-brother's eyes and added, 'I saw someone from her office.'

'No, I don't think so. Well, I don't know really. It may be what they are telling people. Grandpa seems to know more about it.'

'She can't have just disappeared.' He frowned at Julian as if he was accusing him of complicity.

'I don't know, perhaps she's gone off to one of those places they say she went at weekends. Apparently she's been off a lot with some man . . .'

Dickie did not want to hear the lies he and Katie had allowed everyone to believe repeated. He had stuffed his gauntlets into his pockets, now he pulled them out again. 'Right,' he said. 'I'll be back sometime.'

'Is that what I'm to say?' Julian called after him. 'Official?'

'Yep! May not be until after the weekend, or longer.' A message about college went on as he turned back the way he had come. 'I'll be in touch,' he said.

'Don't forget Lord Markham's party next week, Liz said to remind you.'

The lavish weekend planned to celebrate Liz's grand-father's seventieth birthday was low on his priorities, and he did not answer. Once through the door from hall to passage Dickie ran. Julian wouldn't know but he had given him the lead to where Katie just might be, but there was one more person he wanted to see before he set off for Norfolk.

Tommy's curtain twitched again as he retrieved his bike

and set off for the farm. He hoped his grandfather would not be in bed: he needed to borrow some money for petrol, and he hoped he might learn a bit more about Katie's state of mind and what had led up to all this, and to Ken North's astonishing behaviour.

The sound of the bike and the dog had obviously brought Edgar to his door, but he looked surprised to see his elder grandson.

'Hello, young man, this is an honour even if it's late.'

'Grandpa. Are you well?'

'Fine, m'boy, and you? And how's the bike going?'

'Oh! That's great and I did wonder if you'd lend me some money for petrol.'

Edgar immediately put his hand in his pocket. 'Cashed a cheque this morning,' he said.

'I'm a bit puzzled,' Dickie went on as he thanked his grandfather and pocketed the money. 'Just got home and Julian tells me everyone is over at the Wrights, some cock and bull story about Katie having gone missing.'

Edgar pursed his lips and shook his head. 'Not a story I'm afraid, she has done just that.'

'But why? Is she all right, or is she ill?'

'Well –' he paused to shake his head – 'that's debatable. Not ill, I wouldn't say, but not all right either, and I'm not sure how confidential it's all supposed to be.'

'Ma will know if she's with Colleen now, and you seem to know.'

'Colleen confided in your mother first, I understand.'

'Grandpa, for pity's sake, tell me what it's all about.'

Edgar looked at his grandson in surprise. 'For pity's sake,' he repeated.

'I can't bear not to know what's going on.' Dickie felt a generalization was the best cover: he was obviously in danger of giving everything away, perhaps of making his grandfather clam up.

'Well,' he said, 'much to my surprise, Katie is expecting a child. I'd obviously completely misjudged her character, but then—'

'A child,' Dickie interrupted and sat down heavily on to the sofa. 'A child.'

'Seems she's been gallivanting with some chap at the office. He's offered to stand by her, marry her.'

'No!' Dickie exclaimed.

'No,' Edgar went on, 'apparently it doesn't seem to be what she wants at all. Never seen anyone look so disgusted at the thought of marrying someone she's obviously been sleeping with anyway.'

'Grandpa!' Dickie exclaimed to interrupt the flow. 'She's not been sleeping with anyone at the office,' he said, then swallowed hard before he told it all. 'It's my child. It's me Katie's been meeting most weekends.'

'Don't talk so stupid, boy,' his grandfather turned on him, his eyes full of equations about school, and the motorbike, of the suspicions Ian had persisted in, even though Bess had reassured him, had told him, as Colleen had, of the boyfriend at the office.

'Grandpa, believe me, it's our child, Katie's and mine.'

'You can't be certain,' Edgar ruled. 'How can you be, the girl lives in a different world to you. How do you know what she's up to all the time?'

'I know Katie,' Dickie stated, his voice shaking with anger. 'That's enough for me. We love each other, I've told you.'

'I do not believe you, and in any case the whole matter is dealt with, swept under the carpet. The girl has already gone to a clinic.'

'A clinic?' Dickie questioned.

Edgar shook his head. 'You've no idea what I'm talking about, have you. You think you know so much. You're so unworldly, Dickie. She's gone to a clinic for an abortion.'

'No! No, she wouldn't do that.'

'No.' Edgar gave a cynical laugh. 'She probably wouldn't if she saw it was a way to marry into a family that owns half the county.'

Dickie realized that seeing red was not just an expression, and through the haze that coloured his vision he thought for a moment he was going to kill his grandfather.

'Look.' Edgar stood up too and tried to put his hand on the young man's shoulder but he backed away so there should be no contact. 'It's over,' the older man was saying, 'by now it will all be over. There's no need for anyone to know you might be involved. I'm not going to tell anyone, and no one else knows except the girl, and I assume—'

'No!' Dickie shouted. 'Don't assume anything. I love Katie, I'm going to marry her, as soon as I'm eighteen no one can stop me, and now there's a baby I'll just do it sooner, that's all.'

'Don't be a fool, keep your mouth shut. You've had your fun, and I've given her some money and told her there's more if she needs it. No one will know. She can come back home, go back to her job, no one need be any the wiser. This peccadillo need not ruin your future.'

'You've done that!' He turned on his grandfather. 'If Katie, or my baby, come to any harm I'll never speak to you again. You'll never see me again if I can help it. Never!' He thrust his hand into his pocket and threw the notes he had borrowed at his grandfather. 'You can keep your money, all of it, and your half of Leicestershire, I want nothing of it.'

Dickie ran out of petrol just after passing the Norfolk county sign and pushed his bike some way until he came to a small village garage, closed, but the house behind still had lights downstairs.

He parked his bike by the pumps and went to knock at the door. A large man in shirt sleeves came at the third knock.

'I'm really desperate,' Dickie said, 'as well as sorry to disturb you. I've run out of petrol for my bike, and I need to get to Wells tonight, it's so urgent.'

The man drew in his breath, let it out in a long sigh; leaning inside, he flicked a switch which put on the forecourt lights, then pulled the door to after himself. He took keys from his trouser pocket. 'Another ten minutes and I'd have been in bed.'

'Sorry,' Dickie said as they reached the pumps, 'and there is something else.' He pulled his wristwatch off and held it out. 'I haven't any money.'

The man studied him, his leathers, the expensive bike and held out his hand for the watch. He scrutinized this, turned it over in his hand a few times. He took down the petrol hose and indicated Dickie should unlock his tank. He filled it and Dickie screwed back the cap.

'Thanks so much,' he said.

'Hmm.' The man handed the watch back to him. 'Worth too much is that, you come back and pay me some time.'

Dickie took his watch back, then nodded to the man's name and the name of the garage above the door. 'I'll send you a cheque, plus,' he said, 'you're a real friend in need.'

It was two o'clock in the morning when he arrived at the cottage. There was a glow of light from inside, a fire or a table lamp, so Katie was here. His heart lifted. Thank goodness, thank the man at the petrol station, thank everyone in heaven and earth. He took out his key and opened the door, running in, calling.

Katie rose, startled from where she lay dozing, huddled in a blanket before a dying fire. Her eyes large, black circled, she looked as if she had not slept properly for a long time.

'Katie.' He flung himself down by her, gathered her tightly into his arms and rocked her, then felt the slackness of shock, of perhaps a near faint. He lifted her bodily and lowered her gently into one of the armchairs, pulling the wool throw-over round her, kneeling at her feet.

'What were you doing on the floor?' he asked.

'Waiting for you?' she said. 'And is it really you, really, really you? I've waited and waited. I thought you wouldn't come, wouldn't realize where I was.'

'Why did you come here by yourself?' he asked. 'Why didn't *you* wait for me.'

'Oh!' she sighed, bending forward and leaning her head on his shoulder. 'So many reasons. I just couldn't, and I've made up my mind, I'm never going back.'

'I'm here now, don't worry, everything will be all right.' He stopped suddenly, went back on his heels and regarded her solemnly. 'You . . .' His pause was so long she look searchingly into his eyes and he began again, 'You have been here all the time? I mean you haven't been anywhere else?'

'I went all over on trains and buses to get here, but—'

'My grandfather said you had gone to a clinic,' he blurted out.

'You don't really think I'd—'

'No! I told him not.'

'He gave me money. I used it to get away that same night.'

'While I . . .' He related the story of the petrol money and they laughed together, and because they were together everything was all right, nothing mattered, not for that night anyway.

Then he realized she was shivering. 'I'll make up the fire, and shall we have –' he wondered what was left in the cupboards – 'soup? Any bread?'

She shook her head.

'What have you been living on?' he asked.

'Just what was here,' she said, 'I didn't care really.'

'We care now,' he said and, looking round, saw there was no wood inside. He took the torch and fetched an armful from the lean-to shed, piled the hearth and put some of the driest on top of the embers, using the brass bellows hanging beside the fire to blow it into life again. Then he warmed the soup.

He thought she looked thinner and poured extra into her bowl. She noticed and protested they should have the same. He looked at her and grinned. 'Don't you dare,' she told him, 'make any remark about eating for two.' Then she burst into tears, put her head in her hands.

'Please don't, it breaks my heart. After all its only early, I mean we would have wanted children, we're just—'

'Jumping the gun.' She sat, trying to mop up the tears which defeated the small handkerchief she found.

'How serious is it?' he asked and held up the choice of a tea towel or a hand towel.

'You fool . . .' she said now caught between laughter and tears, 'but I'm so happy you're here.'

'Soup first, then happiness later,' he told her.

But that night was the first time they went to bed together and did not make love. He realized she was mentally and physically exhausted, and cold – it seemed he would never get her warm. He wrapped them both in blankets, put two pairs of socks on her feet and held her. After a time she whispered, 'Oh, let me turn over so you can warm my back.'

She snuggled in tight and he could feel the chill of her back through his shirt, for neither of them had undressed properly. He felt really concerned for her well-being. This cottage was not equipped for winter visitors, though with the fire going properly all day it should be warmer at night. He wondered if there were any hot-water bottles? He also realized what a difficult position he had put them in by coming without money.

Then he realized she was at last sleeping, that she was warm and safe in his arms, and he closed his eyes. He still would not tell her what he had done with all his money; he did not regret that.

Twenty

'Colleen has heard from Katie.' Bess greeted Ian with the news when he came in for Sunday lunch. 'They'd been up all night arguing whether they should tell the police or not, then this morning about midday she phoned.'

'And she's all right?'

Relief made their usual stilted exchanges spill over into real conversation over the dining table, and his genuine concern touched her. At that moment, had their split been new, she felt it would have been possible to heal, to come together, but it had become the way they lived. And these days she felt there was other guilt on his side. He was an attractive wealthy man, and her every instinct told her he was not as celibate as she had been ever since they had stopped sharing a bed. Hadn't her own father been guilty of just such a thing many years ago, and well before her mother died?

'Colleen said she sounded sort of reserved, but quite sensible, not as if she was going to do anything stupid.'

'And where is she?'

'She wouldn't say.'

'And has she done anything about the baby?' He did not add with the money your father gave her, but she knew he thought it would have been better offered to Colleen, if it were needed, not pushed into the hand of yet another young person who might, or might not, use it wisely.

She shook her head at him. 'They don't know. Colleen said all she could bring herself to ask was "Are you still all right?" and Katie said yes.'

'Is she coming home?'

'Not at the moment.'

'So there's nothing anyone can do but wait on that one,' he said. 'In the meantime have we heard any more of Dickie?'

185

She looked at him sharply but he held up appeasing hands. 'Just that I'd like to know where we stand with regard to this coming weekend at Lord Markham's. Is he coming with us or not?'

'I understand he's coming, after all it's Liz's grandfather, and he seems to spend more time with Liz than anyone else.'

'Not this last weekend,' Ian said.

'How do you know?' She paused in the act of clearing their two plates.

'Julian saw her in town when he went bowling with his friends last night. Dickie wasn't with her.'

'So all we know,' Bess admitted, 'is what he called to Julian as he rushed away Friday night. Something about the course, but what?

'We could telephone Banford.'

'No,' she vetoed, this was an old bone of contention between them. 'I don't want it known that you still don't trust my son, that we don't even find time to talk to him.' She knew the last remark was unfair: they were always there to be talked to if Dickie ever found the time.

He raised his eyebrows – there was obviously much he could say, but he seemed to have no wish to slip back along the thorny way of disagreement over Dickie. It got them nowhere, was as unproductive as discussions about her father.

She felt him withdraw his interest, shut the door on the subject they never agreed about.

She knew he had never really accepted that there was a reason for Dickie's absence from home at weekends, and that nearly always that reason had to do with Liz. Julian had once undermined her when he had said that Liz was Dickie's 'ways and means' girl, but when pressed by Ian had said it was just a joke.

Ian had not been joking when he had ranted on about what he called 'good old squirearchy', going on to expound the old rights of the squire or his son to take any village girl to bed before her first bedding with her new husband. She had told him he was an inverted snob, obsessed with being a perennial pamphlet-waving peasant. It had been just one of the disagreements that compounded their estrangement.

Katie's predicament, and that bookkeeper's proposal of

marriage, she would have thought once and for all laid the ghost in Ian's mind, but watching him, she felt that in his heart of hearts he still could not exonerate Dickie. Otherwise why the immediate question about his whereabouts when they were talking about Katie?

Bess just looked forward to the day when Dickie would know what he wanted in life, and who he wanted to share it with, and if it was Liz, then no one would be more pleased than Bess's father. Lord Markham's granddaughter he would regard as a real feather in the family cap. Bess considered she would certainly be a better match for Dickie's temperament than anyone like Katie Wright. Katie needed someone more stable, and Bess hoped with all her heart that the father of the child would prove to be just that.

'Well he's only one more full term next year,' Ian said at length.

Bess refocused on her husband and the moment.

'Then we'll have him home for good. We'll know exactly what he's doing then right enough,' Ian concluded, 'and thank God for that. That day will perhaps be our mutual salvation.'

'I hope so, it's not a moment too soon,' she said.

They looked at each other very solemnly, calculations each about the other in their eyes. It would be a new turn in their lives, having the adult Dickie at home.

'Or crucifixion,' he ventured and smiled slowly to show it was to be taken as humour.

She smiled tremulously back, unsure how strong her sense of humour still was. 'I'm going for a hack while the rain keeps off and the light holds.'

'I'll come with you, if that's OK?'

'Of course.' They were on the whole polite to each other – it was what had held the household together. She wondered if they might ever just push one step beyond politeness to real warmth again?

It was dusk when they arrived back, invigorated, but the horses well mud-splattered, needing hosing and drying down. Tommy was there but they stayed to give him a hand. Bess, glowing with the congeniality of the ride, related her child-hood fascination with old Noel Wright, George's grandfather, who as he groomed had sucked his breath in and out with

187

regular loud swishing noises, 'like the tide going in and out,' she said. She and Ian exchanged looks but neither of them made the observation that Tommy just grunted.

She could feel Ian's eyes on her as they walked away towards the house. She knew he had always thought she looked good in the stretchy tight jodhpurs that were the fashion, and she had kept her figure. For the first time she wondered if people who did not have children were closer than those who did. Not so *many* bones of contention, that was for sure.

The sound of a car coming up the drive reached them. They both stopped and turned as it drove into the yard. It was Liz. They both waved and turned back to meet her.

'Trouble?' Ian asked sotto voce as they approached.

'Hi, guys!' Liz greeted them. 'How's the prodigal?'

'No idea,' Ian replied. 'How are you?'

'Fine, fine. You know he's absolutely excelled himself, don't you?'

'No.' There was absolute dread in Bess's voice and she stood quite still, waiting for the bad news.

'No, no,' Liz reassured, 'no, literally, he has excelled. He came absolutely top of his course. Didn't you know?'

When both had assured her they had heard nothing, that only Julian had seen Dickie since last weekend, and then only for seconds, and he had only caught half the message he was supposed to relay to his parents.

'So much so,' Liz enthused, 'that he's being given leave of absence until after Christmas to put into practice all he has learned, to start, in fact, running your estate.'

There was absolute silence while they took this momentous information on board.

'You're pleased, aren't you?' Liz asked. 'I thought you'd be chuffed.'

'I think we are,' Ian answered. 'Just surprised, after all the traumas of him not wanting to continue with his education at all, but, yes, I would say we are delighted.'

'I think you've got to approve the idea, and Dickie has to write a thesis on the experience for his last term.'

'I just wish Dickie had thought to stay around and tell us himself,' Bess said, leading the way inside, 'we could all have celebrated.'

'Never mind, we can do that at Grandpa's party.' She raised a hand to Julian, who appeared in the passage. 'You are coming, aren't you, all of you? I've come really with a further message from Gramps. He knows such as Julian and I won't support the Saturday shoot.' She paused and laughed. 'He says he expects *me* to be in charge of the saboteurs.'

'They don't have sabs at shoots, do they?' Julian asked. 'Only hunts.'

'There's always a first time, I suppose, but not usually. But Gramps said he will set up something different for young pacifists like me and you, Julian, and he's asking what about a cross-country? And he'll put up a decent prize.'

'He's really pushing the boat out, cost him a packet already this weekend,' Ian said, 'what with dinner and a ball, all his weekend guests, a shoot, now a cross-country.'

'He says one's not seventy every day, he thanks God he's survived to celebrate it, and he's taking precautions in case he's too gaga when he's eighty to enjoy his next significant birthday.'

'It will be something we shall all remember,' Bess said. 'If there's anything I can do, perhaps help arrange this horse race? There's not much time.'

'I think it would basically just be people we know would be interested and could phone, and that's the reason I've been sent, to enlist your expertise.'

'The course won't be a problem because we've had cross-country on Lord Markham's estate many times,' Bess said, already involved. 'I'll phone him.'

'Thanks, I think that's what he was hoping,' Liz said, then hooking an arm through Julian's she asked, 'So how's the world of the next Christopher Wren going?'

'Fine,' he said, but he was frowning and Bess thought he looked like a young man who was not quite sure how to take this latest version of Liz. Today she was more boy than girl, Bess thought. Jeans with tartan inserts from below the knee, flaring out to four times their original width to cover her feet completely, black T-shirt and a red pirate bandanna tied tightly over her head completed her outfit.

'Come on,' Liz said to him, 'I'll take you for a spin, then we'll call at a pub for a Coke. That OK? I'll bring him back, honest.'

They laughed and waved their hands, watching Julian slip into the passenger seat and be taken away at speed.

'You've something on your mind,' Liz guessed as they turned out of the drive.

'Yes. Something I found after Dickie left in such a hurry. Show you when we get to the pub.'

'A little way out from where we're so well known, do you think. You can go in the bar then,' she said.

'Great,' he answered with a grin, 'you're such a sport.'

They were the first customers in the bar of the Talbot, some fifteen miles away. They found a corner seat in the low-beamed bar where the panelling glowed with polish and a cheerful fire burned in the grate. Liz fetched two halves of lager and once they were settled, Dickie took out a small folded piece of paper. He opened it out and gave it to Liz.

She looked, then gave out a low whistle.

'I found it after he came home Friday night, it must have fallen out of his pocket. I wondered if *you* would give it back to him. He's not very keen on my knowing his personal affairs, and I don't think he'd want it lying about in the house for anyone to find.'

'This is a serious piece of jewellery, a ring with definite permanent intentions.' She looked at Julian as if wondering how much he might know, or guess about his half-brother's intentions. He obviously knew that she was not the intended recipient, and just as obviously he was, as Dickie always said, 'an intuitive little beast'. 'I think maybe you're right he would prefer me to hand it back to him. I'll keep it safe, don't worry any more about it.'

'He may realize he's lost it,' Julian worried anyway.

'Not likely,' she said, 'knowing Dickie.'

They finished their drinks and Liz pushed through the growing numbers of customers at the bar to buy another half each. By the time they left, others were waiting for tables and she took their glasses away to the counter. 'Big celebrations at your grandfather's place next weekend, I hear,' the landlord said.

'You're right!' Liz said cheerfully. 'Goodnight to you.'

'Goodnight,' he said, looking meaningfully at Julian, 'and to you, young man.'

190

'So much for anonymity,' Julian said with a laugh as they climbed back into the car.

There was no hint of his loss when Dickie did ring the following evening. Julian answered the telephone as he walked in from school, and once he established the call was not about the receipt he halted the flow. 'You'd better talk to Ma,' he said as his mother came from the lounge. 'Liz came yesterday, singing your praises about the course.'

Bess hurried to his side as Dickie still tried to keep his brother on the other end, but mid-sentence he was handed over to his mother.

'Dickie!' she exclaimed. 'Where are you? What are you doing? What's this about not going back to Banford? And are you going to be at Lord Markham's birthday celebrations with us next weekend?'

'I may answer in any order, I presume,' he said. 'First, I'm in a phone box, and my change is limited. I'm with a friend recuperating from all my efforts at being top student. Can you ring Banford and tell them you really want me at home for next term, and yes I am going to be at Liz's do.'

'But—'

The phone went dead.

Julian grinned at her. 'Aggravating, isn't he? You see what I have to put up with when he's home.'

'But you won't mind him being home?' she asked.

'No, I can handle him, and it's fun, you never know what will happen next, and it's always good to have Liz around. She's great!'

She put her arm around his shoulders. 'Come and let's see if Mrs West is having one of her interminable cups of tea.'

Twenty-One

Every day Dickie found some opportunity to try to persuade Katie to go back home with him, to confront both lots of parents with the truth, and say they just wanted to get married. It was a bit early but people would get used to the idea. 'We'll be a nine-day wonder, then they'll forget.'

'Your grandfather has obviously not spread the news.'

'No, he won't, and you know why.'

'I can think of many reasons why,' she said bitterly, 'most of them have to do with being who I am.'

'Or that you took money he thought was for a clinic.'

She had no answer to this.

'In any case, I'm going to tell everyone it's my baby. I'll tell the postman, the baker, the dustbin man, the Lord Mayor. They'll have to let us marry to shut me up.'

He left her without much to say in the way of argument, just a great reluctance in her soul to go back.

'It needn't be a big wedding if you don't want it,' he said on the Wednesday afternoon, as they walked along the beach in an icy east wind, wrapped in most of the clothes they had. 'Registry office'll do me. Gretna Green if you prefer.'

But Katie could not bring herself to face anyone. She had known humiliation at the hands of her parents, at the office, with his grandfather, there was no way she felt she could go back – yet.

'We have to be a bit practical,' he urged. 'You've got an awful cold. We both need more clothes, warmer clothes to stay here, and money. I should never have . . .' but still he held on to his secret, 'come without money, it was stupid.'

'You came, that's all I care about.' She coughed, then sneezed several times.

'You'll feel more like facing people when you're better.'

'And when I look better, without a Rudolph nose and red-rimmed eyes.'

'Your chest's not tight, is it?' he asked.

'And what will you do if it is, Dr Philipps?'

'I don't know. It's what Nannie always used to ask if we had a cold.'

She looked at him despairingly. He could not have said anything less likely to convince her it was time to return home and face everyone, his family at the Hall in particular.

'No!' he exclaimed, leaping in front of her, making her jump. 'I do know.' He steered her from the sea's edge, deserted except for themselves, up towards the empty promenade. 'We'll get some Vicks,' he said, 'I'll rub it on your chest and back tonight. Don't want your mother thinking I don't look after you.'

At the mention of her mother she looked quickly back at the flat grey sea, the grey sky, the horizon lost in the general murk. She felt choked with emotion and began to cough, and then could not stop. He turned her rapidly back towards the cottage. 'We shouldn't have come out.'

'We need something for tea,' she said.

'Oh yes. I'll get something, you go on.'

'No, we'll get something, then we'll both go back.' Their money had to be taken care of: this worried Katie far more than it concerned Dickie.

They had been surprised how quiet the place was, particularly on winter weekdays, and how they stood out as lingering strangers. He took her to the chemist, then on to the small general store – in both places they were aware of much silent appraisal.

The cottage felt cosy after the wind. He had spent hours every day beach-combing for wood, then going up into the pine copse and coming back with branches and pockets full of cones. Later he went back with a bag, and they made patterns in the fire with piles of fir cones. He put twigs and cones on the fire now before he took off his leather jacket – they flamed to immediate life, the fire running and glowing red around each segment of every cone.

'Like living, flaming, Christmas trees,' she said. 'It is like Christmas with the pine logs and everything,' she said. 'We just do things too early, don't we?'

193

'Better than never doing them like some people.'

'Who?' she asked.

'Can't think of anyone off hand,' he said, 'but there must be masses who've never done half what we have.'

'Not so precocious, you mean.'

'Well, not every man gets seduced does he?'

'Dickie!' She lobbed a pine cone at him, and he in turned lobbed it into the fire.

'Shall we make some toast?' he said, reaching down for the brass toasting fork. 'Making it at an open fire is as good as eating it, I think. Oh! I know what we can do.'

He sliced the loaf they had just bought into thick slices, brought two plates and a pile of sliced cheese. As he held each piece close to the fire the yeasty smell of the toasting bread made their stomachs rumble audibly, then he laid the cheese on the bread where it melted very satisfactorily. 'There,' he said, reaching over and placing an apple on the edge of her plate, 'a meal fit for anyone.'

'Hmm, it's great,' she agreed, taking bites of cheesy toast and apple alternately.

'Speciality of the school dorm,' he told her – and she stopped eating.

'That's the trouble really, isn't it?' she said. 'We're from different worlds. You and your nannies and school dorms and posh colleges, me local schools, then a job in an office. Perhaps you should just go home and forget me, and I'll go back and marry a bookkeeper, it would be more fitting.'

'Katie! Don't!' He almost threw his plate into the hearth. 'I long ago made up my mind that my life would not be worth living without you. The only way I can deal with my life, the bloody estate and things, is if I know you are going to be there, by my side, helping.'

His appeal was so dramatic she was alarmed and repentant. 'I just feel inadequate, not worthy, or—'

'Stop it! Stop it!' He held his head, cheesy crumbs lodging in his hair.

'Oh, Dickie! I'm so sorry.' She was on her knees by him, holding him, comforting him now. 'I suppose I'm just looking for reassurance.'

'What else can I do to reassure you?' he asked. 'If I could

marry you this moment you know I would. Perhaps we could try. Should we go to Gretna Green? How much money have we left for petrol? Or should I sell the motorbike, that should fetch quite a bit, then there's my watch. What d'you think train fares would cost?'

She felt guilty, fishing for reassurances, like a flirt fishes for compliments. She had pushed him too far, made him over-react. Her turn to plead now. 'Dickie, stop it, please. I'm sorry.'

'So swear you'll never doubt me again.'

'Never,' she said. 'Never.' She cradled his head and picked the crumbs from his hair. What a mixture of passions he was. 'All right now?' she asked.

'Nearly. Come here and let me rub your chest,' he said.

'We'll not waste this food,' she protested. 'Eat first, rub afterwards.'

He made a lascivious face at her and had her laughing again.

Later when they were in bed with the two hot-water bottles they had bought and her chest and back well larded with Vicks, he said, 'There's another thing you've got to promise me.'

'What's that?' she asked.

'That you'll always wear this perfume so I'll be reminded of this moment,' he said, pushing his hand back up her night-gown to spread the balm ever wider.

'Mind what you're doing,' she said, 'I reckon it will sting in some places. Not that I care . . .'

'I once heard a village woman call another girl a "brazen hussy". I reckon that's what you are, Katie Wright.'

'I'm what you made me, sir, she said.' The words of 'Where are you going, my pretty maid?' had sprung to her mind. Katie felt so much better now she was fed, warm and able to breathe easier and turned to him, tickling and pretending to rub his chest. '"Sir, she said, Sir, she said."'

They slept late the next morning and even when they woke did not get up until hunger and thirst drove them. 'Eleven o'clock, what time is that for an honest woman to be rising from her bed?' he asked as he brought her tea.

'About right, I'd say.' But when he sat on the end of the bed and looked down she asked, 'What is it?'

'There's two things really,' he said. 'One is that we can't

stay on here without money and more clothes, and the other is that I really promised everyone I'd be at Lord Markham's birthday celebrations this weekend. Liz has been such a good friend to us both that I don't want to let her down. Why don't we go back tomorrow, and make our grand announcement at their ball on the Saturday night?'

'Dickie! No!' She was appalled. 'Never! You can't think of taking over someone else's party with something like that. I'll never hear of it. Never.'

He took the tea she was spilling from her.

'But will you come back with me?' he pleaded.

'Certainly not the weekend of Lord Markham's party.'

'Liz would arrange an invite to the party for you,' he said.

'Don't be ridiculous,' she said. She thought she would probably never be invited anywhere after her condition was known, and who the father was. She would undoubtedly be blamed, and ostracized by polite society – wasn't that the phrase she remembered from some high-society play or other?

'I'm not being ridiculous,' he vowed. 'No, I mean it. You might as well become used to going places with me sooner rather than later.'

'Just at the moment I'd rather it was later,' she said, 'but perhaps you should go.'

He did not answer.

'We don't want to upset your parents any more than necessary. If they are expecting you, then why not go Friday and come back on Sunday? You could do that.'

'It's Friday tomorrow,' he reminded her bleakly, 'and it's only the private dinner for family and close friends. It's the big shoot and ball on the Saturday.'

'But I guess your family are all invited Friday.'

'Yes, for the whole weekend, I understand, but—'

'I shall be all right here. Look –' she produced the hot-water bottles, now cold – 'you brought in mountains of wood. I can go to the shops if there's anything else I need, but I won't before Sunday.'

'Then there's more money for petrol,' he said.

'Well, that won't be a problem when you get home, will it?' she stated.

He did not answer. Ready money was something that could

196

be a problem at the Hall – there was always a panic about cash for Mrs West's wages – and he'd emptied his bank account.

He picked up her hand from the quilt and interlaced his fingers with hers, suddenly cheered by the thought of the ring on her finger.

'I'll go on one condition,' he told her, 'that you promise to come home with me immediately afterwards. I could perhaps let your mother know . . .'

'I don't see how you can without telling everything. No. You must promise not to make any kind of announcement, or say anything to my mother without me being there. I'll never go back if you do something like that.'

'OK I promise,' he said, 'and *you* promise about coming back with me immediately after that weekend?'

She looked bleak.

'It has to be faced,' he said, handing back her tea.

'I promise then,' she said. 'Yes, I promise.'

On Friday evening they left it so late to part that Dickie did not arrive back in Leicestershire until way beyond any normal dinner time, so he decided to go to the Hall and put in an appearance the following day.

Tommy as usual saw his arrival, but once Dickie was in the house it was quite strange. He couldn't really ever remember sleeping alone anywhere in his life. He had nearly come of age and never truly been alone anywhere. He knew he had felt lonely many times, or perhaps what he had felt was estranged. Estranged from Julian, and Ian, and sometimes from his mother – but never from Katie. The thought made his heart make a sudden thump like a huge hammer blow. Never from Katie.

He wanted to jump on his bike and go back to her, not be here by himself. Perhaps he might go immediately to join the weekend party, but he felt curiously vulnerable, liable to blurt out his story to the first person who gave him a kind word – his mother most likely – and that would definitely have a ripple effect that would mar the whole weekend, Katie would not like that; and there was Liz. She was so keen to make her grandfather's celebrations a great success.

He wandered from room to room, first putting on the light in the hall, then going in and out of each room, switching on lights, wandering all around, touching this, moving the other, remembering something specific that had happened in each room: in the office, the morning he had taken the locket; in the library, tampering with the gun cupboard when he was about twelve; most vividly, in the sitting room going to jump on his mother's knee and his stepfather preventing him. 'Hold on, young man, you're a bit too big for that now.' He also for the first time remembered his mother's reply, 'Or I am', and realized it must have been when she was expecting Julian.

He wondered if he remembered now because of Katie, and the baby she was expecting, his baby.

He looked all around the gracious room with its expanse of settees and chairs, the long windows overlooking the terraces and the lawns, pitch black now. His family, his and Katie's children, would fill it with life and laughter. He moved further along from the light switches to a covered box. He lifted the cover and threw the master switch which put on all the terrace lights, from one end to the other.

He unlocked the French doors and walked out, going over to the stone balustrade. He stood quite still, absorbing every sensation, hands pressed on the cold stone. He could smell the heavy clay soil in beds and borders, dug over, prepared for the winter, and he listened to perfect silence.

He felt an overwhelming urge to walk down into the garden, to walk to the edges of the light and look back. He went circumspectly down the steps to the lawn, and strolled out to the extent of the light's power and slowly turned round. It was as if he was putting off a treat, an experience. He supposed, if he thought about it, he never remembered doing anything slowly in his whole life; usually the ideas came and he did what he thought.

He turned to view the mansion, a small country mansion in the larger scale of things, but handsome, as pleasing as a painting, an old master with the terraces fully lit, warming the stone, and the outer reaches of the house merging into the night. It looked like a welcoming place, a place to entertain, one that *should* be filled with laughter and children. He and Katie ought to have lots of children, lots, so no child felt isolated, without a peer.

He turned around again and faced the blackness, walked a

few paces away, and further until the darkness enveloped him, then again he looked back. He did this twice more, and the diminishing of the house made him feel like someone saying goodbye to it, when really he told himself, what he must be doing was reassessing, taking stock, in the light of his new circumstances – father to be, father to the child, the first-born, who would one day inherit.

He was not too far from the lake now, and with the feeling that he had some obligation to the father he never knew, he went on along the familiar path until he felt the downward slope increase and he was almost at the water.

He stood and listened again. He could hear the gentle lap of the water on the shoreline, and the slightest of breezes touched and moved the dead leaves beneath the poplars.

The lake had always held a morbid fascination for him, this place where his father drowned. The father whose name he bore, and whose name brought pause in conversations, a swift switching of topics, and glances at him. He recalled the time he had gone to the local Records Office and in the bound copies of the local newspapers found the report of an overturned boat in the lake, the verdict of suicide while the balance of the mind was disturbed. The Honourable Greville Philipps was the only son of Lady Clara Philipps and leaves a wife and a son.' He remembered the words of the coroner: 'an impulsive man'.

Why did you do it, Pa? Were you ill, or just sick in the mind? He wondered if his mother worried that he might be like his father. He had once aggravated Mrs West so much in the kitchen that she had turned on him, telling him he was just like his father 'and would come to no good end.' His school reports had always included the word 'impulsive': 'Richard must try not to be so impulsive'; 'Stopping and thinking occasionally is highly recommended.'

'I wish you could have known Katie,' he said to the black lapping lake. 'She's not impulsive – well, perhaps only in loving me.' He stood for a moment more before turning back to the distant floodlit terraces. 'You would have liked her,' he added.

When Dickie finally went to his bed it was early morning, and he slept late into the Saturday morning. He found he was still alone – Mrs West had obviously been given time off – so he took his bike and rode over to Lord Markham's house. Everyone was already out on the shoot.

He encountered one of the local women helping with the catering, the lavish cold repast which would very soon be ferried out to the wooden shooting lodge at midday, with tables outside for the beaters as it was fine. He helped himself to beef and bread. 'Had no breakfast,' he explained. 'Your loader was sent out with the beaters, I think, but Mr Albert will know.' She led the way to where Lord Markham's butler was in charge of the extra hired help.

'Hello, Albert,' Dickie greeted the elderly grey-haired man who had served the Markhams since he was fourteen. A rare man, his stepfather said, who could serve without being servile, and when the need arose, argue his corner without insolence.

The ice-blue eyes regarded him without fear or favour. 'Thought you weren't coming, young man, your loader's gone off hours ago to help the beaters,' he paused. 'If you want a shot or two before lunch I could try and find someone for you, perhaps one of the young caterers knows how to load.'

'Don't worry, Albert,' a voice called and he turned to see Liz and Julian coming towards them. They were both in riding gear.

'Thought you weren't going to make it,' Liz called. 'Lovely you have.' She came forward and kissed his cheek.

'I was too late for last night, apologies.'

'You're here now. We'll walk down to your stand with you.'

'Neither of you'll shoot,' he stated.

'We're representing the sabs,' Julian told him.

Albert cleared his throat menacingly.

'Not really, Albert,' Liz told him, 'just a joke.'

'Not to those who make their living organizing these sports,' he said as Liz took a bandolier of cartridges from him.

'Well, we'll argue that another time,' Liz said. 'Where are your guns?'

'I'll get them,' Albert offered. 'Lord Markham arranged for you to have the stand nearest the house in case you were late.'

'Living up to my reputation then,' he said.

'Right,' Albert agreed but, glancing at this young man, he was moved to ask, 'Are you all right? You shouldn't be shooting if you don't feel a hundred per cent.'

'Didn't sleep very well last night,' he answered, 'and I might be going down with a cold, but thanks for noticing.' He took one gun from Albert and Julian stepped forward to carry the other.

As they reached the stack of straw bales that were Dickie's official stand, guns began to fire again in the distance, at the far end of the line.

'Were you worried about anything last night?' Liz asked. 'Was that why you didn't sleep?'

'Suppose, sort of,' he answered though he was not sure 'worried' was the word so much as 'haunted', by the past, and his need to straighten out people's perceptions of his future.

'Your first bird's coming over,' Liz said and, pulling cartridges from the bandolier she now had slung around her shoulders, she swiftly loaded Dickie's gun.

'More murder and butchery,' she commented as the guns nearer began to fire, and they saw flight being twisted into falling clumps of meat and feather. Two pheasants came low and terrified over Dickie's stand. He raised his gun and shot, getting both birds with the two shots from his first gun.

'Nice quick job,' he said. 'No suffering.'

Neither Liz nor Julian answered. Liz handed him the second loaded gun. 'We've found something that belongs to you,' she told him and pushed her hand into her pocket and gave him the folded jeweller's receipt.

He opened it with one hand, gasped and frowned. 'I lost this!' he exclaimed. 'I can't believe I was so careless.'

'And you hadn't missed it,' Liz added.

He shook his head. 'But where?' he asked.

'I found it,' Julian admitted, 'it must have been when you pulled your gauntlets out of your jacket, remember. I asked Liz to give it to you, but I meant when I wasn't around,' he added with a grimace at Liz.

'He'd know I didn't find it,' she said. 'Anyway you just wanted to do the right thing, which we have now done.'

'Yes, thanks,' he said to Julian, 'thanks.' Then he hesitated and added, 'Look, I'm going to have to go off again Sunday

201

night, would you keep it for me Liz until, well until I've got things settled, which won't be long now.'

'If that's what you want,' she said. 'No problem.'

'Yes, please –' he nodded again at Julian – 'and thanks.'

Another stray bird arrived and Dickie took it out cleanly with his first shot. Then from the corner of his eye he saw the beaters walking in with their dogs for the mid-morning lunch break; leading the way was Katie's father and talking to him his stepfather. This was the opportunity he was waiting for, though he had in all honesty not given it much thought, but now he was going to do the right thing, in the right manner – surely Katie would approve of that. He was going to ask George Wright for the honour of his daughter's hand in marriage – and Ian was going to be his witness. There would be no way he could say he was being secretive about this.

'Here,' he called to Julian, 'catch.'

Julian looked up, startled, as the gun was thrown.

Twenty-Two

Ian's lips parted in disapproval and he heard George swear as they saw the gun being thrown, tossed in the air.

They saw the arms of one of Ian's sons raised to throw and the other to catch, but then they both stumbled, faltered like partners in a macabre synchronized dance as the report of the gun shattered the lunchtime lull. They saw the two young men both fall, towards each other, as if they were connected by some taut unbreakable thread which someone had stamped on.

It seemed to Ian that everything closed down, that for long, long moments there was no sound, no movement. The girl stood alone, unbelieving, transfixed, then her hands went to her ears. He and George ran now, like men with leaden legs, in a nightmare, into the stand behind the straw bales. The two men reached Liz just as she collapsed to her knees between Bess's sons.

Ian saw, or sensed, Julian move, saw George with the girl. He reached for Dickie. The youth lay flat on his stomach, even his face looked pressed flat into the turf.

He lifted him very gently, just enough to turn him, give him air. He saw blood on the grass as he raised him more, a lot of blood. 'George, ambulance,' he ordered. 'Liz, Dr Michael's in the furthest stand with Markham.' He did not look up, just ordered, 'Go!' when responses seemed slow.

When they were on the move, only then did he take in the extent of the wound, the ragged compaction of black leather, blood and flesh where the lower half of the chest should have been and the smell of butchery in his nostrils.

'Hold on, son,' he told him and for a second Dickie's eyes focused on him.

'Pa?'

'Yes, Dickie, I'm here. Hold on, we'll get you to hospital.'

'I . . .' He half lifted a hand, made an effort, too much perhaps, for blood came from his mouth, a thin but steady stream. Ian felt a terrible cold fear and swept an arm in the air as if warding off something, or someone, he sensed approaching. He held Dickie closer, bent over him as if restricting what anyone could see might make it not true.

'Pa.' The appeal made him look up. Julian was on his feet some paces away. Ian registered that he was not physically hurt, but the thought that came was that Dickie was mortally wounded.

'Find your mother,' he told him, 'bring her here.' He did not move.

'Julian!' he urged the transfixed boy. 'Your mother.'

The boy turned and ran. Ian bent close to Dickie, put his cheek next to his, kissed him, whispered that his mother was coming, and the doctor and the ambulance, there was nothing to worry about.

He thought he caught a look of amusement in Dickie's eyes; he smiled at him, nodding that he was right. If your step-father kisses you, perhaps things weren't quite as they should be. 'I should have done that before,' he said and felt his hand squeezed as Dickie tried to gasp out another word.

He became aware that more people had arrived, but they stood as if on the periphery of some invisible circular barrier, the barrier of those who have nothing to offer, no knowledge, no idea what to do. Then he saw the doctor breaking through, coming without fear to his aid, and carrying his medical bag. He felt his stomach sob with thankfulness. Dr Michael knelt by the boy and the man. 'All right, Dickie, keep quite still. Can you hear me?' Ian made to move out of the way but Michael shook his head at him, then gave an assertive nod that he should stay exactly where he was. 'Just hold him,' he said.

He questioned the doctor with a look. Is that all that can be done? The doctor lowered his head down to his patient. 'Talk to him,' he urged, as he peered closely, then tore open a dressing and placed it over the wound. They both knew it was no more than a gesture; 'cosmetic', was the word that came into Ian's mind.

'Your mother's coming,' he told Dickie as if explaining the doctor's action, then babbled on. 'And thanks for coming, for getting here. I know it means a lot to your mother and Liz, and Julian – and me too that you managed it. Well done. Well done.'

Dickie looked up at him, reminding Ian of someone fighting against an anaesthetic to say something, someone with something important to say. Then his stepson's fingers no longer curled to the shape of his, they fell away and he felt as if he had suddenly gone from his arms: there was no resistance, nothing, no response.

In the distance they could hear the frantic bell of the approaching ambulance and as he looked up he saw Bess and Liz pushing their way through the little crowds. He heard someone say, 'It's his mother.'

She was down by his side immediately, her arm under his, around Dickie's neck, taking possession. As she did so the dressing slipped from the wound. 'Dickie,' her tone was one of reproof as for a naughty child but as she spread her hands, Ian saw the pietà, the Virgin with the dead Christ across her knees, and that same gesture of consummate loss.

'The ambulance is here.' Dr Michael rose, took her hand, and passed her into Ian's care, as he and the ambulance-men skilfully moved Dickie on to a stretcher. Bess was pale as death, and walked with strange jerky uncoordination, Ian supporting her as they followed and climbed into the ambulance with Dr Michael.

They sat and watched as the doctor and the men worked over Dickie, the driver sending messages of urgency ahead of them.

'I don't understand, what happened?' Bess said.

'No,' Ian said, his eyes on the men, who were exchanging glances, and some of the activity over Dickie was less frantic.

'They'll be waiting for us,' one of the men said, catching his gaze.

A wheeled stretcher, two nurses, a white-coated doctor were waiting as they drew in to the ambulance bay before the infirmary. Dickie was offloaded and run at speed through to an emergency treatment room. Ian and Bess were diverted to a side room by a nursing sister; Dr Michael followed. Ian's arm was about Bess and he held both her hands tightly with his other hand, as if he was afraid of what she might do if he released her. He steered her to a chair. She sat on the very edge, like a caged, terrified, creature.

'I don't understand,' she said. 'What happened? How did it happen?'

'I saw,' Ian said. He held her hands tighter, stared down at his feet. 'Dickie threw the gun to Julian. I saw their hands all in the air, then the next moment it went off, and they both fell down.'

'Where is Julian?' she asked, suddenly alarmed for this son's safety too, and looking around the room as if he might be there, overlooked.

Ian shared her alarm. 'I sent him to look for you, but—'

'He'll be with friends,' Dr Michael reassured. 'Young Liz will look after him. They were together most of the morning.

'Will they know anything yet?' Bess asked, her mind back with their immediate worry.

'We have to give them time, m'dear, but I'll go and see.' They saw him outside the glass-panelled door talking to someone for a moment or two, then he moved away.

'I'm still a bit worried about Julian,' Bess said.

'Me too,' Ian agreed, remembering the look on his son's face, fearful, appalling to see. 'I'll go and telephone. Someone should definitely be looking out for him and Liz. Would you be all right while I go? I'll be as quick as I can.'

They both looked up in some surprise when Dr Michael came back into the room. It seemed very quick, this news he had, and neither doubted he had something to tell them, for when they both went to rise he motioned them back down again.

'It's not good news,' he said, coming to sit the other side of Bess. 'He did not make it, I'm afraid.'

'Didn't make . . .' Bess began to repeat his words.

'He was pronounced dead on arrival,' the doctor said very gently, but very firmly, giving no ambiguous messages, no false hopes. 'I'm so sorry, my dear.'

Ian looked at him and realized the good doctor had known, from the moment he saw the gunshot wound at such close range, that there had been no hope.

At that moment there was a noise at the door and Liz burst in. She took one look at the group and waited for them to speak. When no one did she asked, 'What's the news?'

Ian shook his head and she sank on to the nearest chair, saying, 'George said it was bad.' She paused then demanded, 'How bad?'

Dr Michael went to her and took her elbow. 'Shall we leave Dickie's parents on their own for a few moments?'

Though she allowed herself to be taken from the room, they heard her exclaim, and cry out with real anger in her voice, 'Why do all the people I love, or want to love, have to die?'

'I want to go to him,' Bess said urgently, 'want to see him.'

'Yes, of course,' Ian said but when she stood up and made as if to stride to the door he caught her in his arms, held her tight. 'But we must wait until they're ready for us.'

'I don't want him ...' She broke off, bumped her head down hard on to his shoulder and pressed it there. 'I don't want him ...'

'I know,' he said, steeling himself to be supportive and sensible. 'I know. But we should just wait a little, they may be moving him or something.' Then he rested his cheek on her dark hair. 'He called me Pa,' he said. 'I kissed him, and we both knew we should have done all that years and years ago.'

Her arms clasped him – she was the comforter now – and they stood holding each other as if all they had left in the world was each other. The door opened and the sister came in. 'We're ready for you now,' she said, 'when you feel able.'

Dickie had not been moved, he still lay in one of the beds in the emergency department. No other bed was occupied and all had been tidied, all the equipment round about, leads and tubes neatly circled, tucked away, and everything cleared away, spick and span. No urgency now.

The sister led them to the bed, brought up chairs, and they sat side by side. Bess immediately took her son's hand. 'Oh Dickie!' she breathed. 'Oh Dickie.' In the two repeated words were all the boy had been to her, all her loss. 'He's so pale,' she said. 'His colour's quite gone.'

Ian too had been shocked by the complete pallor, the face, the hands, the bloodless skin, so unlike life – so like the marble of memorials to unscathed youth. He's really gone, he thought, and felt tears running down his face. No chance now to make up lost ground, lost confidences. He remembered what Liz had said only a few moments ago. Why did people I love, or want to love, have to die?

Had it really been Dickie and Liz who were keen on each other, lovers, rather than George's daughter as he had believed?

'Oh God!' he exclaimed.

Bess's free hand was instantly on his. 'He drove us apart often enough, now he brings us together.'

His head dropped lower, humbled by her generosity at that moment. 'What fools we were to quarrel,' he whispered. 'What a fool I've been.'

It was only when the sister came to them, stood silently by their side, that they realized it was time for them to let Dickie be moved from this emergency unit.

'He'll be taken to the chapel when you wish to see him again,' she told them kindly. 'Just let us know when you wish to come.'

Liz was still waiting for them outside but with a police-woman and a police sergeant. 'Dr Michael has had another call,' she began.

'Liz,' Ian interrupted. 'Julian? Do you know where he is?'

'I never saw him again afterwards.'

The sergeant cleared his throat and asked, 'Would this be the young man the gun was thrown to?'

'Our younger son, Julian, that's right. We're concerned for him, to know where he is.'

'It was realized he was not in the immediate vicinity when we spoke to Lord Markham, and we have set up a search, along with most of the other people who were at the shoot. I wouldn't think he'll be too far away.'

'He'll be in shock,' Ian insisted, 'he should be found.'

'As you say, sir, but without transport he probably won't have wandered very far. I'm sure we'll hear very soon.' He put his hand to his radio as if to ensure them he was in constant touch. 'This is a terrible time, sir. We've taken a statement from this young lady, who was obviously on the spot, and if we could take some details from you . . .'

'Does my wife have to be involved?' he asked.

'No sir, and if you prefer you could take Mrs Philipps—'

'Mrs Sinclair,' Bess corrected.

'Mrs Sinclair home, we'd be pleased to come and see you there.'

'Could I give you a statement here in the relatives' room, no need—'

'I'd like to be there,' Bess said.

The little party made their way slowly into the room full of neutral colours and upright easy chairs. 'You do realize,' the sergeant said when they were all seated, 'that everything has to go to the coroner, and there will be an inquest.'

'No!' Bess protested.

'It's the same for every sudden death, madam,' the police-woman told her, 'it's procedure.'

'We do know,' Ian put in, not wanting Bess drawn into details of Greville Philipps's suicide. 'Let's get this statement done, shall we, Sergeant, then we'll be free to go and find our other son.'

Liz telephoned her grandfather before they left the hospital; after a few moments she passed the telephone to Ian. 'He wants to talk to you.'

'Ian, my boy, I'm so dammed sorry about this bloody awful thing. But first things first. We haven't found Julian, but Albert remembered Dickie came on his motorbike, and it's gone.'

'The motorbike?'

'Gone,' Lord Markham repeated. 'We're wondering whether Julian could have taken it. Could he ride it, if say the keys had been left in?'

'Yes, I'm sure he could,' Ian said, and it was likely the keys would be in – Dickie invariably left them in at home.

'I've informed the police, thought it the right thing to do. There'll be no comeuppance for Julian in the circumstances, I've made sure of that. All the car patrols have been alerted.'

'Thanks.'

'I think in view of this you should perhaps go back to the Hall, he may be at home even now.'

'I hope to God so,' Ian replied as Bess grabbed his sleeve asking, 'What now?'

They took a taxi home, and sent Liz on to her grandfather's with promises to let her know the moment Julian was found.

Once home, even though Tommy assured them no motor-bike had arrived, they searched the stables, the house, they called his name in the gardens, around the lake. 'Julian! Ju . . . li . . . an!' echoed over the lake.

Ian telephoned George, but he had seen or heard nothing. 'What about the farm, would he have gone there?'

'I suppose he might,' Ian said.

'I'll meet you there,' George replied. 'Lord Markham's keeping Mr Bennett at his place for the night, did you know?'

'I'm coming with you,' Bess said. 'I'll get the key.'

George and Colleen both came by road, their cars following each other along the last stretch of road. Bess and Colleen fell into each other's arms. Colleen cried but Bess was dry-eyed, wanted to embark on a search of her father's outbuildings.

Another car swept into the yard, Dr Michael back from his call and recommending leaving the searching to the men, and prescribing rest and sedation for Bess. She would not hear of it.

'Our children,' Colleen suddenly cried out, 'what's happening to them?'

'I'm going to look . . .' Bess seemed motivated by a new idea, let them into the kitchen and immediately found a large torch. 'No,' she protested when Colleen made as if to go with her, 'just Ian.'

There was silence in the kitchen as the two left, closing the door behind them.

'Bess?' he queried.

'The old barn, the one Pa uses as a machine store, Julian was rebuilding part of it. There's a small hut been put at the back where his materials have been stored. It's been his pride and joy.'

They approached, hardly daring to hope, and yet feeling it could not be just, not fair, that anything had also happened to Julian on this awful day.

The key was in the shed door and the torch caught the wheel of a motorbike propped at the far side. The door gave to their push.

'Julian,' Bess said softly. 'We're here, please come to us.'

There was a slight sound in the farthest corner; Bess shone the light that way.

210

His eyes were enormous in his white face. He sat on the floor, knees drawn up and looked as if he had become an old, old man who just happened to have a youngish face, rather than the opposite.

'We've all been so worried about you,' Ian coaxed.

'He always said he wanted to kill me, but I killed him in the end,' Julian said, 'and what about Katie?'

He repeated the question in the house in front of Colleen and George.

'Katie'll come home when she's ready, I suppose,' George said.

'It slipped through my hands, you know,' Julian said.

'Now I am prescribing for everyone,' Dr Michael insisted. 'Edgar won't mind us appropriating his house.'

Ian telephoned the police, then Liz and her grandfather. Bess spoke to her father, but Ian took over when the questions went on too long.

It was the early hours of the following morning before Ian and Bess took their sedated son home.

Twenty-Three

Katie pushed her case behind the seat in the cathedral garden and sat down, exhausted mentally and physically. Her only satisfaction was that she had arrived in good time, she was there for Dickie's funeral service. She had hardly expected still to be on earth to see this day, so great had been the shock and her grief.

She had thought she would die of a broken heart, but then she had expected she would die of that when he did not come back on the Sunday as promised – she had waited up all night – or the Monday, or the Tuesday. She had felt herself becoming hard, bitter. She had made mental lists of all the reasons *she* could think of why he should not come back. There were many, all connected with her unworthiness. She could hear her father's voice: 'They marry their own kind.'

On Wednesday she had run out of the wood Dickie had stockpiled for her, tired of trying to light the fire with damp wood and gone to buy fire-lighters.

She had been about to use the paper they were wrapped in to make the base of the fire when a headline caught her eye. 'Local heir dies in shooting accident.' So, very casually, not really interested, she had straightened the pages to read. She remembered no more until she came to herself again some time later, still kneeling on the hearthrug, the newspaper crumpled in her lap. She had thought it was a dream, until she forced herself to straighten the newsprint once more.

She had wanted to deny the story, to ring and say they must have got it wrong. It was surely not true, but he had not come back as promised – here was the reason. She did ring. The newspaper referred her to the undertakers to confirm the time of the service at the cathedral, 'followed by internment in the family grave in Counthorpe' she was told. This was how her mother related the story of Edgar Bennett's wife's funeral, the service in town, the burial in the village.

The days had passed in an eternity of lonely walks on the beach, of snacks prepared but not eaten, of the bed tossed about in – a pretence of patterning and spacing the days with normality, a pretence of living.

She reflected that Edgar Bennett was now the only one who knew that Dickie was the father of her baby. She wondered if his reactions to her might be different with his grandson dead, and Katie Wright carrying his great-grandchild? He would be here today, but she shrank from the very thought of meeting him – like her mum said, his eyes were forever judging you.

She shivered with cold and apprehension, knew the sensible thing to do would be to go home. Her mother, probably her father as well, would come to this service. She should wait until they arrived, join their party going into the cathedral, then home with them.

But how could she? How could she be at Dickie's funeral without making a fool of herself, revealing all she felt? How could she go home? Thoughts of bridges over deep swift rivers, or train lines with expresses approaching, came to her and felt like easy solutions, a way to join Dickie – though there was always the doubt about suicides being allowed into hallowed ground, or heaven.

There was some movement near the main gate, and she withdrew further, standing on the grass among a group of closely planted old almond trees, where she could see but not be seen. Men and women, obviously officials of the church, and then early mourners, began to arrive.

She thought she vaguely knew some of the people, though, from where she was, faces were hardly visible unless they turned to talk to companions before they passed under the vaulted arched entrance. The first people she really recognized were her parents, with William, and Tommy the stable lad from the Hall. Her mother looked round just as she entered the church, almost as if she knew someone was looking intently at her.

Katie wanted to cry out, run to her. Her bonny, round-faced, mother looked pale and bleak under her black Cossack-style

213

fur hat, kept at the back of a cupboard and only brought out for such occasions. Katie wanted to hold her, be held, sob on her shoulder, tell the whole truth. Instead she shrank further back, afraid of being seen.

Floods of people came now, too quick for her to do more than register a few. Lord Markham with Liz, who walked stooped-shouldered beneath an enveloping black cloak. Katie was ashamed of the ordinary, everyday grey suit and blue anorak she had travelled in. She felt and was in all ways a disgrace.

Then she recognized the Tophams, the city relations of Dickie's mother, barristers, judges, merchant bankers, people of importance, all sombre in full black mourning. There was a pause now, a pause when all that moved were the leaves dry enough to be blown from the paths, and the black cassock and snow-white surplice of the clergyman who waited at his gate.

Slowly, with due formality, and just as the clock struck eleven, she saw the shiny black tops of cars above the cathedral wall. Slowly they passed, creeping to a halt by the gateway. There was breath-held pause, then she could hear the shuffle of feet and low voices as the right order for the formal procession was arranged.

Then she saw the vicar leading the way to the great doors, saw Dickie's coffin carried by the pallbearers. Tears blurred her vision; she had to brush them away to see at all, push the handkerchief against her mouth to control the sobs. She saw his parents immediately behind, stern, controlled, then Julian with his grandfather, Edgar Bennett, then she heard the vicar begin the intonation as he led the coffin inside to its temporary resting place in the main aisle facing the great altar.

'I am the resurrection and the life, saith the Lord: He that believeth in me, though he were dead, yet shall he live; And whosoever . . .'

She could hear no more. The words became indistinct and then the great doors were closed behind the last of the official party, an elderly man and woman stooped over walking-sticks.

Truly, truly she was bereft, and the words of a Hardy poem learned years ago at secondary school came with sudden and

214

startling truth into her mind. 'She at His Funeral' by Thomas Hardy. She remembered reciting it in class.

> They bear him to his resting-place –
> In slow procession sweeping by;
> I follow at a stranger's space;
> His kindred they, his sweetheart I.
> Unchanged my gown of garish dye,
> Though sable-sad is their attire;
> But they stand round with griefless eye,
> While my regret consumes like fire!

She always felt Hardy had been thinking of a gypsy girl, but everything else in the poem fitted with such exquisite pain.

She could hear the organ and drew a little nearer to the doorway. Everyone she loved, or had loved, was in that building. The congregation doing justice to the well known words of "The day Thou gavest, Lord, is ended . . ." An evening hymn for the end of a life.

Should she just listen for a little while, then drift away, disappear from everyone's life? Or should she after all wait outside, go to her parents when the congregation all emerged? How she yearned to do that. But how would her father greet her? How would it work when presumably they would all be leaving to go to a second service in the village churchyard? Dickie's burial. Dickie of the flying limbs, of the impulsive gestures, of the sudden laughter – her totally loving boy, her entire life. She didn't really care what happened to her now: she felt her life was over.

She went back to sit on the seat where she had left her case.

She had just a short time to decide what she must do, the time to the end of the service. What was the best for everyone? She had no job; the money had dwindled alarmingly. She *could* catch the bus and go home, be there for when they arrived back.

She put her elbows on her knees and pressed her face into her hands.

'I wondered if you would be here,' a man's voice said.

Her head lifted in surprise at being addressed, and it took a moment for her to focus on the man and recognize him.

'Ken,' she said. 'I . . .' She had no idea what to say to the man.

'Are you with your parents?' he asked.

She shook her head and saw him notice her case.

'Just coming back?' he asked. 'I know you've been away. Mr Benbrook telephoned your mother,' he added in explanation.

She nodded.

'Are you going home after the funeral?'

She did not answer, because she did not know.

He sat down by her. 'If I can be of any help, carry your case wherever you wish to go?'

'I don't know where I wish to go, where I'll be welcome. I don't care much anyway.'

There was a pause, then he said very quietly, 'You'd be very welcome to come to my home. Rest, refreshments and no recriminations. There's no one at my house to make judgments.'

She thought it was almost as if he had rehearsed that little speech. 'Aren't you working?' she asked.

'I'm out on an errand. Old Benbrook's at the funeral –' he nodded toward the cathedral – 'didn't you see him go in?'

She shook her head.

'Well, unless you want to wait and see them all come out I've time to walk you to my house, leave you there, and be back in the office before the boss gets back.'

She did not answer.

'Give you time to decide what to do.'

He was wise enough to leave it at that, and when the organ began a second hymn, she said, 'You'd not take it as meaning anything?'

'*No*, of course not,' he assured her.

'I still don't know.' She was so unsure, unsure of herself, and of him, but as the voices rose in the words of the twenty-third psalm, 'The Lord's My Shepherd', she could bear no more. 'All right,' she said.

He went immediately to pick up her suitcase and took her a back way out of the cathedral close, through a shopping arcade to a cobbled passage, then out into streets of terraced houses near the river. 'Number four Garden Street,' he told

216

her, 'so named because the streets either side have just yards, not actual soil gardens.'

Garden Street was superior in another way: every other house had an entry, a shared back way. Ken led her up one of these entries, opened a high back gate and paused to unlock the back door, no more than a stride distant. They walked straight into the kitchen, then through to the middle room. The one thing that struck her again was the slightly strange smell, the peppery smell she had noticed about Ken himself; that, and the tidiness of it all. In the middle room he put her case down and indicated the two wooden armchairs either side of the gas fire. One still had a faded pink and maroon crochet blanket over the back, and must have been where his mother sat.

'Make yourself at home,' he said as he stooped to light the fire, turning the gas-fire on and pressing the automatic lighting button, which worked at the second press. 'There're some biscuits in a tin, and bread if you fancy toast.'

Making toast at an open fire is as good as eating it, Dickie had said.

'Today is my day for fish and chips. I usually call and bring them home with me when I finish,' he said, but she did not answer.

'Well, make yourself at home as I say. If I lock the back door when I go you can always use the front door and pull it to behind you, but I'd be more than pleased for you to stay – as long as you like. There's two bedrooms and a boxroom,' he added with a laugh. 'Give you time to sort yourself out.'

When he had left her to return to the office, she made herself tea and took some of the digestive biscuits from the Petticoat Tail Shortbread tin. She remembered Mary had bought him those for last Christmas, with the comment, 'Poor sod, probably be the only present he'll get.' Shamed into it, she had given him a card with a monogrammed white handkerchief inside.

She found herself washing the cup and saucer and making sure there were no crumbs from the biscuits, restoring everything to its former pristine state. It would be several hours before Ken came home again and she became curious enough to make a tour of the house, going first into the front room.

Here the order of the middle room was repeated, only with more formality, there was a faded uncut-moquette three-piece suite, dark moss green with a scattered pattern of autumn leaves. The fireplace was pink-tiled with a broad wooden surround, a high mantlepiece with an oval mirror above. The curtains too had an autumn leaf pattern and there were heavy nets close to the window. It was all neat; but the nets, she thought, had probably never been down for years, even before his mother died.

He had also as good as invited her to stay the night if she wanted, so she opened the door to the enclosed staircase and went upstairs. The boxroom was just that, a room with an old cabin trunk – two tea-chests stood side by side on top of this, and three cases were ranked in order of sizes under the window.

The room that had obviously been his mother's had an old iron-and-brass bedstead, with pink bedspread and pink eiderdown over it. This room, she also noticed, had a lock, with a key on the inside. The other bedroom she went towards, stood with her hand poised above the knob but then did not enter. She really did not want to see where Ken North slept.

She went back downstairs and sat in the fireside chair with the crochet cover. The radiants of the gas-fire glowed with heat and she began to feel warm for the first time that day, for days and days, and sitting thinking that this was the last place on earth she had expected ever, ever, to be, she went to sleep.

She was roused by a cry of alarm. Ken North was back and, rushing to the fire, he turned it off, then ran to the window and pushed up the sash as wide as he could. Then he turned to her, saw she was stirring.

'Are you all right? I left the fire full on but I thought you'd turn it down, it soon gets hot in a room this size, and you had all the doors closed.'

She swallowed, gasped, felt her face was hot, dry.

'You've been shut in here for hours, there can't have been much oxygen left. It's a wonder . . .' he trailed off at the thought of what might have been.

She got up shakily and went to the window – the air felt good. He followed her and asked again if she felt all right. She nodded. She had been tired, exhausted, but realized that her sleep must have been prolonged by the heat in the room. She breathed in the air, but regretfully. Had he not come back . . . she might have joined Dickie without the stigma of intent.

He insisted she sat down again while he made more tea. 'I don't keep coffee at home,' he said. She wondered why he drank it at the office.

'Look,' he said when he was sure she was recovered. 'I came back before I got my fish and chips, in case you might still be here, and would like some?'

She almost felt ashamed to realize just how hungry she was. 'Please,' she said, 'can I set the table in the kitchen while you've gone?'

'The cloth's in the table drawer,' he told her and left before she could offer him any money.

She stayed that night, in the room with the key on the inside, and he made it obvious she was welcome to stay as long as she liked. He also offered to either go home with her, or take a message if she wanted him to. Whatever he had done in the past, however objectionable she had found him, he went out of his way to make it up to her now.

She stayed on because she was still not sure what to do, and it was so restful all day on her own, Ken coming back in the evening bringing the ingredients for a simple meal, and stocking up with things she could have midday and tea time. She felt she began to see him as his mother must have known him, caring, thinking what to shop for.

After the weekend he returned to say that Katie's father had telephoned Mr Benbrook to ask if he had any news of her. 'Your parents are thinking of going to the police,' he said. 'I think we have to do something about this. They must be desperate with worry, I know my mother would have been if I had been missing all this time.'

'I have telephoned.'

'Not since you've been here,' he said. He sat down in the armchair opposite. 'I think you should go and see them,' he said. 'I'll come with you if you want me to. I also think you should let me tell Mr Benbrook you're safe. He really is concerned you know – and Mary.'

'Yes, I've not been thinking really, not caring.'

'I know,' he said, 'but whether we like it or not life goes on.'

She wondered if he was thinking of when his mother died. 'Do you think I should telephone home first, or just go?' she asked.

He looked pleased to be consulted, moistened his lips several times before answering. 'Why don't I ask for an afternoon off tomorrow and we both go on the bus? If I know anything about mothers it will be easier for you to see your mother first, then before your father comes home from work you will have a lot of things sorted out. What do you think?'

'I think that's a good idea, the only thing is . . .' she hesitated, 'I thought I should go on my own.'

'No problem, but I'll still have the afternoon off, carry your case, see you safely on to the bus.'

'That's very good of you.'

'It's settled,' he said.

When he came back the following lunchtime he had more news for her. 'I did rather have to say why I wanted the afternoon off at such short notice. I have to tell you that Mr Benbrook is delighted you are safe and well, and here, and he wants you to know he'd be pleased to have you back – he's only had a temp in up to now – and Mary really misses you.'

He walked her to the bus station and before she got on the bus he handed her a Yale key. 'To the front door,' he said, 'in case you need it.' She opened her mouth to protest, but he closed her hand over the key. It was the first time he had touched her since he had found her near the cathedral.

Twenty-Four

She could hear her mother upstairs, put her case down and went into the hall. 'Mum.'

Colleen came out of her bedroom, duster in hand, and stood looking down at her. 'Katie?' she queried in disbelief and began to come down, but after two stairs she suddenly sat back on the top step and put her face in her hands.

'How could you do this to us?' she asked. 'How could you?'

'I'm sorry, Mum, I . . .'

'Do you know how much heartache you've caused, when there was so much more? No one knowing where you were, then Bess losing Dickie – you must have heard.'

'Yes, and I was at the cathedral – outside,' she said, 'but I didn't like to . . . well, it felt like intrusion, I wasn't in mourning clothes or anything.'

Colleen looked at her daughter as if she were a stranger. 'What are you talking about?' she asked. 'Where have you been all these weeks? Letting everyone wonder and worry themselves sick. And you were at the cathedral! So where have you been since then?'

'Staying with a friend.'

'A friend?' She studied her daughter doubtfully, then asked, 'Katie have you . . . done anything? I mean about the baby.'

Katie shook her head. 'No, I couldn't.'

Her mother rose and hurried down the stairs and almost snatched her daughter into her arms. 'Katie, Katie, are you really all right?'

'I am, Mum, really.'

'Why did you stay away?'

She shook her head. 'I don't know, I can't explain. It's all so awful now.'

'How did you hear about Dickie, the accident?' Colleen led

her daughter to the kitchen and sat her down, going on before she could answer. 'That really is awful, and now Bess and Ian are both out of their minds with worry over Julian.'

'Julian?' she queried, only vaguely remembering. 'He was involved, wasn't he?'

'He certainly was, and he's not been right in his head since.' She went on to give a graphic description of the accident, while Katie sat eyes down, hands pressed over her ears as her mother turned away to make coffee. She looked up as Colleen brought mugs to the table, saying, 'Dr Michael's up at the Hall every day, and they've got to decide what to do. Something's got to be done.' She stopped there and looked at her daughter as much as to say, yes, and now something's got to be done about you.

'How's Mr Bennett taking it?' she asked to divert her mother's critical gaze.

'Never mind about Mr Bennett, look at us! I reckon you and me both look about ten years older than before you left. Have you any idea what you've put us through?'

'I'm sorry, Mum, perhaps I shouldn't have come back,' she said.

Immediately Colleen's manner became that of a mother chastizing a much younger child, her mug banged back on to the table. 'Don't say that! This is where you belong. You should never have left. Never!'

'I thought things would work out so differently – they nearly did.'

'But they didn't?' Colleen asked, shaking her head in bewilderment.

Then there was a sound outside, a car. Colleen got up to look. 'Your dad? Now what's happened, he shouldn't be home yet.' She went to the door to meet him.

She heard her father say something about having to come home to cool off, before her mother told him, 'Katie's here.'

He burst into the kitchen. 'Katie,' he said, 'thank god! My bonny Katie! Are you all right?'

She nodded, overwhelmed by his immediate and obvious thankfulness to see her. 'I'm sorry,' she began but he waved it aside. 'Makes my row with old Bennett worthwhile now.'

'A row?' Colleen questioned. 'Surely not, not while you know he's so upset.'

'Upset or no, it does not entitle him to say the things he did. I came as near to punching him as I've ever done anyone.'

'We'd have been out of house and home then,' Colleen reminded him.

'Ah! Those days are fast coming to an end. If he can't be everyday civil he can keep his house. We'd get a council house, or something.'

'And another job? That's not so easy these days. The man's distraught with grief for his grandson, his favourite, the Philipps heir,' Colleen stressed, 'you have to make allowances.'

'He wasn't making allowances for me. For all he knew I was distraught about my daughter. I *was* distraught about her, until I walked into this room. Him and his crude references. If he'd have been my mate instead of my boss I would have hit him –' he grinned at his daughter – 'if that makes much sense.'

She did not smile back. 'So what you are saying is that this row was about me.'

'It didn't start out about you, but it certainly finished up that way.'

'What did he say, Dad?'

'Nothing will be gained, but hurt, by repeating it,' George said, reaching for a tea bag which he slammed into a mug.

'I can guess,' Colleen put in. 'I suppose he said like mother, like daughter.'

'Among other things.'

'Other things?'

'Leave it, Colleen.'

'And a bit of humble pie on your side wouldn't go amiss,' she added.

'Not when he insults my wife and daughter. I'd sooner be put out on the street.'

'What did he say?' Katie asked with heavy insistence.

'Bluntly what he said was that he wanted no one gossiping about bastards living in any of his properties.' George gave a humph of disgust. 'The man's twenty years and more behind the times.'

Katie felt something like steel enter her soul. All she was doing here was causing trouble for her parents. She stood up with sudden resolve.

223

'I think you should tell Mr Bennett that he has nothing to fear: I shall shortly be marrying. I've been staying with Ken North the last few days. He has given me a key and I can go back there whenever I want.

'But,' Colleen began, 'I don't understand, why didn't you say all this when you first arrived?'

'And this man, North,' her father said suspiciously, 'you mention his name, but you've never brought him home. You don't act like a girl in love with him, not to my mind.'

'What do you know about it?' his wife asked. 'A woman needs security for her child.'

'I know as much as you, I suspect, and I know my own daughter, and she's not bursting with enthusiasm for this wedding.' He sat down opposite her. 'There's no need for you to marry anybody if you don't want to. Your mother and I talked this over when we first realized, and we're in agreement. You can stay here. Don't worry what old Bennett says. He can't just evict us. I'd take him to court for unfair dismissal, and by the time that happened I'd have found another job and us all another home.'

She glanced at her mother, who looked appalled at the chaos he was describing. She could not look at her father for fear of letting him see how she really felt. 'I've decided,' she said, 'to marry Ken North.'

'When did you decide?' her father persisted. 'When?'

'I'm not sure really,' she lied.

'Well, I don't know.' George sat back in his chair. 'So why all this –' he threw an arm into the air – 'all this going away, all this secrecy, all this unnecessary worry, losing your job, everything?'

'I can have my job back, Ken spoke to Mr Benbrook.'

Her father sighed and shook his head. 'Well, if you're settling on that, you'd better talk over when and where with your mother.'

'What about Ken?' Her mother pronounced his Christian name almost shyly. 'He'll surely have some say.'

'I'll just tell him,' she said flatly. 'It'll no doubt be the Registry Office, and I shall go back tonight.'

'But—' George began.

'I have to,' she interrupted, knowing that if she stayed overnight it would be even more difficult to leave – she would stay and cause them endless problems, endless trouble with Edgar Bennett. The thought of William being home soon too did not help.

'But you've brought your case with you,' George said.

She shrugged.

'I'll drive you back then,' he decided, 'back to Mr North's house, where you've been staying. I'll finally get to meet him – the father of my first grandchild.'

'I'll leave our William a note and come with you,' her mother said, 'then we'll both get to talk to him.'

'No,' George said with unusual determination, 'you stay here and get the dinner for when I'm back.'

Despite all the argument that Colleen wanted to go with them, and all Katie's arguments that she wanted to go alone, George was adamant.

He loaded her case into his red and white Triumph Herald and waited for Katie to climb in. 'See you again soon, then,' her mother said, near to tears again. Katie nodded.

There was silence in the car for quite a long time, then George said, 'So you're happy at the prospect of sharing a bed with this Ken North for the rest of your life?'

She did not answer, tried not to think of such a thing.

'Happy to do his washing, see his personal habits, get his meals, for the rest of your life.'

She remembered the odd peppery smell of him. Perhaps it was just his washing that needed doing – his underclothes . . . 'What are you trying to do, Dad?'

'Show you your future,' he said. They were entering the city now. 'You'll have to tell me which way to go, and in good time, please, there's so many one-way streets.'

'You know where Benbrook's is, you can drop me anywhere near there, it's not far, I can walk from there.'

'Good try, Katie, but I'm taking you all the way.'

'No! I don't want you to.'

'Why not? Is it me you're ashamed of? Am I too down-to-earth? You told me that a time or two when you were still at school.'

She gasped, she remembered she had done that, and was ashamed of herself. 'No, Dad, of course not, I love you, you know that.'

'And I love you, m'gel.'

She never remembered him just saying it outright before – they were not that kind of family.

He suddenly swung the car into a side street, an avenue with trees, and came to a jerking halt. 'And I know something is not right.'

'You're only guessing,' she told him, 'but I'm not when I say that marrying Ken North will solve everyone's problems.'

'Oh! Yes, it'll solve your mum's worries about a baby out of wedlock, it'll satisfy my employer for some reason best known to him, but it won't in the long run make any of us happy, because it doesn't feel right. Your attitude is not right. You're not a girl being married by the man she loves, the man who's standing by her when she's having his child. I did that – you know, you've worked it out – I married your mother because she was expecting you. But we were in love, we wanted to get married, while you—'

'It's not his child,' she said.

'It's not . . .'

'. . . his child,' she finished and gave a sigh of such relief that at least part of the truth was out.

'Wait a minute.' He sat back, reasoning this new fact out. 'It's not his child but he would still be willing to marry you?'

'Oh, yes!' she said. 'He's a pretty lonely man.'

'And you'd marry him?'

'It's a solution to everyone's problems, isn't it?'

'It could be the start of yours. Does he want more children of his own?'

She did not answer. She thought of the bedroom she could not bring herself to look into, of the way he had made her brush against him at the office, of his hand on her arm in the bus station – of his unexpected strength.

'Do you have any feeling for this North at all?'

She swallowed hard. 'No, none, less than none really.'

He restarted the car, turned it round in the next side street and drove out of the city.

'Mum will—'

'Your mum will leave you alone until such time as you want to tell us everything. You're coming home, no questions asked.'

'And if I never do?'

'So be it,' he said.

She sat quietly for a long time, until they travelled between green fields again. 'I think you've just saved me from a fate worse than death,' she said.

He glanced at her, then began swearing, such a string of obscenities as she had never heard before, such as she had no idea he knew.

When he had finished she heard herself sob, half laughter, half tears. 'And that's how I feel about Ken North too,' she said.

He glanced at her with awe. 'My God,' he whispered.

Twenty-Five

When death touched a family so intimately, it seemed to Bess that memories of all losses returned with new clarity. Her own loss felt like a severing of a limb, a whole former life curtailed. Greville, now his son, both deaths so out of natural order.

She also came to fully understand how Ian must have felt when she had left him alone at the Hall. Since Dickie's death she had felt like a caretaker with no employer, her trusteeship ended, she might as well be a mere lodger. Then the family solicitor had come to the Hall to make her financial situation clear. He confirmed that as Dickie had died with no issue then all the property which passed to her with a life interest in trust for her elder son, now became hers to dispose of as she wished.

She felt she would willingly have disposed of the lot without a second thought if it could restore Julian to health. The boy was both depressed and given to wild self-accusation about the death of his brother. He wondered if he had unconsciously pulled the trigger to kill his brother, before Dickie could kill him. 'He threatened me a lot of times.'

'Many people say that kind of thing,' Ian told him, 'it's a meaningless saying, no more. And don't forget, I saw what happened. Dickie threw, you lunged to catch but you had no chance – the butt of the gun hit the ground with force and it went off.'

'But he did nearly kill me once, didn't he, in my pram,' Julian insisted.

Dr Michael was a power of strength through this time, but as Christmas approached they all began to feel it was the worst possible time to be at home and try to pretend things were anything like normal. Dr Michael suggested the two of them should think of Julian's passion for building and architecture.

'He's shown no interest in anything since the accident,' Ian said.

'It needs to be rekindled, *he* needs to be rekindled, brought back to life, and it needs a big gesture to try to do that.'

'And?' Ian queried.

'If he were my boy I'd take him on an architectural tour of Europe. I'd go now before Christmas is here with all its sentimental, emotional nonsense.'

'And all the memories,' Bess added.

'Yes,' Michael agreed wholeheartedly. 'It's a terrible time for the lonely, the homeless, the dispossessed. I've seen so much misery at Christmas time I've often felt it should be banned.' He paused, but saw he had their complete attention. 'In a way Julian is like one of these dispossessed, he's divorced himself from reality. What I'm saying to you, is, if he was mine, I would try to shock him back into his normal self by giving a huge dose of what we know was of such vital interest to him before.'

'I can see the sense of what you are saying,' Ian admitted. 'Be a healthier way than having to resort to drugs or anything like that.'

'We certainly don't want that,' Bess said.

'Look, I've known you long enough to be frank. You've got the money, the resources, the contacts. Buy in the help you need with the estate, and for your father, Bess, then go, without delay. Take him and don't come back until next spring, take six months out.'

When the doctor had gone Ian looked at her quizzically. 'So?' he asked.

'I think he's right,' she said. 'We should go.'

'And your father?'

'I shall go and see him this afternoon.'

'While your dander's up?' he asked.

She nodded. He reached out to her and she slipped into his arms, clung to his waist, just quietly holding each other. It was something they had done a lot these last long, long weeks, during the day and in bed at nights, sharing the hopeless sense of pain and loss. The dressing room adjoining their bedroom had never been used since the shooting.

'Michael said we should make it for six months,' he said quietly.

'I know,' she said. 'Twenty-four weeks, what's that in a lifetime? You're wondering if I can tell him, aren't you?'

He nodded. 'We have to remember he's taken Dickie's death very, very, hard.'

'Then he should consider the health of his remaining grandson more seriously,' she said. 'I'm going now.'

'I'll begin to make some enquiries about destinations.'

She thought his face had some light of normal life in it for the first time.

'Where do you think?' she asked just to see the flicker of interest keep glowing.

'I'm thinking Paris first, Notre-Dame, perhaps down to Avignon, the Pope's Palace, that has towers I feel Rapunzel should have thrown her hair down from. We'll go south into Spain, Barcelona, then in the spring to Granada, the Sierra Nevada, the Alhambra Palace, I've always wanted to see that. Venice, there's a wealth of every kind of building there.'

'I think it might work,' she said.

'I hope so, with all my heart I hope so.'

She reached up and kissed him, and left for her mission to the farm.

She had heard people got angry when they were bereaved, and knew herself it was true, but she felt her father's anger had dawned very quickly and was growing each day, rather than subsiding. It was with a sense of great trepidation that she got out of her car and let herself into the house. She remembered telling Ian years ago that her father brought out the child in her; she took a moment now to remind herself she was a grown woman with a purpose. 'For goodness' sake!' she reprimanded herself.

'Pa,' she called but the downstairs rooms were empty; she ventured upstairs, calling more circumspectly, not wishing to startle him, but there was no one in the house. She went outside and called; the dog answered from nearby and came to greet her from the side of the house. She patted the collie and followed him back to where she could now hear the noise of bricks or slates being moved.

She turned the corner to see her father tidying bricks from

the old barn, the end of which lay looking as if a vehicle had run into it.

'Pa, what's happened?'

'What d'you mean, what's happened? Nothing's happened.'

'Something's happened to the barn.'

'Nothing's *happened*, as you put it. I'm knocking it down, that's all.'

'But . . .' She was so astonished at the act of vandalism she could not for a moment put thoughts into words. 'But it's a listed building, you're not allowed to, and Julian was, had, done so much work on it, beautiful work.'

'It's my barn, I'll do what I like with it, and be damned.' He picked up a large sledgehammer and took another swing at the half demolished wall. 'And as for Julian, he's not going to finish anything now, is he?'

His rough insensitive words made her want to shout and rave at him, allow her own anger full rein. She glared at him, the way he stood with sledgehammer hanging limply from his hands, too heavy for his strength, tackling something beyond his capacity, and against his better nature. He looked defeated, old, and she drew back, swallowed her bitterness.

'Julian is the reason I am here.' She told him succinctly all the doctor had said. 'Ian and I are going to take him on this tour. We hope to bring him back well, able to fulfil all his dreams of building, being an architect and so on, so I'm sorry you've done this.'

'You're going away?'

'Yes, Michael feels it's the sensible thing to do and so do we, both of us. I've come to talk over what extra arrangements you'd like me to make. Colleen, I'm sure, will come more, and Katie might be pleased to do a little.'

'Katie!' he shouted. 'Colleen, is it all you ever think about?' He looked her up and down with disdain. 'I would have thought the Wrights had interfered enough in your life,' he said, 'or have you forgotten what your precious Colleen's brother did?'

She stepped back as if he had struck her. She was never going to forget he knew that.

'Yes,' he acknowledged the shock he had given her. 'They've interfered enough. I don't want either of them here, at all, do you hear me? I've told George in no uncertain terms I want no bastards living in my property.'

'Pa! That's terrible!' She was really shocked by this outrageous statement. 'You can't have said such a thing! It's none of your business.'

'Oh, but I have!' he said, lifting the hammer with a pretence of another strike. 'My property, my rules.'

'You can't punish parents for standing by their own,' she said.

'Is that what you're doing?' he asked her. 'Standing by your own.'

'Yes,' she faced him squarely, 'but this time for once I'm putting Julian first. I can either make arrangements for you, or you can do it yourself, but we shall go as soon as Ian has fixed things up.'

'Go then,' he said, 'I'm getting used to losing people.'

She clenched her teeth against the emotional thrust and added, 'We shall be away for at least six months, so if you want me to arrange for a housekeeper you'd better let me know.'

'Oh! You please yourself what you do,' he said, throwing the hammer down on top of the bricks and walking away. The dog cast one regretful look at her and followed.

She braced herself, determined not to go after him. She stood staring at the destruction of Julian's much talked-about herringbone brickwork. She hated what he had done, but acknowledged that old and bereft of reason as he was, she still loved him for all he had been. It was a burden she had shared with her mother, this love for an assertive, opinionated man – as a child it had been pure hero-worship on her part. She turned away, knowing that she had to devise some scheme of supervision for her father if only to satisfy herself.

When she arrived home she found Ian lingering in the hall, obviously listening.

'It's Liz,' he said, 'come to see Julian. I sent her up. Now I'm wondering if I did right.'

She opened her mouth to say that he had done the same the first time the girl had come to see Dickie, but judged it the kind of comparison her father might have made. Instead she said, 'Well, they're talking, leave them.'

'How did it go?' Ian asked, but before she could answer they heard footsteps on the stairs. They both looked hopefully for their son, but Liz came alone. She was dark-haired, in a black trouser suit, black polo-neck sweater. It all went to make her look excruciatingly pale and ill.

'Liz,' Bess said after a second's too-long pause. 'It's the hair, I wouldn't have recognized you.' She kissed the young woman, and drew her to sit by her side on one of the sofas.

'First time I've been near my true colour for years,' Liz said. 'Julian wouldn't come down with me.' She looked from one to the other. 'He's a bit worrying.'

Mrs West brought in tea and they sat telling Liz about the trip.

'It sounds like a wonderful idea. In fact I was thinking along much the same lines, I've brought a couple of sketch-blocks and some charcoal pencils. I also took some photos of the folly at Banford, Julian was sketching it the first time I met him, but I don't think that was a very good idea.'

'Why not?' Ian asked.

'He just said "Dickie's school", and didn't touch them, just left them lying higgledy-piggledy on the table.'

'Every effort anyone makes for him is worthwhile,' Ian said. 'We just feel he needs something huge and different to help snap him back to some kind of reason. We're banking on his love of buildings, and by taking him right away, showing him some of the splendours around Europe—' He broke off as Bess gave an audible gasp and sat with her fists clenched tight on her knees.

'Bess?' he queried.

'It's just that, it's . . .' She was suddenly appalled and over-whelmed by what her father had done. She told them of the demolition at the end of the barn Julian had worked on.

'What!' Ian exclaimed, and began to pace the room, turning round on her in disbelief. 'What?'

'He mustn't see it,' Liz said urgently, 'Julian mustn't see it, you must get him away. Don't let him go to the farm before you go.' Her conviction was startling.

Ian stopped pacing and stood before the young woman. 'I agree,' he said, his face pale, stern – angry.

'Even so,' Bess said with resignation, 'I still have to satisfy

myself that we're leaving everything organized and well super-
vised as far as my father is concerned.'

'I know who can do that,' Liz said immediately. 'My grandfather. He'd love to keep an eye on the old boy. I think he
finds him good company in normal times, and my grandpa is
a very tolerant man.'

'Do you think he would?' Bess asked. 'That really would
be a solution.'

'And it would play on your father's weakness for the
company of the aristocracy,' Ian said.

Bess thought to let this remark pass, but then decided it
was the time for all honesty. 'True,' she said.

'So now my concerns are for the Wrights, for Colleen and
Katie. Not only did my father refuse to have a live-in housekeeper, but he doesn't want Colleen to go in either.'

'But she's looked after him for years,' Ian protested.

'I mentioned Katie might help, and he just wouldn't hear
of it, wants no bastards in his property, in any of his properties.'

'He means Katie's baby,' Liz said as if speaking it aloud
made it believable.

'He can't throw them out,' Ian said. 'He can't dismiss
George, he's a good and faithful manager, he—'

'Apparently threatened to punch Pa's head in if he wasn't
civil about Colleen and Katie. I don't want it blowing up while
we're away, leaving the family insecure.'

'There's the old Dower House,' Ian said, 'time it had a new
tenant, offer them that, and we could make a job for George
on the estate, he'd be a valuable man to have. We've got one
or two near retirement age.'

'I could tell them, so they knew they need not stay in the
old Paget farm if things got unpleasant, or worse.' She paused
and looked doubtfully at Liz.

'Don't worry, if my grandfather was worried about Mr
Bennett he'd be in touch with Dr Michael at once. And I shall
be in close contact with Katie. Katie and I have a lot in
common.'

'I didn't realize you knew Katie that well,' Bess said.

'I've been in touch since we lost Dickie, and I intend we
shall know each other a whole lot better, be bosom friends,'

Liz said. She knew she could not reveal what she guessed about Katie's baby – that was Katie's prerogative to tell or not to tell – instead she revealed her own story.

'The only thing is Katie has kept her baby. My family, well my mother really, made me have an abortion, you know.'

'No,' Bess said carefully, 'we didn't know.'

'They've kept it pretty quiet, the family, unsuitable sire, don't you know.' Her voice was full of bitterness. 'You know, like when the pedigree hound gets out and mates with the village mongrel. I wanted my baby, but I let them win. Katie's got more spunk.'

She saw them both look at her with a dawning of new understanding. Now they knew why she kicked at the establishment and lived with her grandfather. She saw Bess dig deep to find something appropriate to say.

'Katie has a supportive mother and father.'

'Yes.' Liz smiled with gratitude. 'That is true. And you can rest assured I shall support Katie. She and Dickie were good for me, gave me faith in people again.'

She knew she must have left them a bit puzzled but they had a lot of arrangements to make, and as she drove away from the Hall she knew she had two missions, both to do with Dickie and to do for him.

Twenty-Six

The first time Liz visited Katie at home was two days after the Sinclairs had left on their European trip.

Katie had the sewing machine on the kitchen table when she arrived, and rose flushed and confused when she saw who it was.

'Hi,' Liz said, placing her handbag on to the table like one come to stay, 'not interrupting anything, am I?'

'It's lovely to see you,' Katie said, her face flushed, and her mother standing behind Lord Markham's granddaughter looking somewhat bemused. 'No, I'm helping out making curtains for a friend in the village.'

'Work at home?' Liz queried.

Katie nodded. 'Need to keep busy, and earn a little.'

'I'll put out feelers. Is it just curtains you do?'

'She's not a bad dressmaker,' her mother put in. 'You sit down and talk while I—'

A figure passing the window drew their attention, and Katie and her mother drew in their breaths sharply.

'It's Mr Bennett, isn't it?' Liz asked as she saw the other two shrink a little at the coming encounter. 'Would you let me open the door to him? I'd like to do that.'

Before either of them could answer Liz was at the door opening it, to their landlord's complete astonishment, though he pulled off his cap with some alacrity.

'Hello, Mr Bennett,' she said, 'how nice to see you. My grandpa was talking about you only this morning. I think he intends to call, either tonight or in the morning, not sure which really. Shame if you're out.'

'I'll not be out for long,' he said morosely. 'Surprised to see you here, young lady. Didn't see your car. Are you just leaving?'

'On the contrary, just come. Left my car on the road, but this will be the first of many visits if Katie and her mother will have me. We have such a lot in common, Katie and I, which I suppose you know really.'

'Do I?' he questioned and frowned.

Unsure, but worried, was Liz's summing up of his expression, certainly not wanting a direct answer to his own question as he immediately asked if George was in.

Colleen came to the door and, without greeting, answered that her husband had gone to fetch the sterilization fluid for the milking parlour, which had been missed off the delivery lorry.

'Ah!' Edgar frowned, but at Liz, who was clearly foiling his real intention. 'Yes, I'll see him later.'

'Anything else we can do for you?' she asked.

'Not at the moment,' he said and, nodding to Liz, he turned on his heel.

'He'd come to make trouble,' Colleen said, 'as soon as Bess is away I thought this is what might happen.'

'Well, you have her offer of the Dower House if you need it. A suitable place for you all, I would have thought.' She raised her eyebrows at Katie, who gave no sign of having any idea what she implied.

'You know about that, then?' Colleen asked.

'Yes, I do, but I don't think Edgar Bennett is going to be a problem to you, my grandfather is going to keep an official eye on him. He's going to invite him for Christmas and the New Year so he'll have to be a good boy,' and added affectedly, 'we can't have scandals at the Lord's house.'

'Dickie always said you were . . .' Colleen hesitated over the word.

'Incorrigible, probably,' she supplied.

'Yes, that was the word,' Katie agreed with a brief fleeting smile.

Liz linked arms with them both. 'Can I invite myself to a cup of coffee?' she asked.

Liz became a regular visitor at Katie's home. She kept herself busy on Katie's behalf, finding her customers for the sewing she had taken up, and running her out and about in her car, delivering the finished orders. The extra income meant a lot to the family with her mother no longer employed, although she helped with some of the necessary hand finishing of the sewing orders.

Liz and Katie became very close, and when they were alone, Katie began to talk about Dickie, things he had said and done during their secret times together. She told of his mad ideas, which usually became outrageous schemes he involved her in. 'It's been the same ever since we were children,' she said, then corrected herself. 'It was the same.'

'He was quite a guy,' Liz gently agreed.

One day as they had struggled to the car with a load of heavy velvet curtains, Katie said, 'I've something to ask you, and you can say no if you don't want to, I would understand.'

'Ask away then,' Liz told her, starting up the car, and expecting a request for a run into town for material or some such.

'When the baby's born, will you be a godmother?'

Liz was so astonished she stalled the car.

'I didn't mean to upset you.' Katie was immediately repentant. 'I shouldn't have asked, it's ridiculous, it could be awkward for you.'

'Ridiculous! Awkward!' Liz exclaimed. 'Nonsense, I'd love to be, thanks so much for asking me. I feel . . .' She paused to assess her true feelings, 'I feel so honoured, yours and Dickie's baby, my godchild.'

'You must be the only one who really knows, apart from Edgar Bennett, but he obviously wishes me and the baby . . . well, a long way from here.'

'Why don't you tell?' Liz urged. 'I'd back you up.'

'It won't bring Dickie back,' she said, 'and the baby will be all mine if no one knows.'

'There's a lot of money and land . . .' Liz reminded her.

Katie shook her head at her friend. 'Doesn't always go with happiness, does it?'

'No, you're right,' she reflected. 'I might have had my baby – well my toddler by now – if there had not been so many "earthly treasures" involved.'

'Your baby,' Katie said hesitantly, 'was the real reason I wasn't sure about asking you.'

'No, it makes me feel better actually. I'll be involved officially with a baby.'

'A love child,' Katie reminded her.

'The very best kind to have.'

They squeezed hands.

'I tell you what I would love to do before the baby is born,' Katie said, 'I'd like to go back to where Dickie and I were most happy.'

'No problem,' Liz told her.

Before the following spring, Liz had seen off a dozen or so sorties by Edgar Bennett, and all this was reported to Bess, who telephoned Colleen every week.

Colleen was also able to tell her that Lord Markham went over to see Edgar at least once a week and, she thought, because of his aristocratic visitor he now had Mrs West's granddaughter – 'you know them as used to keep the village shop' – to go in and clean him up once a week. 'She tells me your father's got all the postcards you've sent him lined up on the kitchen dresser.'

She heard the relief in Bess's voice as she answered, 'That's something. He doesn't have much to say to us when we telephone him.'

'He doesn't have much to say to us either,' Colleen said, 'I reckon my George'll be ready for a change when you come home, but he says he won't rock the boat while you're away.'

Bess's reports on Julian after several weeks of 'nothing' and 'no difference' began to change. 'Julian wanted to go up to the top of the tower'. 'Julian's sketching!' 'Julian is asking questions.' He and Ian had a real discussion about the miracle of men vaulting stone ceilings over enormous spaces inside the great old cathedrals. All they had hoped for, as time and the ever changing interests of new places, new wonders of man's works impinged on him, was happening, and he was becoming himself once more.

'You'll see a big difference in him too,' Bess told her friend, and whispered into the telephone that his voice had broken. 'He's looking and sounding like a man.'

Liz took Katie on her long requested trip to the Norfolk coast one bright windy day in early March, about a month before the baby was due. Katie directed her to the cottage. She found the key under the flowerpot, let them in. Liz watched her wander around from room to room, touching, tidying, remembering.

'Just one more place I want to go,' she said. Liz held her hand as they went down the scramble path to the beach. Once on the sea's edge the wet sand was firm and Liz let go of her arm. She seemed to have her eyes firmly fixed on a group of rocks at the far end of the beach. The nearer they walked, the more concentrated Katie's attention.

'I'll let you go on alone,' Liz suggested.

Katie glanced at her and nodded.

Liz stood watching as she made her way a little erratically, sometimes veering on to the dry sand, pausing here and there as if reliving some other time. When she reached the rocks she went from them back to the sea, stood and looked out towards the horizon, once reaching out an arm as if to embrace her memory more closely. Eventually she went back to the rocks and sat down.

Liz watched the still figure on the rocks for a long time. Then she stirred herself, knowing this was the right moment for something she had previously thought would be appropriate after Katie's baby was born, but now she changed her mind. This was the moment.

She walked on to join Katie, going slowly so she had full time for her memories, but finally coming to sit on the rock by her side. Katie took her hand and held it. 'We swam here, and made love here,' she said, 'did you guess?'

'I did, and I am guessing this is exactly the moment Dickie would have wanted me to give you this.' She pushed a small black velvet jeweller's box into her hand.

'Dickie?'

Liz nodded. 'Open it.'

Katie did very slowly, then started back almost with shock at the sight of the beautiful solitaire diamond ring. 'But,' she said, 'how?'

And Liz told her the story. 'I'm sure he intended it for your engagement on the day of his eighteenth birthday.'

'Yes,' she agreed. 'But it must have cost a fortune.'

'I'm sure it did,' Liz said and left her own hefty contribution untold. Katie needed this to be entirely Dickie's gift, as indeed it would have been had he lived.

Twenty-Seven

She wore the ring in secret at night, imagining Dickie was with her, with this ring he had chosen, he had touched.

She held it up to the moonlight and let the rays catch the stone and, moving her finger very slowly, she took it through its rainbow. She paused as each colour sprang from the diamond, like coloured fire, red, orange, yellow, green, blue, indigo, violet, and she remembered sheltering beneath the tree near the Red Pool. After the storm the sun had shone out and the raindrops had hung huge on every twig and sparkled in all these colours.

'As soon as I am eighteen I shall buy you an engagement ring that catches the light like that.' She remembered his exact words. 'And you did,' she breathed.

'I'm frightened, Dickie,' she told the ring, 'frightened of having this baby on my own. I'd be frightened even to show this ring. They'd think I'd stolen it. I'm a real coward, I lost my daring when I lost you, my darling Dickie.'

She felt the child stir within her, and she put her hand on her stomach as the activity increased. 'A real live wire you've got in there,' the midwife had said on her last visit. 'If it stops you resting you want to put your hand on your bump and tell it to be still, you're trying to rest.'

'Does it work?' she had asked.

'Don't see why it shouldn't, everything else is connected up to you.'

She tried it now, spreading her left hand as wide as she could.

'Shhh,' she whispered. The activity slowed and the child was still. She was amazed, and awed by the thought of a bond with a baby not yet born.

She drifted into the outer edges of sleep, only to be fully

awake again in less than an hour, aware of an ache in the bottom of her back different to, and more persistent than, any other ache she had ever had. She remembered another thing the midwife had said, 'As soon as you think you've started, ring me and get your father to take you straight to the hospital. I don't want any ambulance dashes out to old Paget's farm.'

She went to her parents' bedroom and woke them. In no time, the whole household was astir and Colleen, George and Bess on their way to the hospital, William calling after her to wish her luck, 'and make it a boy, Sis, please!'

It was only as she was entangled with the hospital procedure and her parents despatched to await news at home that she admitted to herself that she had all along meant to wear the ring while she had their baby. She had turned the stone so it lay inside her hand.

The labour was long, painful, and she was sure it hurt much more when they asked her lie down. It was when she was transferred to the flat hard bed in the delivery room she heard one of the young nurses snigger and remark, 'Don't know why she bothers to wear that ring, it has to be false and we all know she's not married.'

Richard George Michael, seven and a quarter pounds, was born the following morning at six o'clock. 'Well, young man, for one so active in the womb you've kept us all waiting long enough,' her midwife greeted his safe arrival. 'Now your mum can relax for a bit.'

The midwife put her baby into her arms and, opening Katie's left hand, twisted the ring the right way round. 'I know a real diamond when I see one,' she told her, 'I know you heard what that nurse said, she's a spiteful madam.' She touched the ring, admired the setting with the stroke of a finger. 'He must have really loved you, even if he's not around now,' she said, then nodded to the baby, 'so you be proud of him.'

She was proud, for he was a bonny child, and before she left the maternity unit her midwife paraded him all around for everyone to see – but Katie hid her ring again.

Everyone who made their way to Paget's farm in the following weeks said Michael was a beautiful baby, and as he lay out in his pram under the flapping lines of washing she saw her parents, and William, tiptoe to peep at him.

Liz came with a most beautiful hand-crocheted shawl. 'Swish, my old nannie, did it,' she told Katie. 'I have to take lots of photos of my godchild and let her see him.'

'He must have the shawl on then,' Colleen said, 'I've never seen such fine lacy work, it must have taken –' she tried to imagine – 'forever. It'll be a real heirloom.'

The one visit Katie was not looking forward to was Dickie's mother. They had been away over seven months, but were now on the way back. She knew that Bess would come to see her mother as soon as ever she returned – it was the way they had always been, best friends, running to each other at every event in their lives. She tried not to remember that Bess was just as much Michael's grandmother as her own mother. If Dickie had lived, if things had been different, they might have celebrated a mutual grandson. If. If.

The day before they were due back, cakes and scones were baked, and the kitchen, Katie noticed, was kept extra tidy, the ironing basket put in the pantry, the sewing machine banished for the afternoon. She was tempted to say it would all be for nothing if they didn't come, but by two o'clock Colleen was up on her feet at the sound of a car. 'Here they are,' she announced and went out to greet Bess and Julian.

They looked tanned and well, but Julian had grown so tall and, as his mother had said, his voice had dropped several octaves. He had gone a distressed boy and come back a sober but level-headed young man.

'Oh, it is good to see you!' Bess declared and Katie thought she never would stop hugging her mother. Julian shrugged his shoulders at all this emotion and came to kiss her on the cheek, then Bess enveloped her with a warm hug and kisses. 'So where's this baby?' she asked. 'Everyone tells me what a beautiful boy he is.'

So the moment she had dreaded had come. Dickie's mother wanting to see his baby.

They went outside to where the pram was shaded by the emerging deep-pink blossom of the apple tree and protected by a cat net. Katie pulled the net aside and the baby was just stirring, stretching himself awake, pushing up a fist.

'Ooh!' Bess sighed, and extended her arms towards him. 'May I?' she asked. Once he was in her arms, Katie watched, waited.

'Hello, young man, you really are beautiful.'

Katie was amazed to see her baby make a conscious effort to open his eyes and look to see who talked to him, and once open, he stared fixedly at who held him. 'My,' she whispered to him, 'you'll certainly know me again, won't you?' She turned to Colleen. 'Just look at him, I feel as if he'll be asking me questions in a moment.'

Once more her baby had astonished her: if there had been any recognition, any struggle to make contact, it had been on the part of her baby, of Bess's grandson.

'Have you seen your father yet?' Colleen asked as they all walked back to the house, Katie pulling the pram back after the two friends who were certainly not going to give the baby over to be laid down again.

'George says he's making a rod for his own back with the local youths,' Colleen went on. 'He started by shouting at some of them for riding their motorcycles too fast, as he thought. Now they've begun to plague him by joyriding over his open fields, particularly that ridge and furrow near the road. George has told him he'll have to fence it before it'll stop, but he says it's been like that since "time immemorial" and he won't, he'll catch the youths and see they're prosecuted.'

'We're going there now,' Bess said, looking at Colleen, a question in her eyes, and her friend shook her head minimally, so she gathered that the barn had not been put to rights.

'I'd like to walk over,' Julian said, 'it'll be good to see the old ways again.'

'You've not been away that long,' Colleen said, 'nothing much has changed.'

'It feels like a long time,' he said very soberly.

'I'll walk part of the way with you,' Katie said, 'I can fill you in.'

'I'll see you there then,' Bess said and, still holding the baby, she watched them go.

'She'll tell him,' Colleen said, 'so it won't be such a shock.'

'Why didn't I just tell him?' Bess agonized.

244

'Because as always you don't want to let your father down.'

'It's stupid,' Bess declared. 'I am stupid. If I hurry I can be round by the road and meet them before they reach the back of the farm.'

'Don't worry, those two have both come through fire and survived. They'll be all right,' Colleen said, 'and you and Ian.'

There was the lightest of queries in her voice.

Bess looked down at the baby. 'Yes, we're fine.' A choke of tears came to her voice and her eyes were full of tears. 'It's just,' she began, 'poor Dickie, he feels so close to me now we're home.'

Colleen relieved her of the baby, who was asleep again now, and put him back into his pram. 'You get off to your father's now, it won't hurt if you're there before Julian sees the barn.'

She parked, then ignoring the house, walked straight through the farmyard, to the barn behind the stables and sheds. She found herself shaking her head once more at the wilful destruction of what had been a machine store and before that the barn where when she was a child the harvest suppers had been held.

She was there first, but only just – she could see Julian and Katie coming through the orchard. No more of the building had been knocked down, and in fact she was sure the sledge-hammer still lay where she had seen her father throw it months before.

Katie had obviously told Julian but even so he was clearly upset, surveyed it with disbelief, walking round the bricks, up and down the devastated sections.

Bess went to where Katie had stopped some little distance away, but when she went to link arms with her, Katie shook her head. 'I'll go back now,' she said and turned on her heel. Bess wondered what had sent the girl scurrying away, then turning saw her father emerging from behind the sheds.

'Pa,' she greeted him, but anything more effusive was stopped by his manner and his stance, aggressive, upright, his walking-stick stabbed into the ground in front of him, both hands white-knuckled on the handle.

'You look well,' she said, 'good to see that.'

'Grandpa.' It was acknowledgment and question as Julian waved a hand at his destroyed work. 'Not what you wanted?'

'None of it is what I wanted,' he declared, his voice shaking with either anger or emotion. 'None of it. Was that the Wright girl I saw?'

'She walked over here with me,' Julian said, 'just for company.'

'She knows she's not welcome here, don't encourage her.'

'I won't,' Julian said, 'I can always—'

Bess silenced him with a shake of her head as they followed the old man back into the house. She noticed there was no sign of the postcards.

Her father slammed his walking-stick flat on to the table. 'Twenty-nine weeks you've been away,' he said, 'what am I supposed to say to you?'

'Welcome home,' Julian supplied.

'What's to welcome you back to?'

'Quite a few people seem pleased to see us,' Julian answered.

'You've found your tongue while you've been away, as well as other things. Think you're a man now, do you? You'll be wanting to ride *your* motorbike around my fields, will you?'

'Pa!' Bess shouted, then took hold of herself. 'No, this won't do. I think it will be best if we go now, we've had a tiring three days travelling. I'll come and see you properly tomorrow.'

'You can just please yourself about that. Is my minder off duty now?'

'Your minder?' she queried but he turned away.

Once in the car, she tried to make excuses for him, but Julian said, 'It's all right, he's just angry with himself because he's done wrong.'

In the weeks and months that followed, Bess kept going to her father every day – for one thing, because he refused to have even Mrs West's granddaughter in the house to clean and cook now she was back. She did what she felt was her duty by him, but there was no joy in the doing and no thanks.

One fine October morning, during the half-term break for the local schools, she was on her way to the farm when she heard the sound of a car and shouting. She stopped to listen. The high-pitched scream of an engine, interspersed with near silences, then another spurt of high whining speed, and somewhere in between all this someone shouting. 'Pa!' she breathed and began to run.

She reached the roadway and could see on the rising land which formed the open fields, a blue Mini careering wildly over the old bumpy ridge and furrow. A real exciting fair-ground ride for those who cared neither for the food source for farm animals, or for the vehicle. So high were the revs the driver was giving the car, it seemed fairly to leap from ridge to ridge – and, looking like a comic figure from an old film, her father was in pursuit, waving his walking-stick.

She called and waved but neither the carload of teenagers nor her father were looking her way. She caught her breath when the car turned as it reached the hedge, and in the moment of turning was slowed down in one of the dips. Her father advanced on them, obviously thinking he had them at last. The car engine revved and revved, then as if the tyres suddenly found purchase it leapt forward, and Edgar Bennett had no chance. There was a sound like a gigantic bat hitting a gigantic ball. Frozen with horror, Bess watched as the Mini went on but her father was no where to be seen.

She ran uphill to the spot without any sensation of either effort or being breathless. Her father lay spreadeagled on his beloved land. His eyes were open and he knew her as she knelt by him.

'Bess,' he said, struggling to pull breath into his chest.

'Don't talk, Pa, I'll get help.' She stood up and saw one of the youths from the car some distance away but at least coming back.

'Get an ambulance and a doctor quickly. Quickly!' she yelled at him.

He nodded and ran back towards the car. She heard it start up again and skid on to the road. She just had to hope they were going to the nearest telephone box.

She knelt again by her father.

'Bess . . .' he began again. She shook her head at him, but he insisted. 'No, I have to. Katie Wright's baby –' he lifted a hand briefly as if he needed her much nearer – 'it's Dickie's, he told me . . .'

Though she stooped closer she did not catch the end of the sentence. She grasped his hands and he rallied again. 'I didn't want to believe it,' he said and a rueful smile curved his lips for a painful second. 'You'll make it right?' he asked her urgently.

'I will, Pa,' she promised though her mind was in turmoil.

'That baby's Dickie's heir.'

'Yes, all right,' she told him, 'rest easy.' She put her cheek next to his and there were tears on both their cheeks.

After a moment she lifted her head to look at him again, and he looked deep into her eyes, and it felt as if he said, 'My daughter, well done.'

'I love you, Pa,' she breathed in his ear, this man who perhaps had loved some things too deeply, too exclusively – her mother, his land and, she realized, his daughter, for he had wanted everything for her. She looked at him again and saw a change. 'Pa.' The word was both goodbye and complete understanding.

She stooped and laid her face against his once more.

She had pulled the last strands of grass from between his fingers where he had taken a final grip on his land, closed his eyes, and knelt by him for a long time, when help all came together.

An ambulance siren sounded in the near distance, then a voice called her name and Ian was running to her, kneeling by her.

'It's over,' she told him, 'and you were right all the time, Katie's baby . . .'

'Dickie's,' he said. He held her to him for long pondering seconds, then added, 'So he has left us much more than memories.'

The ambulance came bumping up the field, followed by Dr Michael's car. Ian pulled her gently to her feet and slightly away as the doors of the vehicles swung open.

'You know?' Dr Michael asked them, after he had knelt briefly by her father. 'Go home then, there's nothing more you can do here. Take her home, Ian,' he instructed.

Ian began to walk Bess away but he said, 'I think we should go to see George and Colleen, and Katie.'

'Yes, now,' she agreed. It had been her father's last wish for her to put things right, and it was her husband's idea to go at once, things coming together.

248

She leaned into him as he walked her away from the hillside, where it was possible to overlook all their farmland. She looked ahead and knew that the love she had for her father from her childhood on, and the love she had for Ian, were very separate things, as was the love she had for her two sons. The difference between life and death hardly mattered when it came to love.

'Each person draws a different love from you, don't they?' she said.

'So this new baby?' he queried.

'He's already made his claim,' she said.